The Making of Angels

A Novel by

Terri Michel

To Adrienne —
The angels of the Lord
encamp around those (Ps. 34:7)
who fear Him —
Love and blessings
Terri Michel

Hope Publishing, LLC
Denver, Colorado

Hope Publishing, LLC
Elizabeth, Colorado

Cover Design and Format by Shelby Soto, ˘
Ingenious Design

Photo Credit: www.comstock.com

Library of Congress Number 2010912272

ISBN 978-0-9765532-2-9

endorsement

This is truly a day that God is using all of the Arts to communicate the gospel. Dance, Music, Drama, and other forms of artistic expression are being powerfully used to paint the picture of God's love and grace. The book, *The Making of Angels* by Terri Michel is a gospel-based fictional writing that will cause the reader to embrace the realities of Heaven and Hell.

Terri Michel was an active member of Word of Life Christian Center of which I am the senior pastor. We have one of the fastest growing churches in this part of the United States, so I have the privilege of working with many, many people in the work of the kingdom. Terri was a dependable, committed, and devoted part of our congregation, and had in a multiple of ways used her gifts and compassion for people to change lives. I believe this book is a product of heartfelt revelation that God has imparted into her life. I believe you will be blessed as you read, *The Making of Angels.*

God bless you.

Dr. Tim Bagwell, Senior Pastor
Word of Life Christian Center
Denver, Colorado

dedication

As a child, I knew Jesus was the Son of God, but didn't know him personally. I didn't realize forgiveness rested in His hands. By accepting Him as my savior, I was born again. What greater gift than this was there?

I wanted to share this gift with my family, friends and people whom I've never met. Because of this, I wrote this story.

The story is imaginary, however, truth remains. It is not forsaken.

acknowledgement

Lord, I thank you for helping me capture my thoughts and ideas. I can't count the number of times I turned to you for wisdom. The Bible speaks of seeking wisdom and there were times my search for the "how" seemed obscure. You shed Your light on my path and provided the way.

Bill, I appreciate the hours you spent reading and re-reading the first manuscript and your suggestions, which helped shape the outcome. As my husband, you showed me great support.

I have to mention our children, Ereina, Carmen, Paige, Gary, Jr., Jennifer, Sam and Renee, who were my raison d'être, my motivation.

Also, Roxanne and my daughter-in-law, Chris whose perspectives and observations affected the content of the original book.

My heartfelt thanks to Maggie Bazan Gleeson whose expertise, time and guidance molded the words on the pages of this revision.

I owe my gratitude also to my writer's group, Words for the Journey, Rocky Mountain Chapter for their encouragement and knowledge.

And last, but not least, to my oldest daughter Ereina for her final read and suggestions.

The Lord provided the canvas, and each of you were brush strokes in the final work of *The Making of Angels.*

contents

contents

galaxies 1

Lev would discover the training manual didn't cover everything. He strolled along the pure glass-like road in the City with a careless strut.

A showcase of glowing colors shot across the sky. Dazzling hues of magenta, Caribbean green and golden yellow streaked into the atmosphere.

His large white wings hung motionless and a slight smirk crossed his lips as he picked up his gait near the intersection of Promise and Trust Way.

A young girl stood, statue-like, amongst the busy multitudes passing by.

Her dark curly hair glistened as her head turned from one side to the other. She lifted her chin to the horizon and an expression of wonderment fired from her clear brown eyes.

Tall buildings that arose like white candles against the multi-colored heavens stood before her.

Lev noticed another angel standing next to her with his hands on his hips. He peered to the right and then to the left. With each quick turn, his green eyes flashed as he searched the lively street.

Lev almost tripped over the girl. "Excuse me, little one."

She turned and fixed her gaze on his bronze smiling face and warm copper-hued eyes.

He patted her head and then addressed the angel by her. "You look troubled."

His palms turned upward and then he dropped them to his

sides. "We arrived from earth several moments ago and I can't find them."

"You're an accompanying angel aren't you? Tell me, what is your name?"

"Yes, I am, and it's Daniel, sir."

Lev chuckled. "You don't have to call me sir. I'm only an angelee and most likely as old as you. My name's Lev."

"I'm glad to meet you, Lev. Then you must be in training?"

"Yes, I and five others are in preparation. But, who is it you can't find?"

"The young girl's parents were supposed to be here a couple of days ago. I was instructed to wait here, at this corner. I don't understand." He raised his hand to his mouth. "I think I goofed -- big time."

Lev thought a moment and then snapped his fingers. "I know. I met a transporting angel here two days ago with a man, woman and a young girl. I bet they're the ones. The angel's name was … "

Just then, a gust of wind blew above them. Lev and Daniel gazed with mouths wide open as a sizeable life form hovered above.

He descended gently to the ground. His rounded chest and twelve foot height made him look like an oversized football player.

"Sunergos … it's you," Lev blurted.

"I see you've met my new assignment."

Lev's grin widened. "I knew she must have something to do with you."

"Yes, I'm to transfer her to another planet today."

"Great! That sounds exciting, traveling through space."

"It is."

Sunergos' eyes set a steady gaze on young Lev. "Would you like to come along?"

Lev brushed his wheat-colored hair aside and stared at Sunergos with an incredulous look. "Me? You want me to travel through space. I mean, how? I'm not able to fly. I've never been away from the Magnificent City."

"Simple. I'll hold the girl Superman style and you can hop on my back. You're going to have to hold on tight."

Lev thought a moment. He had studied the subject of galaxies and this would be a fantastic opportunity. Slowly, a Cheshire-like grin peeled from one side of his face to the other. "I think that would be great. What about you, Daniel?"

"I wish I could, but I have another appointment. Otherwise, you couldn't keep me away."

"Are you sure?"

"Positive. I appreciate the help you've given."

Daniel waved and surged into the azure blue sky and Lev watched longingly until he disappeared from view.

Sunergos leaned over, gathered the child and cradled her against his chest. She giggled and held him with a tight grip.

Her thin white arms clashed against his thick bronze neck. Her eyes searched his quizzically. "Are you taking me to see Mommy and Daddy?"

His hazel eyes revealed a gentle softening. "Yes, we're going to see them today. Are you ready?"

She nodded eagerly.

"How about you, Lev?"

Lev's heart thumped wildly beneath his breast. He shook his head in affirmation and hopped effortlessly onto Sunergos' back.

His legs glided on the smooth garment beneath him. With his arms outstretched, he grasped the arch of each of Sunergos' wings and squeezed his eyes closed.

"Ready?" Sunergos announced, like a pilot preparing for lift-off.

"It's a go," Lev responded.

Lev pressed his cheek against Sunergos' back and would have given a thumbs-up sign, but he wasn't about to release his hold.

Sunergos pushed lightly on his toes and they lifted, slowly at first, and then suddenly rocketed with a forceful thrust into the heavens.

"Are we taking her back to earth?" Lev shouted into the current of air swirling around them.

"No," Sunergos answered. "We're on our way to earth's twin planet."

"We're going to Venus?"

"No, that would be earth's sister planet. We're going to Tobe."

"Venus sounds like it would be a great place to visit," Lev responded.

He was unaware he originated from the angel-dusted planet of love, Venus.

His name meant heart, depicting his extraordinary capacity of affection.

A fluttering sensation quivered within him as they flew through space. Bright lights of every color, size and intensity dotted the vast horizon.

With half-closed eyes, he clung to the arch of Sunergos' wings as they flew at lightning speed through space.

They wove back and forth appearing like a tiny speck among the heavenly bodies.

The velocity they travelled at pulled on his cheeks. As they rushed through the air he shouted, "Whoa!" The young girl laughed.

They approached a large white glow, which merged into luminous pink shades. The blush tone deepened to lavender, darkened to purple and then faded into the black universe.

"How many galaxies beside Qodesh have you been to?" Lev asked in the stillness that surrounded them. The seat of the heavens, Qodesh, was home of the Magnificent City. Those who accepted the king's invitation resided there or elsewhere in the universe, as they desired.

Sunergos laughed and replied, "Well, Qodesh is one of thousands."

"Really?"

"Yes, which is minuscule in view of the fact there are about a hundred and twenty five billion."

"Incredible! Boy, do I have a lot to learn."

"Since they're constantly formed, there will be others. Forever is more than enough time to visit them.

"So, did you keep a log of the ones you've been to?"

"No, I've never kept a tally. I know there have been many of them through the ages."

He lifted his chin and peeked over the side of Sunergos'

wing. "What are they like?"

"They're magnificent! There's this one I nicknamed blue feathers. Blue stars spiral out from the center like a fan. You know, young stars are blue to begin with.

Lev attempted to envision this spectacle of wafting colorful plumes in the darkness of space. "It sounds like an interchange of conglomerations."

"I guess you might say that. Together they form a cluster of galaxies. Earth and Tobe lie in the Milky Way Galaxy."

Suddenly, a huge bright object popped up. Sunergos made a razor-sharp turn and Lev's mouth dropped open. "That was close."

"Sorry." Sunergos continued, "I guess I would have to say my favorite, beside our own of course, is Hoag's Object. I like the massive blue stars, which encircle the huge bright, yellow star."

"Where is that?"

"Hoag's is … about six hundred million light years from earth, a little farther from us."

Lev began to calculate. *One light year is about six trillion miles.*

Nearly impossible to multiply six trillion miles times six hundred million light years as they flew through space, he vowed to figure it out later.

They tilted left and an enormous light beige ball came into view.

"There it is. There's Tobe."

"Wow, I wish the others could see this."

Sunergos continued on his often-traveled path. He had served the kingdom in the capacity of transferring immortals from earth to different galaxies for generations. He swerved from side to side veering past asteroids and stars, which contrasted the immense darkness.

They approached their destination. Blue and silver striations ringed the globe with red elongated moons, far different from what circled Lev's home.

The threesome circled the aptly named planet. Its name meant bounty, cheer and ease and it personified those qualities. It appeared earth-like, except for a deep royal blue atmosphere and thin silver clouds. Hills inundated the plains like waves.

As they neared, Lev realized the atmosphere and clouds caused the streaks of blue and silver he had observed from space. Below, a large silvery lake summoned a restful dip in its waters.

They came close to the receiving port and Sunergos maneuvered the group with expertise. He landed with care on the reunion pad where spirit beings waited for their loved ones.

"This is my favorite part," Sunergos announced.

The young girl leapt from the angel's arms and shouted, "Mommy! Daddy!"

"Salena, you're here!" They echoed back.

Salena's sister jumped up and down. "I'm so glad to see you!" She cried out. Her voice halted with each bounce.

Salena's father rushed to her. "We didn't know until a few moments ago we'd see you so soon. I'm glad we didn't have to wait!"

They held hands and danced in a circle. Then, her father knelt and gathered his family in his arms. "This is wonderful," he said softly. His wife wrapped her arms about them, reaching partially around. "I'm so happy we're together again."

Salena's dad pulled back. With a broad smile he asked, "Guess who's here?"

She blinked her long-lashed brown eyes. He laughed. Rarely did his little chatterbox remain silent.

"That's alright. You don't have to guess, I'll tell you. You're going to see Grandma and Grandpa!"

She hadn't seen her grandparents for a while and her face lit up like neon on a marquee. The announcement served as extra frosting on the cake of their dear, sweet reunion.

An almost tangible joy permeated the group. Flushed with goodwill, Lev felt as if his heart would burst.

They lingered as long as they could, but knew they needed to return home. As they left, the grandeur of the cosmos amazed Lev again. He laid his head back, eager to get his last view of the glorious blue and silver stripes.

That's when it happened.

His legs swung to the side and he slid from Sunergos' back,

toppling through space like a ragdoll out of control.

His voice echoed a languished cry into the cosmos "Sunergos … help!"

standing 2

Austin knew his favorite spot for lunch would fill quickly and so he left the office a bit earlier than usual. *Got to feed the body as well as the soul,* he surmised.

He tossed his Bible on the seat next to him.

He angled into a parking space and as he opened the door, he caught sight of two young women.

The one on the right looked up and smiled. She wore a chocolate brown cardigan that matched her eyes. He stared and sank into his seat.

He sat for a moment and rubbed his face. An urge to leave mounted within. Thirty-five years was a long time, and this woman barely looked thirty.

It can't be her.

He started to pick up his Bible but pulled his hand away. Instead, he reached for the door and exited.

The quaint ambiance of the café beckoned with its restful lighting and music. A calmness wrapped its arms about him.

"One or two?"

Caught off guard, he signaled *one.*

He walked to the table and searched for the mysterious woman. White crisp linens with napkins set in water glasses donned each table. He surveyed the patrons that sat and spoke with each other assuredly. Two females sat across from his table, about twenty feet away.

The woman that drew his attention sat with her right side toward him dressed in three-inch heels.

Her skirt parted at the knee, revealing smooth, tanned legs.

He couldn't take his eyes away and his brow furrowed. Maddie would never wear her hair swirled that way.

He envisioned Maddie's warm smile and as he closed his eyes, he could almost smell her perfume.

He opened his eyes. The realization that today would have been their wedding anniversary sobered him.

The woman's friend pointed toward his table and he glanced away quickly.

"Are you ready to order a drink?" Austin gazed at the waiter standing by his table.

"I'll … have an iced-tea, thank you."

"Coming right up."

He held the well-known menu before him and glanced around it from time to time. The women smiled and conversed with one another easily. *It's not Maddie, it's impossible. Why did I have to run into a "look alike?"*

"Here's your tea. Do you know what you'd like for lunch yet?"

He gave the waiter a stare as cold as the ice in his glass. The waiter stood, paused.

"Actually, this will be it thank you. I'll just take it to go."

An expression of surprise crossed the attendant's face. "Are you sure? If you're in a hurry, I can get your order out to you right away."

"No, I mean, yes, I'm positive. It isn't anything you've done, please believe me."

"Okay. You're the boss." He scribbled something on the pad and handed it to Austin.

"Thank you. I'll just take this up front and get a glass to go."

At the podium, Austin placed the bill with his payment on top of the counter. "I have a to-go cup of iced tea."

The host exercised a curious frown. "Is there anything wrong?"

"Not at all, I just realized I can't stay."

"Certainly."

Austin paid, leaving a generous tip. He pushed the door, started to glance over his shoulder but turned quickly as he exited.

One more time and I'll quit Becky rationalized.

She walked a few steps to the elevator and found a hand-written "out of order" sign taped to the narrow door.

She hurried to the stair entrance and pushed her body against the heavy squeaking door. She hiked three flights of stairs in the dimly lit passageway, dreading each dark landing.

The muscles in her legs tightened as she trudged along the corridor. It reeked of cigarette smoke and grimy carpet. Finally, she reached the familiar yellow-stained door.

Her small, light-skinned hand rapped against the door. It opened a crack and a man peered through the narrow slit. "Oh, it's you," he said as he opened it the rest of the way. She slipped past him, anxious.

Becky's straight blond hair shed a ray of light in the bleak, grayish room. She tucked her shirt in and wiped her clammy hands on her well-worn jeans.

Unkempt bodies straddled the unkempt room. She avoided making eye contact with the others. It wouldn't be long before she would be off in her own world.

Relentless August heat stifled the already muggy air. Two small windows on one end of the room offered little relief. At the bottom of one sat a large non-working cooling unit.

Dingy white metal cabinets appeared bright against the dull, smoke-layered walls in the kitchen. Half-filled glasses of water, dirty dishes, pots and pans littered the countertops. A cockroach scurried from a plate and into a drawer, unusual for daytime.

The disheveled man stood next to her. "Got the money?"

"Sure."

The man took her hard-to-come by cash and handed her a packet. She bared her arm, popped her fingers against her skin and looked for a good vein. *It won't be long,* she thought as she closed her eyes.

She drifted into a stupor and everything faded from view. She would do anything to escape reality. Drugs veiled her conscience, her character and her deeds. However, the truth remained.

The lie bound her with the illusion she had control, when all the while she lived in bondage to her weakness.

❖

Austin and his wife, Anna, ate a little later than usual that evening.

They sat at the round table in the corner of their kitchen. His grayed temples appeared grayer and he had a faraway look.

"How was your day?" Anna asked.

He cleared his throat. "Fine. Where's Haley tonight?"

"She's at Mackinsey's, spending the night."

The aroma of Moussaka, a Greek eggplant casserole, one of Austin's favorites, and garlic-mashed potatoes filled the kitchen. Anna planned yogurt with honey for dessert.

She held her every-day plate in her hand and served the delectable meal, placing it on the table.

Five minutes passed. They both picked at their food.

"You aren't eating very much," she announced, breaking the silence.

"I guess I'm not hungry."

She picked up the saltshaker and sprinkled it lightly. "Isn't it something about the tornado they had in West Virginia?"

"I didn't give it much thought," he responded. "I've been thinking about … Jacob."

"Oh." She didn't look up as she drank her water and then went back to her pretense of dinner.

A softening shrouded his light hazel eyes. "I haven't heard from him since I wrote. I hope he understood what I meant."

"Maybe it was too much."

"What do you mean?"

"Well, I know you try your best and I know you want to help him but there are times you go to extremes when you explain things."

"I didn't go into great lengths about it. I just wrote a short note."

"Oh, I didn't know. I assumed it an exhaustive discourse."

Her comment grated like barbed wire on a fence.

She continued. "I'm not saying it's your fault. But you know he's not a child and there comes a time you have to let go. He is twenty-seven years old."

"Twenty-eight, Anna. Even though you're his step-mother, you should know how old he is."

"Twenty-eight, alright, I stand corrected. That's not the point. I mean, it's like you are co-dependent and you … you coddle him."

"Coddle? What do you mean coddle?"

"You try to take care of every detail in his life."

His fork flew across the dish. "That does it!"

Startled, her head jerked up.

"At least I communicate with him. When did you talk to him last?"

She sat silent at first and then answered, "I talk to him."

"Sure. He calls the house and you say two words and hand the phone to me."

"Austin, I've tried. I'm sorry; I guess I shouldn't have said what I did just now but maybe it would have been better to talk to him instead."

"I wrote the letter because I felt there wouldn't be any mistake about the whole situation. I wanted him to know where we stood and so I put in on paper. This way, there isn't any doubt. He's visual, like me. I like to see things in black and white. Besides, it allowed me to pull all my thoughts together."

"But it's not like a conversation. He couldn't respond to you right away."

"True, but I knew he wouldn't want to hear what I had to say and I had to answer him, right?"

"Well we didn't refuse to go because we don't love him. I hope he knows that."

"Maybe I could've been a little kinder, but what's done is done. He's defensive and bringing up the subject is like walking on eggshells without breaking them. I didn't want to get into an argument and have either one of us say things we would regret."

Silence fell.

"I guess you're right," she conceded. "I just don't know. It may have been better to go to the wedding and not say anything at all."

Austin looked forward to the day his son would marry. He thought a lot about having a prospective grandson. The announcement should have been one of the happiest days of their lives. Instead, it brought devastation. His eyes misted. He didn't want to think about the future anymore. In a quiet tone he said, "I didn't know it mattered to you."

She leaned forward and squeezed his hand. "Of course it matters. He's a part of you and I love you."

"Funny, I thought Haley meant more to you."

"Haley means the world to me but because she's my biological child doesn't mean I love her more. You love them both the same don't you?"

Austin thought a moment. Of course, he loved Haley, but Jacob was older and Austin's pride and joy. Oddly, Jacob resembled his stepmother. They shared the same olive complexion and umber brown eyes.

Throughout his young adulthood, Jacob excelled. He carried a high-grade average in high school and college and he had a position as an architect for a good mid-sized firm. Austin couldn't have been prouder of his son's life achievements.

Austin's nurse, Destanee, told him Jacob called and wanted him to return the call right away. Jacob didn't call the office often.

He couldn't get a break between patients. A half-hour later, he called his nurse. "Destanee, hold my appointments. I'll be on a private call for a few minutes."

He dialed Jacob.

"Dad, I've got something to tell you."

"It must be pretty important."

Austin remembered Jacob didn't sound like himself but he brushed it aside.

With an impassive tone to his voice, Jacob informed him of the future event.

He couldn't believe it. What he feared had happened. In a

way, he wished he could say, "It's all right," but knew he couldn't.

Words continued to play through his mind.

He went through the rest of his appointments in a systematic manner and at the end of the day slipped back into the solitude of his office.

"Are you working late tonight?"

"Yes, but don't worry about staying, Destanee. I have a few personal items to take care of." His voice sounded mechanic-like, even though his mind raced.

Finally, his psyche settled, and he prayed, *Lord, what am I to do?* He sat with his head in his hands. *I have to find an answer.*

He searched the Bible, compiled a list of scriptures and scribbled his thoughts below the list.

Whole pages of notes stared back at him. He knew Jacob's reasoning came from the man's way of thinking, not God's.

He probed diligently through all the references. The note shrank as a sweater washed in hot water.

Jacob: I have to tell you—you surprised me. We've discussed at length the morals of your present circumstances. This marriage will not make your arrangement honorable and though we love you, your mother and I don't see how we can attend. We love you very much, Dad

He folded the written statement and addressed an envelope. He sat back in the large, black leather chair gazing at the first letter he had ever written to Jacob.

He heard Anna's voice, as if in the distance. "You don't do you?"

Tears formed in his eyes. "What?"

"You don't love Jacob more than Haley, do you?"

"No, of course not."

"It should be easy for you to see I don't either, even though Haley is our child, I love them both. I'm just afraid for him because he doesn't think there are consequences …"

She placed her hands over her face.

He fought the emotional pull and reserved his pain. With a sturdy yet soothing hand, he wiped her tears. "Don't cry. We've made it through a lot. We can make it through this."

"I know but Austin, it seems so hopeless."

"Well, we've done all we can."

"I know. I … I wish we weren't going through this."

He took a deep breath and reached out for her hand. "I never imagined we would be."

"I guess all we can do is stand in faith, like you said. We've prayed about it, and I guess there's nothing else."

They sat a moment, preoccupied with their thoughts.

"I don't know what happened," Austin remarked.

"I don't either. You did a great job raising him."

"We did, not me. You helped raise him through his teen years."

She shook her head. "I hope he's not lost. What if he's stubborn and ends up in hell?"

Her words flared like the fiery inferno itself.

"Anna, what are you saying? We've taken a stand and we're not going to budge. It may seem like there's a chasm between us now, but things are going to change. We're not letting go. We've got to hold on and believe no one in our family will be banished to that Godless existence."

Anna prayed under her breath, *Help me, Lord. What promise do I hold onto?*

They had attempted to walk their Christian faith. Sometimes they exchanged angry words. At times, Anna's selfish motives ruled and Austin's sullen attitude emerged but they forgave each other and went on.

Tears streamed down her face.

Austin held her chin and said in a gentle tone. "I don't want you to cry anymore, you hear?"

She looked up and smiled. His gentleness and kindness fulfilled her need. She mimicked back to him, "Ya hear."

Her eyes engaged his and with a smile she murmured, "You are my strength."

"No, I'm not; hon. God's your strength."

"Yes, you're right, He is."

"And Jacob will be all right. We're going to keep praying for him and for Haley. They're both going to make it."

The telephone rang a familiar chime. In general, Anna would let it go through to the answering machine, but this time she picked it up.

"Anna? It's your sister."

"Mackinsey, how are you?" Anna said cheerfully.

"I'm all right, but everything else isn't."

"Is Haley okay?"

"Yes, she's fine."

"Then what's wrong?"

"I need prayer."

Anna thought about her niece, Rebecca, or Becky as they called her. Becky left home at the age of sixteen and lived on the street. Her two siblings, Hannah, fourteen and Mark, thirteen were a handful.

"I'm sorry Ryan's not there to help you."

"I know. He tries, but, well you know, it's hard to get a hold of him."

"What's wrong?"

"I found something in Mark's room."

"What?"

Austin stood next to Anna, waved and gestured in an effort to get Anna to tell him.

She covered the mouthpiece. "It's about Mark." She returned to Mackinsey. "What did you say it was?"

"A ... magazine."

"Oh, Kinsey, I don't know what to say. I'm sorry."

"Well, you can imagine, I'm in shock."

"Yes, I can."

"What about the girls? Are they all right?"

"Don't worry about them. They don't know anything about it."

"Are you sure? You know they can come and stay here tonight instead. You can bring them over or we can pick them up."

"No, that's fine. Their chatter is therapeutic. It's good to have them around me. I just don't know how to pray."

"Well, we'll pray Mark sees it is wrong and changes."

"It sounds simple but you know we've been praying for Becky for such a long time and it hasn't worked."

"We may not see it happening but God is at work and He will answer."

"I guess he will. There are times I'm strong and times a feather can knock me over. I mean, shouldn't we ask the Lord what His will is?"

"Only if you mean you're asking if He's happy to do it."

Mackinsey paused and said, "I'm not sure I know what you mean."

"I think what you're saying is if we say 'thy will be done,' and nothing happens we can say, 'I guess it wasn't His will after all.' But that doesn't take faith. I attended a bible study on this not too long ago and learned the word 'will' means His desire or pleasure. Do you think it is His desire to help Mark?"

"I don't see how it wouldn't be."

"Right, when things come up, find a scripture you can stand on. Like, 'the battle is the Lord's,' which David yelled at Goliath before he hit him between the eyes."

"You're right, Anna."

"Are you ready to pray?"

"Yes."

Anna closed her eyes. "Father, help my sister. Help her to be strong and to know the battle is yours. Help Mark to see this is wrong, straighten his path, and I pray he will make the right choices. And Lord, I pray Becky will stop trying to destroy herself with drugs and will come to you. In Jesus Name, Amen."

She opened her eyes. Austin stood next to her with his hands raised as he prayed along with her.

"Okay?"

Mackinsey let out a deep sigh. "Yes. Thank you. I appreciate it."

"What are sisters for?"

"Thanks. I'll talk to you later. I love you and say hi to Austin."

"We love you too. Likewise, give our regards to Hank."

She set the phone in the cradle. "Wow. I think I needed that more than she did. It seemed as if I prayed right into our situation. You know, I need a scripture to hang onto too, and I need to rely on the Lord to take me through the battle."

Austin embraced Anna and held her close to him.

With her chin raised, she gazed at him. "I wanted to help her and I ended up helping myself. A few minutes ago, I prayed a short prayer about my faith, and then the phone rang. I don't know why some answers take longer than others do but I guess if I knew that, I wouldn't need faith.

They hugged again and a sense of peace enveloped them. Anna smiled and rocked lightly in his arms. "Thank you for your agreement, Mr. Connor."

The phone rang again.

"Anna?"

"Yes, what's going on, Mackinsey?"

"I just got a call. I have to leave for the hospital."

"What?"

"I got a call and it sounds terrible. It's Becky."

"What happened?"

"I don't know but they said I had to get to the hospital right away! Can you meet me?"

"Of course."

"Okay. She's at St. Luke's."

"We'll be there."

With a tremble in her fingers, she replaced the phone in the cradle.

"We have to go. Something's happened to Becky."

I'll think about it 3

Doug's excuse for an office sat in the corner of his bedroom. He snatched a few manila folders and shoved them into his mom's old safe. The West Virginia humidity caused beads of sweat to form on his brow. He jerked a grayish handkerchief from his pocket and wiped with a fervent motion.

Dabbing his face, he walked to the living room and pulled the curtains. He peered through the double pane windows.

Evening approached, and a blackened sky and wicked wind confirmed what he had heard. Earlier, he laughed at the possibility of a tornado.

He quickly stuffed his shaver and a change of clothes into an old army bag. He looked around the room and then seized his belongings.

Crack! A thundering clatter from the bellowing storm snapped overhead, like an elevator coming to a stop mid-floor.

The house went dark. Doug groped along the walls, searching for the door. Finally, a cold metal knob rested in his palm. He exited into the flooded street as the wind slammed the door behind him.

Doug scurried to his sedan and threw his now saturated bag on the front seat. Lashing rain pelted the metal bubble. Inside he felt safe.

Lightning shattered the dark sky again and thunder roared its battle cry. He flipped from one radio station to another until he found the news.

In a casual tone, the announcer stated, "Not since the seventies have we seen weather like this. Champlain and surrounding towns have lost power. The storm is moving west, folks. It's probably a good idea to stay home in a basement, if you have one. If you must go, your best direction is to go due east, or northeast."

He sat drenched in his jeans and t-shirt. A tremor slid down his spine.

He ran his fingers through his wet, straight hair. His wire-rimmed glasses fogged and he removed them with great care.

He wiped them and replaced them with a strange air of control. His square jaw set, determined, as he yanked a crumpled map from the side pocket.

With a steady finger, he traced the best road heading northeast, Route 50.

He heard a rap on the car window. A hooded figure stood outside in the downpour. Carefully, he lowered the glass.

"It's me, Mrs. Olson," the woman blurted, grasping a rain jacket with both hands, over her head. "Are you leaving town?" she yelled into the wind.

"No, I mean yes. I'm leaving for the night, until this blows over," he shouted back.

"Oh." She gazed a moment as if mesmerized.

He leaned toward the open window. Rain splattered into his face. "Why?"

"I didn't know if it would be foolish to try and leave. I … I thought I would leave, but I have to wait for my daughter."

Relieved, he shook his head. "Yeah, that's probably best."

"Do you think a tornado could touch down?"

"Who knows? You should get inside, don't you think?"

The woman stood quiet for a moment, and then replied, "You're right." A light courtesy smile crossed her lips. "Hope everything goes well."

Her departing words lingered as he raised the window. *Hope everything goes well. What are you thinking? We're in the middle of a thunderstorm and possible tornado.*

He reached into his bag, grabbed the first piece of material he could find, and dried his face.

He maintained a good speed at first, even with restricted

visibility.

Then a downpour released sheets of water. If anyone else were on the road, he could at least follow their taillights, but he had to go it alone.

He struggled as the car became self-propelled at times.

Wipers snapped, click, clack, click and clack, as fast as they could.

They couldn't keep up with the water-covered windshield. The windows fogged and his ability to see, worsened.

He leaned forward, turned the defroster up as high as it could go and wiped the inside of the windshield.

Condensation invaded the glass as fast as he swabbed. *I'll get through this, even if it kills me.*

Doug lived outside of Talbert, West Virginia, southeast of Champlain. His parents moved there during the 1930's.

He loved the town.

Downtown consisted of a few blocks, enough to satisfy his shopping desires.

Rows of houses lined the streets with elms in front of every home on his block. The seasonal changes pleased him.

As a child, he rode the sidewalks at first and then the street. Now, it disturbed him to hear the clicking sounds of neighboring children's wheeled toys.

Life remained uneventful until the day he came home and found his mother standing by the front door.

"Can you come here a minute?" Her voice sounded pressed.

His books landed in a soft hush on the cocktail table. He followed her into the kitchen on the unusually warm October day. Sunlight shimmered cheerfully through yellow chintz curtains, glazing the top of dishes drying in the rack. He sprawled into the dining chair and fidgeted with the spilled salt on the tablecloth.

"I have to tell you what's been going on," she said.

She turned away.

He thought he heard her whimper.

"I'll be right back." She marched out and an empty dread filled his being.

She returned, wiping her reddened nose with a handkerchief.

With a grave pitch to her voice she announced, "There's something I have to tell you."

A slight quiver shook her shoulders. She wiped her reddened nose with a handkerchief, and with hoarseness in her voice announced, "Dad and I ... decided we're getting divorced."

The familiar word echoed a foreign tone. His mom and dad had never exhibited any signs of incompatibility. His mind slipped in and out of reality in a dream-like state as he struggled with the news. The warm, hospitable kitchen generated a stark contradiction to this cold, harsh information.

She turned and walked away, muttering something about being sorry. Doug had stared out the window. If there were some warning, maybe it wouldn't have been so hard.

He recalled his father moved out and his vacant feeling. From then on, he didn't trust his emotions.

After this, things changed dramatically. His dad had always said before, "Wait until you have to hold a full time job. Your life will change, big time."

But he didn't have to wait. Carefree school days ended and he became responsible for taking care of everything.

In addition, when it came to work, he found he disliked the constraints and doldrums of work. Mornings rolled around too early for his taste and Doug found he dreaded Mondays.

❖

"Another one?"

The men knelt beside the crumpled figure on the ground. Lights from squad cars flashed in the pre-dawn darkness. The vicious event seemed almost common with yellow crime tape strung around the scene. A man opened his window open and yelled, "What's going on down there?"

The officers ignored the question.

Sealy stood over the recently discovered victim's body quietly while police officers shouted orders to one another. He took a drag on his cigarette and exhaled slowly.

"When are you going to quit?" His partner, Owens, chimed.

Sealy held the cigarette inches from his face. "Why should I now?"

"I thought your doctor ordered you to."

"Yeah, well, he doesn't have to deal with my frustrations or my divorce, now does he?"

Sealy's two daughters were born close together. His wife's career as a nurse required crazy hours, which proved a detriment. The menagerie continued until the day Sealy received a call.

He answered and barely recognized the woman's slurred voice.

"Yes, *detective,* I have a gross negligence I want to report."

"Joann? What's going on?"

"The thing is, John, this isn't working."

"Hon, get hold of yourself."

"I've gotten a hold of all I want. Do you know you were supposed to be here at noon?"

The realization he had forgotten his promise again wedged in his throat like a chunk of banana.

"I'm … I'm sorry."

"You're sorry? I was supposed to be at work at twelve-thirty. That's it, John. I can't take it."

"Hon, listen. I'll try harder. Just give me another chance. You know the workload … Hon? Are you there?"

Silence followed. The end of their marriage occurred soon after.

Motionless, he stood over the corpse. "This is the fourth one," he announced to his partner, Owens.

Owens uttered an expletive and both men remained fixed over the cold and lifeless fourteen-year old girl. The marks on her back revealed she must have suffered.

Sealy and Owens were veteran detectives with about twenty-five years apiece. Detective Bailey, who had been with the department five years, approached them with an outward constitution of iron.

"We'll try to wrap it up as soon as possible. Looks like lacerations …"

Sealy raised his hand. "Enough. I don't need to hear anymore."

Bailey shrugged and walked away.

Owens took notes on his pad as he watched Bailey and the

others comb the area for clues. He tapped the pad vigorously with an unconscious twitch. "We need to get a lead, and fast."

Sealy looked back with tired eyes. This job made him feel older than his forty-five years. "It's incredible. I don't know how one human can do this to another."

"How long has she been dead?"

"Well, it's just a guess, but from the looks of it I'd say about two hours."

"Great, that means everything's fresh."

"Yeah, we have an opportunity to learn a lot."

"Database time, huh."

The men remained by the young girl's possessions folded neatly in a pile next to her body. They could imagine the anguish she must have experienced when the perpetrator methodically set her things in order.

"She doesn't look like someone from the streets. It's going to be hard one to tell the parents."

"They're all hard."

"Yeah. You're right. They all are."

Summoned by the Ruler of the Realm, Jonathan crested the highest point of the city, the Temple Mount.

Invisible from the plains, the Mount peaked at 7,920,000 feet, about 270 times higher than Mt. Everest, the highest mountain known to man. The outside boundary was also 7,920,000 feet in length and breadth.

A river flowed from the peak of the Mount and split into four tributaries.

Clear water bubbled over rocks while schools of fish swarmed beneath. Spinner dolphins spiraled in the air, squealing with delight alongside those swimming in the refreshing river.

The king's request piqued Jonathan's curiosity. After his last visit, the king ordained a special visitor to the class, resulting in termination of the entire crew.

Jonathan wondered if the upcoming lesson would include another special visitor as well.

If so, they would be in for another wild ride.

He arrived at the outer courtyard and entered the majestic hall.

Statuesque figures, eighty feet tall with forty-foot high brass column pedestals lined the walls. The pedestals held large vases of spectacular flower arrangements.

Numerous banquet rooms branched from the hallway corridor. The rooms brandished marble floors with gold overlaid ceilings. Intricately decorated red and blue linen curtains hung in the portals.

A pure gold lampstand stood on each of the numerous beautifully crafted wooden tables, topped with delicacies.

Luxurious gold and silver transparent draperies hung across the arched windows, tied together five at a time.

Cherubim, made of pure gold, decorated the spaces above the ties.

With graceful lines, delicate, almost translucent, white porcelain pomegranates garlanded each side of the room.

Jonathan's soft shoes slid across the marble hall floor.

His gaze fixed on magnificent works of art on the corridor walls. He passed the doorways and glanced at the masses of people gathered around the tables.

Those of every race and nation, who had escaped the control of Nachash, congregated..

Jonathan overheard a proclamation, "Isn't He wonderful?"

"He is. We're fortunate to have a king that rules with such grace."

"What do you think he has in store for the future?"

Unfortunately, he couldn't hear the response.

He wished he knew what would happen next but even he, a timeless entrusted servant, didn't.

He stood at the doorway of the palatial room behind the angel who served as a Sergeant of Arms, and waited.

A mist enveloped the room. Often, the king's spirit manifested itself in this manner.

He peered around the angel's shoulder.

A halo of emerald color radiated behind the magnificent throne.

Soft red, orange, yellow, green, blue, indigo and violet rays glowed around a sapphire blue threshold.

He beheld the Ruler of the Realm and his son, Arnion.

Thunder pealed and lightning clashed. Jonathan remained courageous.

Near the throne stood living things, with eyes that covered their body in order to see in front and behind them.

They bowed continually.

Jonathan stood, awestruck, as the creatures cried out, "Holy, holy, holy Is God our Master, Sovereign-Strong, The Was, The Is, The Coming."

The guard announced, "Your Majesty, the angelic being, Jonathan."

A sensation, as if suspended in air, overcame him as he neared the throne.

He struggled to keep his body upright as he approached the magnificent chairs of the two monarchs.

Overwhelmed, he fell prostrate with his face to the ground.

The Ruler of the Realm spoke. His voice sounded like rushing water and at times, the king's voice made the earth tremble.

"It's good to see you, Jonathan."

He raised his head and stammered, "The honor is mine, my King."

"You may rise. I have instructions for you concerning the special emissaries which will be sent in the final days to open the seals and blow the trumpets."

"My King," he said as he stood up slowly.

"This is a special mission. The angelees will first be visited by one of my high angels."

The King continued, **"I will also allow an emissary from the enemy's camp to visit."**

Jonathan bowed in acknowledgement that he would oversee the coming trial. His chest heaved heavily as he sensed the privilege of this duty.

"Thank you, your Majesty. I know you will take into consideration the youthfulness of this group. They so lack experience and development compared to others in your service. But as always, I will endeavor to complete all of your wishes."

He bowed and waited for a response.

"Chosen are the foolish things to shame the wise and weak things to shame the strong. Therefore, the lowly things are chosen so that none can boast before me."

"My King."

"Go in peace."

Though invigorated with this new responsibility, Jonathan didn't want to leave the king's presence. Would his young angelees be able to withstand the task?

"Thank you, your Majesty."

His descent through the City seemed to take less time. He surveyed the city and thought about their Master.

How can one begin to comprehend what the extent of His knowledge is? It is unsearchable and goes beyond anything any mortal or spirit can imagine.

Jonathan surmised all should be well.

At least those on earth had time to prepare before the final blow of the trumpets.

He looked forward to meeting with the six ingénues again.

on the way 4

"Wait! Wait for me!" Elizabeth shouted.

She caught sight of her classmates long white robes sweeping behind them as they marched ahead.

Nathan, Shay, Abigail and Gordan, pronounced with a soft "J" sound, like Jordan, ambled down Boulevard Glorious on their way to their next session.

The angels in training were all about the same height, except for Shay. He stood about six inches shorter.

Elizabeth had earned her nickname, pokey.

She wished it stood for something regal like Pocahontas but it portrayed her daydreaming tendencies.

Her shouts to her colleagues went unheard.

She picked up her white robe and dashed down Gideon's Golden Fleece Pathway, exposing her calves.

Her face reddened and her cheeks resembled a polished peach with a deep orange-red glow.

She enjoyed the wind blowing through her long white hair and loved to run, although she couldn't keep up with the others.

Maybe someday I'll leave a swirl of power behind me. Maybe, if I race a human I'll disappear before their *eyes.*

White winged doves flew overhead. Elizabeth had halted as a small flock of warblers fluttered past.

She looked back at her own, motionless wings and remembered their instructor, Jonathan, promised they would all receive flight to their wings after their class today. As Jonathan phrased it, "you'll flit and flutter, like baby birds out of their nest."

The group of birds attempted to land on the slick golden street.

Their tiny legs skidded across the slippery surface. Finally coming to a rest, they scooted and picked at chunks of goodies for their fare.

One looked up, cocked its head to the right and to the left. Without notice, it flew to a garden on the other side, looked back and chirped wildly.

The tiny-feathered creatures filled her with delight until she realized the others had gone on without her.

Oh, my, I've done it again.

Nathan looked around. "Elizabeth's still on her way. We'd better wait."

His long flaxen hair glistened in the bright noonday light. Nathan's lake-blue eyes fixed a steady gaze on his fellow angelee, Pokey.

"There she goes again," Shay uttered.

His bluish-green eyes twinkled as he tucked his thumbs into the sash wrapped around his plump stomach.

His eyebrows moved in a Groucho Marx type fashion and he added, "The clue of the day is: Why is the shortest one ahead of one who's a head taller?"

His tease went unnoticed.

Unfazed, he stretched his hands out and wiggled his fingers.

He intended to exhibit their recently acquired flame throwing technique.

He couldn't wait. If he did it right, fire would propel from his hands and incinerate his intended object.

He vacillated between two nondescript bushes and chose the one on the right.

Without warning, another pair of hands covered his and pressed them away from his intended target.

"Don't get your curly mop of red hair fired up."

"Oh, shucks, Nathan, I just wanted to have a little fun while we waited for Elizabeth. Shouldn't she have a bright object to light her way and celebrate her being last?"

"The practice of ignition isn't for our pleasure. And, Elizabeth is not the last one. Someone else isn't with us."

Shay poked his chin around and counted heads. Nathan, himself, Abigail and Gordan made four, and Elizabeth added up to five. "You're right!" he exclaimed as if he made the discovery of the century. "Lev's not here! Has anyone seen him?"

Gordan shrugged his shoulders. Abigail followed suit and then Nathan. Shay followed and exclaimed, "I guess it's official. No one knows where he is."

Elizabeth reached the group, gasping with her hand to her chest.

"Oh my, oh my, I don't think I've run this much and this fast in all my existence! I'm out of breath from tip to toe."

She leaned over with her tongue hanging out of her mouth.

Abigail shook her finger. "Elizabeth, I can't understand why you're never on time. You know, when we're given assignments, we'll have to keep up with mortals." She watched to see if the stern approach worked.

Abigail and Elizabeth had alabaster skin and gray-blue eyes, but Abigail's blue-black tresses contrasted against Elizabeth's snowy white curls. Together, they reminded one of salt and pepper.

Upset for being off track with time, Elizabeth's expression seemed to say, *I know I goofed and I'm sorry.*

However, she didn't admit it and answered with exuberance, "Our assignments! Yes, I can't wait! You know they won't give us any they think we can't honor! I wonder if we'll be assigned to a mortal and maybe appear in his or her dream!"

Her face beamed and her eyes gleamed brighter.

Nathan cleared his throat. "We may be called to war."

Without acknowledging Nathan, Elizabeth continued. "I just can't wait! We might visit other planets and stars! Just think about it. I think I'm going to burst with delight!"

Abigail gave up and chimed in. "You're right Elizabeth. I can't wait either. By the way, have you seen Lev?"

"No, I haven't. Why, is there anything wrong?"

Nathan responded, "I don't think so. We noticed he wasn't

with us and as a rule he is prompt."

Her countenance flashed with a questioning look. She exclaimed, "Well, he has to be around somewhere."

She attempted to skip ahead of the others but Nathan caught her by the shoulder. "Elizabeth."

She turned. "What is it? Do you know where Lev is?"

"No, but I must issue a caution. You spoke about our assignments being fun, however, we may receive one which may be, and well … it may be difficult."

"I know, but I trust whatever we do will be admirable because we serve an honorable king and that's why we've been created." Her curls thrashed about her head as she bounced with enthusiasm.

Gordan came alongside. "You expounded on that excellently, Elizabeth."

"Yes, well said," she heard another.

Shay stood behind her with a curious smile. He thought about adding, "and thanks for bringing up the rear," but restrained himself. Instead, he nudged Abigail, and said in a cockney accent, "Ain't that right, Miss Abby?"

Abigail was usually unflappable. In fact, she kept the rest of the group from distractions.

On one occasion, Shay, Gordan and Nathan decided to play football with another group of angelees.

Abigail knew that they didn't have enough time and secondly, they had made a poor choice for their football.

They chose a vegetable similar to squash. It was the right size, but it had ripened too long.

Absorbed in the scrimmage, the players didn't think about what would happen if they missed a pass.

Abigail stood in the middle of the field, held one of her hands in the air and with the other, placed two fingers under her tongue and blew a high-pitched whistle.

The shrill sound jolted them and they came to an abrupt halt. She pointed to an imaginary watch on her wrist, tapped it and said, "Gentlemen, I'm calling a two-hour timeout in order to facilitate our appearance which is due in two minutes."

But this time, Shay unnerved her. She squared her shoulders, raised her chin, and in a cool tone responded, "Usually I agree with you, Master Shay but must I verbalize it also?"

She leaned close and whispered to Elizabeth, "Well said, Pokey."

"Thank you so much," Elizabeth answered. She glanced from one side to the other.

Where can Lev be? "Do you think Lev's already in class?" she asked as they turned and strolled along Pearl of Great Price Boulevard. No one seemed to know.

The troupe turned once again and headed down Mount Sinai Avenue.

As they climbed the hill, glorious colors streaked across the horizon.

"Look how beautiful *Reflections* are today," Abigail proclaimed.

The others stood silent beside her.

"I love when the rays from the king's throne echo against the wall's foundation gems."

"Yes, and the way they mirror against the smooth gates and return into the heavens." Nathan chimed.

Colors changed as they remained at the top of the hill. A kaleidoscope of hues – lavender, pale green, pink, yellow and blue filled the atmosphere.

"This is one of the most awesome displays I've seen," Gordan uttered.

The beauty calmed Shay. "We are fortunate to dwell here."

They drank in the dreamlike scene for a moment more.

Nathan cleared his throat. "We could stay all day but we really need to go."

Shay walked backwards as they marched to their class. "I heard we're having our instruction in the garden of Moses' home."

"Yes," Nathan agreed. "Jonathan most likely awaits us even now. I hope he doesn't have his arms crossed in front of his chest and his foot rapping the floor and I hope Lev is there. But if he isn't, I expect he has a good reason."

Elizabeth interjected, "I wish I knew why it happened."

"Why what happened?"

"Why did it have to go wrong in the Garden? They were so happy."

"The Garden is our example. Jonathan told us that it served as the foundation of humankind and their relationship with the Creator. When mankind began, man's response to the king's commands were documented, remember?"

"But it was perfect."

"Well," Nathan explained, "As I see it, when He 'formed man out of the dust of the ground ...'"

Adam, the Man appeared.

Tall and muscular, his reddish-brown skin complemented his chestnut-hued hair.

Groggy, he awoke, and remembered the Creator told him a deep sleep would come over him for a short time.

He tended his domain named Eden. It meant delicate, delight, and pleasure – a perfect description.

The Garden exemplified paradise on earth, a model of the Creator's celestial home.

It displayed His handiwork.

Before, an empty wasteland covered the sphere in total darkness.

The Ruler of the Realm uttered the word "light," and darkness fled before Him like a stampede of wild stallions.

Adam's pale blue eyes searched the horizon for his creature friends. He gazed deeply into the sun as its rays filtered through the trees.

Birds sang and monkeys, springing from branch to branch, rattled and rustled.

A tiny bird came and flit its wings in front of his face.

He chuckled. "Good morning, little hummingbird." He had named all the creatures. This little one was a favorite.

The river shimmered with silvery peaks as it flowed past.

It seemed quieter than usual.

Adam moved to the bank, knelt and splashed water on his face. Perhaps a refreshing spray might awaken him.

He took a quick drink. The cool moist swallow satisfied him

right away.

He focused on the highest tree towering above him.

He wondered what it would be like to be lifted, high in the sky.

He heard a call, "**Adam, where are you?**"

Joy surged through him as the voice beckoned to him.

"I'm here, Father. I've been asleep," he called back.

He peered into the mist and watched as two figures approached.

The one he called Father and another being, unfamiliar to him came near. The creature with his Father walked upright on two legs.

Adam remained speechless and then cleared his throat. His voice cracked. "Fa … ther."

"**I've brought someone to see you.**"

"Yes, I see. But you've brought … brought me many creatures."

"**Adam, you know I created all of the sea creatures and birds and every beast of the field and there wasn't a suitable helper for you.**"

He heard the words faintly as he stared at the wonderful vision before him. He shook his head and in amazement, walked around the creature.

"**When you slept, I took a rib from your side and formed your helpmate. But you must remember what I told you about the trees.**"

He stared, captivated, and once again strolled on all sides. When he came around the second time, he stopped. Their eyes met.

He placed his hand on her shoulder. A slight blush rushed across her face and she returned the gesture.

Then Adam did something strange. He leaned forward, brushed his lips across her cheek, and put his hand on her stomach.

She looked at his strong hand.

"You have a womb," he said, "you're like me, but you have a womb."

They stood beneath the tree. Clouds drifted across the sky creating soft shadows.

Adam drew a deep breath and declared, "This is now bone of my bones and flesh of my flesh: she shall be called Woman, because she came from man."

Love bloomed as they gazed and drank in each other's existence.

They were not aware they were the cradle of civilization or that humanity would emerge from them. Nor were they aware of the test that would affect every man, woman and child born thereafter.

Life would never be the same. An altered destiny and an eternity, poles apart from the original plan, would transpire.

broken commandments 5

Wind whipped the sides of Doug's automobile. He steered away from the worst of the storm and pounded his fist on the dash with glee. "I knew I could get through it."

Then he saw a single bright beam. The brightness intensified, and Doug leaned closer.

It headed straight for him, and horror struck.

He jerked the steering wheel, but his efforts to turn were lost as the waterlogged street refused to surrender.

His body stiffened. He closed his eyes and yelled, "God!"

His body plummeted through the air, as if liquid sucked through a straw. He gasped and everything went black.

Stifling heat enveloped him as he regained consciousness.

A dark coal-colored blanket surrounded him.

Thick silence presided until a sharp knife-like shriek shattered the atmosphere. He sprang upright with a wild look in his eyes.

Stillness followed. It reminded him of a late-night walk he took through a cemetery. He had hoped to find his father's headstone, although he didn't know why.

"Who's out there?" The question sounded ridiculous. Moments passed without a response. "Is someone there?"

Time lapsed by, then he heard a moan.

"Who's there? Can you hear me?"

More silence.

Doug struggled to recall what had happened.

He remembered his body seemed to funnel through the air. *Could it have been a tornado?* The possibility fascinated him.

Another bounding half-human, half-animal howl exploded. He vaulted to see where it came from. The black curtain of darkness surrounding him made it impossible to see.

"Okay, Doug, be rational," he said aloud. "You could have fallen into a cave. That would explain the strange noises. You may have been out for a while, which is a good thing. A rescue party is probably on the way."

Wouldn't that be something if a tornado hit right at the time of the accident? It's a wonder I didn't die.

He stood and shifted his weight from one side to the other. Moments slipped by and with each passing one, his optimism faded. Thoughts of Larry crept in.

Larry! STUPID Larry, it's all his fault. If it weren't for him, I wouldn't have had to hide the files. That would have changed everything.

He sat, pulled his legs against his chest, wrapped his arms around them and rocked back and forth. The swaying motion reminded him of the chair on the front porch of his house.

The size of the town appealed to him the most and the way folks took pride in their small berg, particularly seasonal displays.

Doug thought they kept it interesting. Spring decorations presented pink and white Easter bunnies, although Talbert Park, which consisted of a square block, brimmed with children for the annual egg hunt.

In summer, vibrant planters dangled from light posts, depositing a sweet aroma to the air.

Fall exhibits, along with autumn leaves scattered in the streets, involved pumpkins, decorative orange and black cats and straw scarecrows greeted shoppers. The townspeople like to go all out.

Christmas dressed its best. Porcelain angels replaced scarecrows and lights twinkled in store windows.

"Alright," Casey Murray would say, "how much am I bid for this gem of an ornament?"

The prize consisted of whatever price it fetched. The town's setting offered an appealing assurance.

Something scuttled across his foot. He jumped and stood in a boxer's stance with his eyes flaring and clenched fists.

He glanced down and tapped his foot. *It's a rock. How did I get on top of a rock?*

He touched his face. *My glasses, where are they?* Then he reached and patted his foot. *Where are my shoes?*

Austin and Anna scurried into the lobby at St. Luke's and made their way to the family waiting room.

Anna poured over the crowded room searching for a spot to settle in. As she searched the chairs, something caught her attention.

A woman, about seventy-years old, sat with hands folded in her lap.

She wore a pink organdy dress and patent leather shoes resembling a young girl's baby doll. With light blonde hair, combed into ringlets, rouge and heavy lipstick, she sat with a quizzical expression on her face.

She glanced at Anna and then looked away quickly. If the season were Halloween, there could have been an explanation but the end of summer ticked away on schedule. Anna yearned to know her story.

Anna found her sister in a corner, sitting on the edge of her chair with hair uncombed, wearing a loose housedress.

Though only a few years younger, Mackinsey's figure appeared matronly.

Mackinsey stood and embraced Anna and Austin. Her grip tightened as she released her relief.

Anna drew back and looked at her pensively. "What did they tell you about Becky?"

"They said it was an overdose."

Anna clutched her chest. "I'm so sorry."

"But they said she's going to pull through," Mackinsey added quickly.

"Have you been able to see her yet?" Austin asked.

"No, but it won't be too long."

"Thank the Lord," Anna whispered.

"I'm grateful she's alive," Mackinsey responded with a shaky smile.

Austin held Mackinsey in a brotherly-hug. "You know, it's probably going to be awhile. Why don't I go and get some coffee?"

Mackinsey grasped Anna's hand as they sat, both perched on the lip of their seats.

After a pensive moment, Mackinsey stated, "I'm glad we prayed earlier. If we hadn't, I don't think I would have the strength to be here. As I drove, these words popped into my head."

"What was it?"

"It was about how He created all things. I don't know why, but I kept thinking about it and the more I did, a deeper sense of peace came over me."

"I think …"

"Mrs. Porter? You can go in and see your daughter now."

The women bounded from their chairs and headed down the hall. An odor of oxygen permeated the wide, sterile-like hospital corridor. Mackinsey continued seemingly impervious to the smell, glancing into each room they slipped past.

They approached Rebecca's room and the nurse announced, "You can see her for a few minutes." She turned on her heel and walked away.

Mackinsey walked slowly into the room and pulled the half-drawn curtain aside.

Becky lay helpless in the bed, with tubes attached to her arm. Mackinsey leaned over and kissed her daughter's forehead.

"Mom?"

"Yes, Becky. Don't try to talk."

"I'm glad you're here."

"I'm here and Aunt Anna and Uncle Austin are too."

Anna walked guardedly to the other side. She didn't know what to say but managed to utter, "How're you feeling?"

"Pretty stupid, right now." Her words sounded muddled through her thick tongue.

Mackinsey stayed close. She searched her daughter's face. "I'm happy to see you're alright."

"Can we get you anything?" Anna asked.

She shook her head and uttered a weak, "No."

"Was anyone else with you?" Mackinsey asked.

She frowned as she thought about what happened. "I think . . . I think Pam was."

"Pam?" Anna and Mackinsey looked at each other. "Who's Pam?"

"I am."

Startled, they turned to see who spoke. A large black man leaned against the doorway. He wore dark gray slacks, a red shirt, and a black full-length coat. With his hands in his pockets, he looked calm, unflustered.

"You're Pam?" Mackinsey asked.

"Yeah, that's my name." He sauntered into the room, stopped at the foot of the bed and said, "How're ya doin' Beck."

Rebecca flipped her hand from side to side. "So-so."

Mackinsey and Anna, opposite from one another, gawked into each other's faces.

Mackinsey's nerve rose. "Were you with Rebecca last night?"

His eyes remained steadfast on Rebecca. He shook his head in affirmation. "Yeah, we were together for awhile," he drawled.

Rebecca's body squirmed in her hospital bed. "Mom, Pam's a good guy. He watches my back."

"Then why did this happen to you? Mackinsey said softly.

"You know, ma'am ..."

"You can call me Mrs. Porter."

"Yeah, Mrs. Porter, you can't tell when something's gonna go down, you know what I mean? There's so much stuff out there, it's kind of like playing Russian roulette."

"Then why do it?"

Quiet loomed like a concrete block penetrating the room.

Austin whistled in through the doorway. "Hi everyone."

The women stared at him. He set the coffee down and gazed back. "I'm sorry; I didn't know Rebecca had another guest. I would have brought another cup of coffee."

"Don't sweat it," Pam replied.

Austin extended his hand. "Austin Connor, her uncle."

Pam didn't move. He glanced down to Austin's shoes and then back up again.

"Name's Pam."

He shifted his feet and in one quick second, exclaimed, "Hey, girl, I'm glad to see you're doing okay but I gotta run. I just came by to see what was up."

He held the toe of her foot gently, nodded in Austin's direction and then strolled out.

Mackinsey's eyes followed him as he left and then she threw her hands up in the air. "Where did this guy come from and why do they call him Pam?"

Becky's face revealed a slight smirk. "It's his nickname from the streets because he thinks he's slick."

"Oh," Mackinsey grunted.

"You've got him all wrong. If it weren't for him, I wouldn't be here. The last thing I remember, Pam had his hand on my face and shook me as he called my name. I know he must have called 911."

Mackinsey stood in a stupor.

What if no one had called? What if this man had arrived an hour later?

A shiver went down her spine. "I see," she said weakly.

She stood quietly for a moment, grateful the worst had not happened.

"Rebecca, I know you owe a lot to Pam but I believe prayer had a lot to do with it."

"Sure, Mom, whatever. I think I need some rest if that's okay with you."

"I love you hon."

She didn't respond.

The awkward silence made Mackinsey uneasy. She glanced at Anna and Austin and motioned for them to go. They tiptoed out.

When they neared the waiting room, Austin proposed they go in for a minute. "I want to talk to you about something, okay?"

"Sure."

The threesome found a quiet corner.

Anna noticed the woman in the pink organdy dress had left.

"I wanted to tell you," Austin explained, "when I went to the nurses' station, I told them I was a doctor and Becky's uncle. I asked for her chart. Becky's lips and fingernails were blue from shock when she first arrived and they revived her."

Mackinsey's head fell with a forward motion. "I thought she felt clammy."

"She doesn't understand," he continued. "She could have had cardiac arrest and never woken up. She would have drifted off and who knows where ..."

"I know," Mackinsey said quietly. Anna put her arm around her and held her.

"I'm sorry," Austin said, "but I thought you needed to know how serious it was, so you could talk to her."

"I don't think she'll listen to what I have to say. Becky's been away from home for a while. I don't know why, but I believe she'll be all right. Thank you both for being here with me."

"We wouldn't have it any other way," Austin responded.

"Are you sure you're all right?"

"Yes. I'll be fine now. God bless you both. I'll call you tomorrow or if anything new happens."

Anna and Austin held hands as they strolled back to the car.

"Do you think this will make a difference for Becky?"

Austin lifted his eyes and he peered into the dark night.

The heavens spread before him like a planetary exhibition. Bright stars sparkled above.

He followed a flash of light flickering across the sky. "Yeah, see."

"What?"

"A star exploded. That must be a sign. Maybe it's an angel telling us everything's going to be fine."

"Yes, well, at least Becky's alive and the call wasn't to identify her body."

special visitors 6

Elizabeth lingered, mesmerized with her vision of the first man, Adam, and the woman Eve.

She felt a tug on her robe.

"What?"

"Com'n, wake up," Nathan remarked. "No wonder you're always late. I walked along, talking about our last class, and the next thing I knew you were behind us, staring at a tree. Come on, I'm sure Jonathan's begun class already."

"I'm sorry, truly, I am."

"Honestly, it's a wonder you get anywhere," he muttered as he tugged at her elbow and quickened the pace.

She galloped the stairs two by two, trying to keep up with him. "That's right! We begin our special class today. I'm soooo excited," she squealed.

They arrived at the largest mansion on the boulevard.

Columns graced the front portico, which lead to a glass prism doorway.

Nathan and Elizabeth trotted through a huge gate on the side, onto the grounds of the outdoor garden.

As they entered, they stood in amazement. Three of the others were there. One of them exclaimed, "Inconceivable!"

Three levels of pools cascaded into a delicate waterfall. Gazebos stood on each level, with pockets of tawny grasses tucked between them.

Large trees shaded much of the garden with tête-à-tête benches nestled beneath the trees.

White chiseled statues adorned the sides of the pools with backdrops of eye-catching pink and white shiny-waxed begonias tumbling over the walls. A bed of violet and blue flowers surrounded the outer edge of the grounds.

The angelees remained motionless as they listened to the restful sound of the falls. Then they burst into a traffic jam of chatter.

"I've seen beauty before …:

"How come I haven't seen …"

"Where was I when …"

Their babble ended abruptly when they realized their instructor, Jonathan, stood beside them, with his arms folded across his chest. "I wondered where my squadron could have disappeared to and I see five of you have made it."

"We were admiring this splendid array of horticulture," Shay said in a professor type manner.

"Of course. I hope I'm not mistaken about my initial opinion about this group. I've said this squadron is as good, if not better than the others are. Even though there is no "peer" structure in place, my commendation for the job you all have done thus far should make you feel good. I have thought highly of my former classes but there is something special about this group. I can feel it in my wings."

They mumbled to one another and entered the classroom. Thus far, they had taken three courses. Jonathan gazed at the zealous students as they situated themselves in their chairs, set in a semi-circle. Shafts of light filtered through from the trellis above, casting a golden hue in the room.

Jonathan eagerly announced, "Well, students, today's class promises to be challenging."

"Yes," Nathan replied. "Are we waiting for Lev?"

Jonathan peered at the seated child-like angels. "That's odd he's not here. Does anyone know his whereabouts?"

The angelees gazed at one another. Jordan spoke up. "Well, no, we don't. We thought you'd know where he was."

❖

Lev's cry grew faint as he tumbled helplessly through the

cosmos.

Flashes of light continued to flicker past him as he plunged further into the dark void.

His lifeless wings and robe flapped around him, resembling a parachute jumper in freefall with outspread hands and feet.

It never occurred to him until now he could be lost in space.

He gathered his strength and shouted with every force of his being, "HELP!"

Suddenly, a billowy surface enveloped him. "What's this?" He stammered.

Turning, he found his newfound friend. "Sunergos am I glad to see you!"

"I haven't lost anyone yet."

"How did you find me?"

"Good fortune, I guess. I have to say, you gave me a fright. There are devouring black holes out here."

Lev had heard about the monstrous regions in space. "I guess I am fortunate! Aren't they millions times larger than the earth's Sun?"

"They can be billions times larger. That would have been a terrible fate."

Lev thought about the sun and earth.

His curiosity centered on the special globe, earth.

Out of all creation, the home of mortals in their initial life held a special place in the heart of the Ruler of the Realm.

"It appears blue because of the surface waters. It's also called the Blue Marble."

Lev liked the idea of a marble, crystalline and unbreakable. However, he knew earth would not last forever.

In the lessons he and his comrades attended, they learned of an evil plan initiated by Nachash to misguide mortals and keep them from their eternal habitat. The battle existed and raged for eons. Nachash's objectives resulted in horrendous episodes and catastrophes.

Lev and Sunergos moved at a rapid speed, their course illuminated by celestial bodies and solar dust.

They approached the outer atmosphere of their homeland.

Hardly discernible from earth because of interstellar gas obstruction, when visible Qodesh appeared as one bright blue object.

Scientists knew the triple-star system as LBV 1806.

The vivid beam caused Lev to close his eyes. *I hope Sunergos has his open.*

Warmth from stars around him flooded his back and the tilting motion made him drowsy. He remembered his recent fall through space, tossed his head and shook it off.

Alert, his eyes became accustomed to a darting light racing by him. As they neared their objective, their speed increased.

The most extraordinary experience Lev has ever had mingled his thoughts.

The voyage helped him understand the scale of the incredible Universe the King created. Love for his Master swelled within.

His heart pounded faster as they neared the base of the city. *I can't wait to tell the others!*

Magnificent mansions peaked from the middle of the celestial city, reaching into the stratum. A massive wall surrounded the city, making it appear like a gigantic white fortress.

The wall's support consisted of twelve types of precious stones. The first base consisted of jasper, but not the clear type like the wall, but a dramatic green jewel.

Next, a deep and beckoning blue sapphire and copper-like chalcedony followed.

Emerald's green dazzle came fourth and sardonyx and blood red Sardis composed the fifth and sixth rows.

Seventh was chrysolyte, also known as peridot. A bluish green colored beryl adjoined and ninth, a pale green topaz.

The last three foundations were a yellowish green chrysoprasus, a dark blue, verging on black jacinth, and a brilliant purple amethyst.

The stones were similar to those in the breastplate of the Older Kingdom High Priest's. The last row of the High Priest's garment, jasper, mirrored the first foundation of the wall, like a continuation of their Kingdom.

From the center, the next set of buildings pyramided down. The pattern repeated, in calculated dimensions, resulting in a skyline that resembled a majestic bow, from one end of the city to the other.

As well as order and beauty, the shape facilitated minimal travel time in the huge municipality.

Lev soared through the atmosphere clinging to Sunergos. They arrived as a mist dispersed over the city, revealing a lustrous, glistening City, as bright as a star.

Sunergos glided effortlessly over the wall and descended slowly as he landed exactly at the same place where they took off.

"What an awesome trip," Lev said grasping Sunergos' hand.

"I'm glad it wasn't too memorable."

They spoke a few more minutes, and then Lev watched Sunergos lift off the ground.

He sauntered through the city and joy flooded his soul. Memories of his wonder-filled flight permeated his being. He had mixed emotions now that his excursion in space ended. He looked forward to his session today but visions of the incredible sights he encountered burned within.

Birds chirped happily in the trees while others flew in and around the palaces. As far as one could see, fields of flora covered the ground from the edge of the city to the border of the wall. Flowers curiously popped through the ground to see what event took place: roses, peonies, buttercups, carnations, orchids, gardenias, tulips, daisies, and delphinium, to name a few, released perfumed aromas into the air. A glorious sight of row upon row of colorful blooms in full display filled the landscape with pathways between them so all could walk among them. *Our city is glorious. I'm so glad I'm here.*

Lev realized time had elapsed and he hurried along. *I wonder where the others are. And they're probably wondering where I am.*

He chuckled to himself. *I'm going to have a blast telling them about my ride with Sunergos.*

Animals roamed the outskirts and mingled together in harmony.

It would take thousands of years to domesticate a wild animal completely on earth and then there would be no guarantee the creatures would not revert to their fallen nature. Here, it occurred naturally.

A huge Grizzly played with a kitten and long legged

giraffes safely drank at the river without fear of attack from lions or hyenas. Even the mighty white tiger stalked no one for the king declared, **"The creatures shall not hurt or destroy in all My Holy Mountain."** With his proclamation, fear of pain, tears, and death no longer held their grip.

Music filled Lev's ear as he hurried along the boulevard. At first, melodic sounds from an exquisite voice, singing strains of a beautiful melody saturated the air.

He continued as musicians played a concerto in the plaza. The tones drifted throughout the streets.

Lev picked up his pace. *Gosh, I'm going to be late for the very first time. I hope Jonathan understands.*

"We'll have to get started without him," Jonathan stated.

Shay wiggled into his chair and announced, "I'm hungry."

He peered to see if anyone had brought some food.

"You're always hungry," Gordan responded.

"I could go for some milk or cheese right now."

He rubbed his stomach and licked his lips with the vision of how delicious even a morsel of this scrumptious snack would taste.

"Don't you want some manna to go with it or how about sautéed purple bananas?" Nathan teased.

At the sound of the delectable offerings, Shay's eyes widened. "Or Minglings! That would be great!"

Minglings were a type of fruit prepared by dipping in honey and baking until the honey crusted in a finely crystallized cover.

"And Gordan can fix a wonderful sauce to go with it," Nathan prodded. "Man, no one can make anything better except if they add a loaf of baked bread on the side. Perfect."

"Maybe Lev will bring you some," Jonathan chimed.

A look crossed Shay's face as he realized they were joking. He decided to change the subject. "Where is Lev, anyway?" Before anyone could answer, he changed the subject again. "Hey, my man, Jon, how's it goin'?"

Jonathan chuckled. Shay's colloquialism's always entertained him. Everyone else could take them or leave them but they amused Jonathan.

"Well, young Master Shay, it is 'going' just fine. And has it gone anywhere for you today?"

"Yes, Jon. In fact, I guess I'd say I'm quite 'gone'."

"And did Elizabeth keep you today?"

"Uh, yes, she did. You know, it's amazing how Elizabeth gazes into space. That wouldn't go too well if we had an important message and it didn't get delivered in time."

The air seemed motionless after he uttered these words.

Shay waited, and then immediately addressed Jonathan. Perhaps he wouldn't notice his *faux pas*.

"Jonathan, maybe Lev's here but he's made himself imperceptible."

"If he were here and made himself invisible, I would know it," Jonathan replied. "It is unusual though. I'm used to him being the first one present. Knowing him, he's probably out there trying to help someone."

Shay's eyes widened and his mouth opened as he formed the letter "o."

Jonathan continued. "And regarding Elizabeth's tardiness, perhaps, the fault lies with the star from which she was birthed."

His ears perked at the mention of their creation. They had never discussed their origins, although they surmised they probably came from a star.

The sacred writings said, "when the morning stars sang together, and all the sons of God shouted for joy'?" and "There shall come a Star out of Jacob," which they knew was the son of the king.

Shay leapt from his chair and gulped. "Her star? Why? What star did she come from? Is it a close one? I know it's an honor to be associated with heavenly bodies, but, wow, tell me all about it."

Jonathan chuckled. "Yes. Well, we'll have to discuss it some time, now won't we?"

"Discuss it sometime? Uh, well, why not now, OKAY?"

As if he didn't hear, Jonathan stood at his podium nonchalantly rearranging his papers.

Shay would not be shuffled aside. "Jonathan, you know everything, I mean e-v-e-r-y, everything. Com'n, spill the beans."

"Spill the beans? Jonathan laughed quietly again. "Shay,

Shay, Shay," he said shaking his head. "You surely pick up the most modern vernaculars. Is it because you're listening to the immortals so intently or because of the star from which you were fashioned?"

"My Star! All right Jonathan, now you're talking. What Galaxy am I from? Is my star out there? What's my P.O.O.?"

Jonathan smiled. "Your P.O.O.? Whatever do you mean?"

"My Place-of-Origin. Com'n, Jon. You can't just get me going like this!"

The instructor let out a good hearty laugh and then gave Shay a 'calm down and don't have a hissy-fit' look. "I can see you're quite interested in this star talk and, of course, in your P.O.O. Let's see if you can keep your interest during our next class and perhaps we'll discuss it then. Moreover, if we don't get to it by the end of this class another time will have to suffice. When I said this class would be a memorable one, I'm referring to the events we have scheduled at the end of class. However, I've been informed we have special visitors slated for a visit."

The angelees sprang to attention and sat with their hands in their lap, like overgrown schoolchildren.

Jonathan surveyed the angels gathered around him in the classroom.

He cleared his throat and announced, "Welcome, angelees. It's an honor to have you in class once again. As you all know, we're here to carry on with your education. Before we proceed, we are going to have a review to make sure we're all up to snuff."

A collective "nooooo" erupted from the group, interrupted by a flurry of jabbered words. Shay, excited about the prospect of finding out about his origin, chattered about various stars. The rest discussed their understanding they were going to launch into a new course.

"That's disappointing," Nathan said.

"I thought this would be an unforgettable class," Abigail offered with a pout.

Gordan piped, "We didn't think we would do another review, Jonathan."

"We'll never get back to finding out about our stars," Shay whined.

Lev had not arrived yet. Though the group had been together a short time, he endeared himself in a short space of time. His overabundant compassion, love and tenderness made him special.

Gordan cleared his throat. "Excuse me, Master Jonathan."

"Yes, I know, Lev hasn't arrived as of yet. We just need to be a little more patient."

As he concluded his sentence, Lev walked in, with a curious smile on his face.

Shay rose to his feet and stood with his hands on his hips. "Where have you been?"

He held his hands up and exclaimed, "Guys, I just had the most fantastic experience!"

Together they responded in a chorus. "What?"

"On my way to class today I met a young girl, about five years old. A carrying angel named Daniel transported her from earth. He may have been new because he didn't seem sure what he his next step should be. The little girl had that look on her face, you know, that awestruck look mortals get when they first arrive. Anyway, her parents had left earth a few days before, along with her sister. The angel who brought her was a little confused and of course, she didn't know what to do. I just happened to stumble upon them and there they were."

Nathan stood close to Lev. "So what happened?"

"I found them!" Lev exclaimed.

"Oh," they drawled in unison.

"How did you do it?"

"It was neat, Abigail." Lev said with a tremendous smile. "I met Sunergos, a transporting angel, a couple of days ago. He had transported a couple and a young girl. Then today I ran into Daniel with this other young girl and he said he was going to look for her parents. I thought, there has to be some association. In my spirit, I had a strong feeling about their relationship. Then Sunergos appeared and confirmed my hunch."

"What happened then?"

"We transported her."

"Where did you take her?"

"We flew to the edge of our galaxy and it was awesome. I

saw stars, asteroids, planets and meteors. It was incredible."

"You flew?" Elizabeth said. "How did you do that?"

"Oh, I went on Sunergos' back and he held the young girl in his arms. What a ride! We reunited them on the planet Tobe."

The prospect of traveling through the cosmos invigorated them. "Awesome," they repeated to one another.

"Yes. But I did have a scare."

They stopped abruptly, unaccustomed to the idea of fright.

"What do you mean?" Shay said.

"Well, I ... sort of ... slipped off Sunergos' back."

"What did you do?" Nathan said.

"I fell."

An outburst of laughter permeated the room until Lev held his hands up and said, "No, I must say, I was fortunate Sunergos found me in the vast spread of space. I'm amazed he did. He's quite good. Think about it. This all happened because I ran into Sunergos and made his acquaintance just a couple of days ago. What a coincidence."

Jonathan looked up, pursed his lips, and said, "I don't think coincidence is the term, Lev. These things rarely are."

Lev thought a moment. "Of course," he said, as he snapped his fingers. "You know, it's cool how things are orchestrated."

"Yes it is, Lev," Jonathan said. "Now, how am I going to get this class back into a receptive frame of mind after all this?"

Elizabeth blurted, "Lev, you're so sweet, you're like butter and sugar."

The angelee looked sheepishly around. The group exploded and howled, "Ooooh, butter and sugar," teasing him mercilessly. His face reddened.

Jonathan tapped the podium.

Abigail waved her hand vigorously. "Jonathan. Sir." The classroom filled with a commotion so loud, one could barely hear her.

He tapped harder a couple of more times. "Class. Please, let's have some order." After a moment, calm began to transcend among the rumpus.

"Yes, Abigail?"

"Well, dear Instructor Jonathan, now that Lev is here, we can most likely continue."

Jonathan glanced up but held his tongue.

She continued. "I thought we were to resume this class with new material. As you know, you told us this was to be our most important classes. Could it, by chance, have to do with receiving flight power to our wings?"

"Patience, patience," Jonathan said as he walked to the front of his podium. "First we are to have some special guests, whom you have not made an acquaintance as of yet." Then he added, "And yes, flight will be awarded at the end of this session."

Flight. They sprang into the air and yelled in unison, "Flight! Right on," they shouted.

The commotion resumed to a higher level than before.

Shay tramped up and down with his fist in the air. "Yahoo!" He shouted like a cowboy at a stampede.

Jonathan tapped the podium energetically but they babbled among themselves relentlessly.

"Did you hear that?" they chattered in exhilaration. Lev's grin broadened.

"Quiet, quiet, down please," Jonathan said as he tried to institute some sense of composure. "Please, Teleiotes Squadron, we have to settle down so we can go on."

One by one they sat in their chairs, which looked minuscule compared to their size. They beamed at one another other, pleased with the good news. Finally, quiet prevailed.

Jonathan turned to Shay. "And Shay, you may be interested to know, one of our speakers originates from the same star you do."

Shay bounded in the air again, put his hands over his head and snapped his fingers like a flamenco dancer. "Cucamonga, Cucamonga, from my star! Who is he? Is he as tall as me?" He wound like a top. "I'm going to meet someone from my star? Whooooo!" he wailed like a train. "That's the sound of my train, comin' home. You know I love trains. Whooooo, whooooo!"

Jonathan closed his eyes a moment and then opened them again, slowly. "Yes, well, we'll see how far we get with our discussion young Shay. Now let's settle down, please everyone.

This is a serious portion of your instruction."

Sitting in their chairs, they jostled high fives amongst themselves. The hearty news warmed them. All was well and they felt as if they were on top of the mountain. It couldn't get any better.

A gust of wind rushed into the yard without warning and a brilliant light appeared directly behind Jonathan. The light intensified until their vision became impaired.

When their eyes adjusted, the most beautiful luminous form with white wings large enough to embrace them all stood before them.

They were awestruck and didn't utter a word but sat with their mouths gaping wide open.

The essence smiled, turned slowly and looked intently at each of them. He knew of their existence from the time they began their instructions.

Jonathan observed their look of wonderment and knew their first guest had appeared. He turned and bowed in acknowledgement to the creature that entered from behind.

"Class," he announced, "I would like you all to meet our first special honored guest. This," Jonathan said reverently, "is the highly honored Arch-angel, Gabriel."

The trainees gasped. They had learned about Gabriel and revered what they'd ascertained. This was almost like having an audience with the Ruler of the Realm.

Gabriel's wings swooped behind him slowly and came to rest. His face gleamed so bright, it was hard to see his features. He placed his hand on Shay's head. Shay's body wobbled as a rush of glory went through him. Next, Gabriel turned and set his hand on Lev's shoulders. Glorious tones emitted, as he spoke. "**I am pleased to be with you here this morning, young angelees. I've come to impart wisdom to you in all you do. I've come also to give you understanding in your achievements and strength in your trials.**"

The magnificence of his presence and his words charged through Lev like a bolt, rendering him unable to respond.

The squadron remained enraptured by the visitation and they gazed at the marvelous angel, who stood in the presence of the Ruler of the Realm and His Son, daily.

They had received instruction about how Gabriel appeared to Daniel and to Zechariah long ago on earth and carried the message to a young girl named of Mary.

Shay attempted to speak, but Gabriel continued. **"Blessings to you children."**

He disappeared before their eyes in a dazzling gust of wind. They gazed longingly to see if they could by chance catch a glimpse of him again.

No one spoke for several moments. Then Shay meekly said, "Am I from the same star as Gabriel?"

"No, Shay you aren't," Jonathan replied.

the review begins 7

In a euphoric state, Shay blurted an unintelligible sentence, his face lighting as he spoke.

Jonathan laughed softly. "I see you're speaking in your angelic tongue. I suspect you'll interpret so that edification will occur, as mortals do. Or are you speaking to edify yourself?"

A sheepish expression shadowed Shay's countenance. He surveyed the rest of the group to see if Nathan or anyone else noticed what had happened. Nathan busily talked to Abigail and Elizabeth. Gordan and Lev remained active in conversation.

Shay surmised this might be his only opportunity and leaned forward. "Psssssst. Hey, Jonathan."

Jonathan looked up. "Yes, Shay, what is it now?"

"Well, I apologize, I know I got carried away but wouldn't this be a great time for us to practice our fire power?"

With an eager expression, his fingers wiggled and he licked his lips like a child in a confectionary factory.

The mighty angels possessed the gift and ever since Shay received it, he could hardly contain himself. "Com'n Jonathan, I want to liven things up and go 'Whoosh.'" His eyes widened at the thought of how glorious it would be. "You know, like, like …"

Jonathan's arms folded across his chest. He looked sternly at Shay. "The only reason I don't chastise you for this master Shay," Jonathan said quietly, "is because your motive is not one of malice or retaliation. As you know, the disciples wanted the power to destroy men who had rejected the Son. They believed if they used Elijah's name, the Son would consent. Instead, he reprimanded them. This power is not given lightly nor is it for jest but it is to be used when the king's Son calls you to use it."

"Yes, sir, I understand," he answered meekly. He looked around. Nathan had stopped his conversation with Elizabeth and Abigail and waved his finger at him as he mouthed the words, "I told you so."

"So be it," Jonathan announced. "Now, we must get on track with our class." He looked beyond the angelees toward the back gate and saw the other guest had arrived.

The guest stood behind the group of pupils for some time, awaiting acknowledgement. Jonathan nodded for him to join the group.

He proceeded to come forward and Abigail looked back. "Oh!" She cried out startled.

Shay peered over his right shoulder to see why Abigail's white face had waned even more. "Whoa!" he exclaimed.

The others turned, one by one. A strange figure hobbled toward Jonathan's podium. The young novices spun around and fixed their eyes on Jonathan, their teacher and benefactor.

"Please, come in and sit with us," Jonathan said, "We've reserved a place for you in front."

He moved with a strange gait. He passed by the shocked angelees and his weight shifted from side to side: left, right, and left. They sat stunned.

Dressed in black, his garment contrasted theirs sharply. The sight of him repulsed them. He resembled a huge crow with smooth, slick black wings that appeared as humps hung on each side.

Words written in another language covered him and he reeked of a strange odor. It would have been improper to hold their nose and so they refrained from being rude.

The creature turned toward Jonathan, bowed a short bow and sat next to the podium, facing the group. They were eye-level now.

Instead of beautiful almond-shaped eyes the angelees were accustomed to, he had two narrow slits. They revealed dingy gray pupils. The whites of his eyes were mustard yellow.

62

"It's good of you to invite me Jonathan," the guest drawled with slurred speech. His mouth contained a thick, saliva-type liquid, making it difficult for him to talk. He continued. "Even though this is tedious for me, I'm pleased to come and see what I may glean, I mean gather."

'Being glad' might have been the least expected comment. He came from a place of darkness. When he went on his missions, it exposed him to light and it had a peculiar effect on him. In one way, he longed to be in the light but he also hated it because he knew he couldn't stay there. The dilemma tormented him.

"You'll have to excuse me Jonathan, my eyes aren't accustomed to all of this light," he added.

Jonathan gestured for him to proceed with a wave of his hand.

"I do have a question."

"And what would that be?" Jonathan replied.

"I know this is a special class and this squadron is one of the most elite, so to speak, of squadrons," he replied, "if they weren't, would I be here? But, my question is this: Is there a way we can dispense with the review this time?"

"Dispense with the review? No, I don't think so. You know we have the review to refresh our candidates. So, both apologetically, and at the same time, happily I must say, no, we cannot dispense with the review." Jonathan glanced at the podium quickly and shifted his papers.

The specter replied, "Well, as I said I know this is a most elite squadron and you, Jonathan, are the best instructor there is to teach this unique class. I've never asked before and I wouldn't ask now but as you know, I've attended these instructions for some time."

"Yes, I know."

"Well, I've reviewed and reviewed and reviewed and I guess I would have to say, I'm tired of it. Not tired exactly, but well, you know Jonathan you've been through this, as many times as I have and it would save time. It seems we could at least dispense of it this one time. You can't blame me, can you?"

"Blame doesn't lie with me and as far as getting tired is

concerned, I've taught this review every time you've been here and I find it *more* intriguing each time. That's all I have to say."

The visitor's murky eyes stared at Jonathan.

"As I said, we will commence with the review." The proclamation seemed definite as Jonathan raised his chin, signifying his final decision.

"Well, if you say so, of course, Jonathan, I defer to you," the visitor replied. "After all, I am your guest." Then he jerked his head around as if bothered by a gnat. "Confound the noise!"

Jonathan looked right and then left. "The only noises I hear are shouts of joy from the Magnificent City. We deem this as a melodious sound, not noise and I would have thought you were accustomed to it by now."

The visitor purred a low grumble.

Jonathan surveyed the squadron who appeared dismally shocked.

Shay shriveled in his chair, staring straight ahead.

Jonathan cleared his throat and said, "I . . . I know you all wonder who this is and why he's here. Previously, I advised you all about the relevance of this class. As we continue with our review and through its conclusion, you will all understand the significance. As you know, I can be trusted, implicitly."

Jonathan words soothed the afflicted angelees much like sipping a cup of hot chocolate on a cold night.

The presence surveyed the group, searching their young faces in an effort to discern where frailty laid. If he could find a weakness in one of them, it could annul the entire mission. Other groups attempted this preparation in the past and he successfully aborted those instructions. He championed himself as the master terminator, the best.

Lev broke the silence.

"Jonathan?"

"Yes, Lev?"

"Well, we trust you Jonathan, don't get me wrong and I don't want to be rude but my question is what can our guest possibly have to do with our review? Or with us? He has all of these names written on him, which none of us comprehend. I don't understand why he's here."

"Good question, Lev. As I said, we're going to cover this in our review."

"Oh." Lev glanced away quickly so as not to make eye contact with the guest.

"You will understand, shortly," Jonathan continued. "Our guest has been here many times, as you heard earlier. He's been through many of our reviews and he will have a lot of input."

"Input? From, from this …?" Shay stammered. At this, the group erupted in chatter amongst themselves.

Lev spoke again. "Jonathan, what about all these words written all over him?"

"Yes, exactly, you will see how all of this will come together. For instance, one of the words written on our guest pertains to our first lesson and as we enter our discussions our guest will have input which pertains to those words which are written on … on him."

Another voice called out, "Jonathan, Sir?"

Jonathan surveyed the group and found Gordan, waving his hand in the air. "Yes, Gordan?"

"In our first lesson about the Garden of Eden, we talked about Adam and Eve's disobedience. Since our guest wasn't there, I don't know what kind of input he would have."

"Yes, we covered Adam and Eve's wrongdoing," Abigail added almost mechanically. Her eyes stared at the black creature before her. She couldn't stop staring. They had received instruction about the underworld but she never thought they would come face to face with an entity from "that place" in the Magnificent City. At least, she surmised, that must be where he is from.

Gordan continued in a seemingly unaffected manner. "It was terrible. They were in the Garden, a piece of pure bliss itself."

"Yes, you're right," Jonathan responded. "It started at the formation of earth and it had everything to do with Adam and Eve's defiance. This is totally in line with our review."

Quiet hung like a heavy theater curtain. It seemed they would have to interact with the undesirable visitor after all.

"But wasn't it the disobedience of the serpent?" Gordan asked.

The group let out a collective sigh.

"Yes," Jonathan said, "you all most likely have had the thought in the back of your minds. In a sense it was and as you all recall insubordination originated with the serpent, and the … the serpent's …"

"Lies!" Nathan spouted.

Strangely, the angelees calmed as the word *lies* rang in the air.

"Yes, class," Jonathan continued, "you see if the serpent had not spoken to Adam and Eve, they would not have been enticed. Eve did not perceive the impending jeopardy. We know reptiles are the most dangerous creatures known to man and they kill more mortals than any other living thing on the face of the planet."

The visitor sprang from his seat. "Sir, may I interject?"

Over the years, Jonathan grew accustomed to his visitor's method and answered, "Of course, proceed."

"Well, as I recall when the serpent, who may I remind everyone was a created creature by the Ruler of the Realm, was he not? Well," he continued, "this poor creature came to the two magnificently manufactured beings created in the Ruler's own image. This sorrowful creature, which you maligned and called a serpent, spoke with them and merely tried to befriend them. He didn't have any bad intentions and he didn't tell them anything that wasn't true."

Jonathan looked up and peered with narrowed eyes. He had never heard his visitor take this stance before and didn't like it.

Pleased, the visitor allowed his comments to sink in for a moment. He continued, "As I said, he didn't tell them anything that wasn't true."

He then sat with his arms and legs crossed, proud he made his point.

Finally, the silence broke. "And how is that?" a voice beckoned.

Lev stood with the bottom of his robe wrapped around one arm, looking much like a Roman aristocrat.

"Oh, I'm happy to hear a reply at last. Your name is Lev, is it not? I'll consider your silence to mean it's affirmative," the guest continued, "and may I say you are most astute for asking this excellent question. Would you mind repeating it Lev?"

Lev glared at the black caller. His shoulders shrugged when he heard his name but he proceeded. He looked directly at him and said, "My question is: how can you say the serpent didn't say anything that wasn't true?"

"Well, you see, Lev, when the serpent spoke with Eve and by the way, the word serpent doesn't mean what you think it does."

"It doesn't?"

"No, words were translated differently by those scholars from long ago and serpent actually means one who is 'soft spoken'."

"You mean one who whispers or hisses don't you?" Jonathan exclaimed.

The mustard-yellow eyes shot a penetrating look at Jonathan and replied, "Sir, I believe this is my point and intervention is to be minimal on your part?"

Jonathan's eyebrow rose. "Of course."

"As I said, perhaps you could say 'whisperer' and doesn't that mean 'soft spoken' after all?"

The guest took a quick breath but before he began his next sentence, Nathan countered. "Excuse me, but I think we're getting off track."

"Oh, of course," he responded with an ingratiating tone. He stood with his finger pointed toward Lev and with a strange intense gaze he purred, "Dear Lev."

"Sir I would appreciate it if you would not address me as dear."

"Yes, of course … Lev. I'm sorry but as I said a creature is not a serpent, per se, but we won't belabor the point. Well, the poor creature actually spoke the truth. You see he wasn't very well-liked and wanted to make friends with Eve and Adam and well, he had a conversation with them to get to know them better."

"Yes, you covered much of that but please answer my question in regard to why you said he didn't say anything that wasn't true."

"Yes," the essence carried on as he waved his hand. "The statement he made was, as you remember, 'Yea, hath God said, ye shall not eat of every tree of the garden' is a true statement, is it not?"

They searched within for an answer and didn't know what to say. Jonathan did not attempt to help them this time but then Abigail answered. "I believe the statement by the serpent should have been 'of every tree of the garden thou mayest freely eat: But of the tree …"

"My point exactly," he interrupted. "You see the soft spoken one merely reiterated there was a 'but' there and they were told not to eat of every tree, isn't that right?"

Their eyes flashed back and forth between them as they sought each other's help for a response. No one seemed to have an answer.

Finally, Lev answered, "I believe you may be correct in what you're saying."

Jonathan's heart sank but he didn't correct Lev.

An odd, slight curl of a smile crossed the guest's face. He sat down and crossed his arms.

Lev continued, "Suppose it is correct, about the tree I mean. It stands that the serpent tempted Eve and Adam ate of the tree as well."

"Oh, but he didn't tempt them at all," the presence answered. "He merely *informed* Eve."

"But … if Adam wasn't beguiled then how did he end up eating of the tree, which he was told not to eat," Lev asked, confused.

He pounced on back on Lev's statement. "Well it wasn't the soft spoken one's fault; he merely told them what would happen."

"What do you mean?"

Jonathan's gaze shifted between Lev and the visitor but held his tongue.

The visitor continued. "The soft spoken one said, 'your eyes shall be opened, knowing good and evil' and they did know good from evil, correct?"

Shay's ears perked up and he blurted out, "Wait a minute! No, you left out something important."

"And what might that be, my little friend?"

"Well, in the first place, as Abigail said the serpent misquoted the commandment."

"Commandment? Oh, please, this wasn't a commandment but merely an instruction."

Jittery as he faced the creature, Shay stood opposite him.

However, he wasn't alone. Nathan's large frame suddenly appeared next to him and he announced, "We seem to be off subject once again."

Shay stood at the front of the classroom. "Yes," he continued, "The serpent didn't quote exactly what Adam was told and when he did this he confused Eve. She added, "Neither shall you touch it, lest you die."

The guest snorted in disgust and answered, "What difference does that make?"

"Well if Eve believed she would die if she touched the fruit and was alive after she picked it then she certainly would go ahead and eat it. The old dragon has made disobedience appear as if it has no consequence for centuries when its consequence is death. He lied to her."

The others joined in unison and said, "That's right."

"BUT, did she die?" the guest declared. Then with a lilted, taunting manner he repeated, "Did she?"

A moment passed, which seemed like forever. Shay finally replied, "Yes, she did."

"Master Shay, how can you say this being you and I are from the same star?"

"Sir, I am not a master and as far as my origin is concerned I'm sure there's a very good explanation of how we can be from the same place and yet be so entirely different. Environment is not judgment. However, to get back to your statement, Eve did die. Adam and Eve both died *spiritually* and I think you know this!"

"Me? Well, not for a moment. I am looking at the facts as you are and I simply see Eve and Adam, for that matter, conversed and carried on after they did this supposedly terrible thing of consumption of the fruit of this tree. For what purpose they were told not to, I have no clue but there they were and they went on with their life. They didn't seem very *dead* to me and they continued to talk and operate pretty much as they had before."

Shay thrashed a sideways look at the black visitor. "It stands to reason you're going to say you didn't see them dying," he replied. "But, if they hadn't eaten from that tree they would have eaten from the Tree of Life. It was there in the Garden and they were told to eat of every tree except the tree of knowledge of good and evil and had they eaten of the Tree of Life, it would have given them …"

"Hold on, hold on" the guest said with his hands raised in the air. "You're making me woozy jumping from tree to tree. With all your gibberish about trees, the confounded noise and the bright light around me, I can't concentrate."

He threw his hands up and covered his eyes, which made him look more grotesque because of the long black hair that covered his hands.

Shay persisted. "…It would have given them eternal life. Therefore, you see the serpent, who I don't think was particularly soft spoken, did speak lies mixed with truth. In addition, lies are lies no matter how much they're mixed. The whole objective was to mislead and misdirect. In doing this, it cost humanity their magnificent eternity and it would have remained that way if the Ruler of the Realm had not instituted another plan.

At the mention of the Ruler, the presence recoiled. Saliva drooled from his mouth and down his chin.

The group ignored what they observed. They cheered Shay heartily and resounded, "Good, Shay. Way to go, Shay."

The visitor appeared unhappy. "Yes, good, very good. Our common origin must drive your oratory abilities, which are excellent

Shay ignored the remark and glared straight ahead. In one way, he felt vulnerable but in another, he felt strong.

The guest abruptly stood on his feet. His long bony fingers pressed against each other and he drew them up to his pursed lips. "We've said the same thing. Lev agreed earlier it's just a question and the question was correct, wasn't it? It wasn't the whisperer's failing; it was the woman's decision in the end, wasn't it?"

Another voice, clear and strong interjected. Elizabeth stated, "Sir, we discussed the statement in regard to what Adam and Eve were told, not whose fault it was. They carried the responsibility for their action but the fact remains lies emerged regarding the outcome.

They could have asked the Ruler if it was true, but they didn't. They listened to the tempter and as stated earlier in this conversation, he told Eve she would not die. That was the first lie spoken directly to her. They did die, first spiritually and then later physically and as you know, their bodies returned to dust. The words, 'you shall not surely die' are the exact opposite of what happened. As Shay stated, the Tree of Life grew in the Garden. They wouldn't have died spiritually or physically because the Creator said they could eat of every tree. Their spiritual death, which separated them from the Supreme Being, happened instantly. The Holy Book says 'you were dead in your transgressions and sins.' This kept the Tree of Life from them and banished them from the Garden. It would have been wonderful if they had remained as they were created: innocent – unaware of evil. They were like children but when they ate of the tree, they received knowledge."

An incredulous look crossed the visitor's face. "And what is wrong with that? Why shouldn't they know what's good, beautiful, kind, bountiful, merciful, joyful, precious and loving?"

Elizabeth, stumped by his reply, didn't know what to say. Her eyes blinked at a rapid pace, as if they stuttered.

Abigail came along side her. Under her breath she said, "Let me get this one, Liz." Then she responded, "It's a two-edged sword. The Creator wanted them to know goodness. However, he knew with this knowledge they would also become aware of wretchedness, trouble, grief, adversity, calamity, affliction, distress, hurt, sorrow, wickedness and wrong. That's the definition of evil. They would have the know-how or the knowledge of how to commit evil."

"Just as the Ruler did?" the presence retorted.

Jonathan flinched.

Nathan, who had returned to his seat, stood up again.

The tone of his voice quivered slightly. "The Ruler of the Realm has NEVER committed evil, sir. You are quite wrong to insinuate this could be the case. In actuality, as Abigail and the others have expounded, He protected them. Since they didn't possess a divine nature, He knew they would not have the strength in themselves to resist evil if they received the knowledge of evil.

"And furthermore," Elizabeth said, reinvigorated, "It's

written 'but I fear, lest by any means, as the serpent *beguiled* Eve,' and it's also written 'but the woman being *deceived* was in the transgression.' You can't be beguiled or deceived without a lie!

The visitor sat and his eyes rolled. *This Elizabeth come lately has started to be a nuisance. In fact, they all are.*

She didn't stop there. "Adam and Eve brought destruction to every future being that would have life."

"Aren't you being a bit melodramatic, Miss Elizabeth?" he retorted.

Her eyes sparkled. "Sir, you know this is correct. Adam and Eve were perfect without sin but when they didn't keep the vow, they corrupted what they were and every mortal born thereafter was born in sin."

His nasal passages flared. The angelees noticed a liquid run down his face.

He replied in a sarcastic tone, "I say it was not the soft-spoken one's fault." He stuck his chin out and fumed. When he did this, the odor of sulfur filled the air and the angelees held their breath to avoid the repulsive stench.

Jonathan stood and his unexpected movement alarmed the squadron. They almost forgot his presence. "This topic seems to have been covered sufficiently," he proclaimed.

The visitor pouted. He wanted to continue to talk about it. When he wanted to talk, he wanted to talk then. He scowled at Jonathan. "Oh, sure, fine. We'll not discuss this subject further is that it? It seems to be about what you want, doesn't it?" He put his hands to his ears. "Can't somebody stop that confounded noise?"

Jonathan dismissed the visitor's goad. "Yes, it seems the subject has been covered sufficiently and we have other things to review. Apparently, you've become less and less tolerant to the so-called noise. You've been here many times and I don't know why it bothers you more now."

The guest didn't answer.

"Shall we proceed?"

The visitor glared at him and answered, "Surely, Jonathan, whatever you say. This is, after all, your instruction class?"

Shay regretted the discussion ended. He had another "and

furthermore."

Obviously, their guest tried to lighten the subject to make it look acceptable.

The fact the Holy One and the serpent were 100 percent opposite of each other wasn't even touched but Shay deferred to their instructor, Jonathan.

But he wanted to talk; he really wanted to.

place of torment 8

Something slimy slithered across Doug's foot.

He leapt to his feet and fought a wave of unsteadiness.

He held his hand to his head and waited to regain his equilibrium but the feeling remained for several minutes.

He closed his eyes. A moan arose from his inner being. He squeezed his eyelids together as hard as he could until he shook.

"It can't be, it can't be," he repeated to himself. "What do I do now?"

His nostrils swelled from the stench. Pinching his nose closed, he breathed in deeply through his mouth.

The vulgar sulfuric taste caused him to hack. He sputtered from the objectionable taste. "Help, somebody," he gasped.

Moans and words that sounded like, "I'm sorry," filled the air. The muffled tones made it hard to discern what the voices said. He thought he heard men and women talking.

His voice regained some strength and he croaked as loud as he could, "Help me, someone, please!"

No one answered.

Doug wiggled his toes and thought about Larry's well-polished loafers.

Larry, a slight framed man with small-rimmed glasses, mild mannered and quiet on the surface, had a wily nature.

Everyone thought him to be harmless and the façade often duped people.

Larry's job enabled him to dress well. His shirts looked expensive, the kind you'd find in an exclusive men's shop.

He wore pressed pants and tie. No one would guess his humble origin.

He hailed from a hot, dusty town in the southwest.

Most of the homes built in the nineteen twenties had problems by then with pipes and fixtures, not to mention the lack of air-conditioning.

Larry hated it and resolved he would move.

One of these days, I'm going to have a lot of money.

Through high school, Larry bused to another school, which rescued him, at least in the daytime, from his dreary environment. He loved the active environment of the new school and had a group of new friends and his teachers liked him.

"Why don't you run for class president?" His friends suggested. The idea enticed him.

"Nah, it's not for me."

Doug had been at the bank a short time before they met. He sat in the employee lounge with his usual sack lunch. His job as a teller didn't pay much so he economized wherever he could.

Larry walked up and greeted him.

Doug mumbled something as he pretended to read.

Larry pulled up a chair and grinned, which left the small gap between his teeth exposed.

"Yeah, Doug, how's it going?"

"Fine," he responded gruffly.

A moment passed and Larry put his arm around his shoulder. "Doug, my friend, I've got a *great* deal for you."

Doug glanced at Larry's arm. It made him uncomfortable. He scooted his chair a short distance away from him. "What about?"

Larry lowered his voice. "Well, I've thought about this for awhile," he enunciated deliberately, "and I can't see where we can go wrong."

Doug's quizzical look said it all. "What do you mean, 'go wrong,' it sounds like something's wrong already."

"Wrong? Well, maybe, but it is sweet."

Doug remembered the positive tone of voice but at this

moment, he wished for intervention. *I don't know how I let myself in for all this. Trying to be something I'm not, I suppose.*

Doug had observed Larry pull his chair closer to him. Interested, he asked Larry, "What kind of a deal?"

"It's like this. We meet up with a woman and talk her into letting us buy her a fur coat."

"Ha!" Doug's drink snorted out through his teeth. He couldn't believe his ears. "Talk her into it! Are you kidding? I don't think you would have to talk too long!"

"No, listen to me." Larry said as he peered behind Doug. "We buy this coat. Most furs are in the range of maybe five to eight thousand dollars, right?"

"Maybe … I don't know but this sounds like stupidity with a capital 'S' to me."

"Hold on a minute. We report it stolen but we get it back from her."

Doug's brow wrinkled.

Larry continued with the plot. "Of course, we insure the fur, for like say, double what its worth. We pay her off and we have the coat to boot – which we can sell. I'm telling you, it's beautiful; it'll work."

Doug stared as he pondered the proposition. "It sounds too smooth. Something's bound to go wrong."

"What do you mean?"

"Well, what if she wants the coat?"

"Wants the coat? Where would she get off with wanting the coat? We're the ones who put up the money. I'm telling you, we can triple our investment. Just think. We can pull this scam across the country. That way no one will be wise to us. A bunch of furs won't disappear from one place. The beauty of this is, she can buy her own with the money we give her."

Doug fiddled with his sandwich. "Where are you getting the money to buy the coat?"

"I've got money," Larry whispered as he leaned closer.

"Yeah, but you'll be ripping off insurance companies."

"It's not like they don't rip people off. Look at the premiums they charge. Think about it, Doug. After a few of these, you won't have to work this lousy job either. I have a good gig here but I hate to come to work. I'd like to be able to enjoy my life more, you know. I'd like to fish or golf. Wouldn't you?"

"I don't know. Why … Why would you want to do this when, like you said, you have a good job?"

"This isn't going to give me the money I need. I even thought about doing the same thing with diamonds."

"Diamonds?"

"Yeah, people lose diamonds all the time. You know, in areas where it's too warm for furs. The great thing about all of this is, it's not you or me losing them, it's whoever we get to go along with us."

"But, what do you need me for?"

Larry looked around. He sat back, tilted his chin up and said slowly, "I've kept my eye on you Doug. The way I see it, you … well you have a look people trust."

Flattered, Doug responded. "Well I think you do too. But, back to my question, what do you need me for?"

"It'll take two of us so the gals we pick won't be able to identify one person. Come on, what do you say?"

It didn't make sense to him and but he replied, "I … I don't know. I'll think about it."

"You don't want to be stuck here all your life do you? That would be so boring, day in, day out."

Doug appreciated this job, at least up to a point. But the thought of a free existence and not having to work from nine-to-five appealed to him more. Doug surmised Larry had a point.

"So, what do you think?"

He looked at the half-finished sandwich. *I'll probably never have to bring my lunch again.* Intrigued, he proclaimed, "I'll think about it."

"All right! Way to go, Doug. Don't think too long. Many people would like to cash in. I'm telling you this is sweet."

Doug recalled the gapped grin on Larry's face as they shook hands.

He found a sucker didn't he?

Larry entrusted the paper work to Doug and made him the main contact for all the deals. "You're so good at it," he had told him.

❖

Doug reached, grabbed some skin and pinched. "Ouch!" *Well, I'm not dreaming. Why did I have to tell him I would think about it?*

I wish I could see him for five seconds. Five seconds is all I need. I wouldn't be here if didn't have to hide all those files.

He sat and stared motionless for a moment. *I have to find a way out of here.* He cupped his hands around his mouth and shouted, "HELP!"

Something approached him and he froze.

"There you are," he heard. "How did you go unnoticed? You must have slipped through the cracks, somehow."

He stared into the thick maze. A hand with a long pointed finger came through the mist. The smell of sulfur grew stronger and he leaned forward. Then he stopped in his tracks.

It resembled a woman. A narrow drawn face with bristly long hair, large owl-like eyes and leathery skin, creased into huge folds stared at him. Her hands seemed disproportionate, larger than normal. It pulled its hair in an attempt to make itself presentable.

It held a black, charred lump on a platter.

"What's this?" he asked startled.

"It's your din-din."

"I don't think I understand."

"Just a small luscious morsel prepared just for you but it may be a little old now. I had a trial finding you."

"Who are you?"

"I'm your guide, Sir Lancelot."

"My what?"

A strange curdling sound emitted from the creature. "Your escort my dear, and now eat up like a good boy."

"What is it, pheasant?"

"Pheasant? I haven't heard that word for thirty or so years. No, it's your special reception meal readied just for you. You'd better savor it because you won't get another one like it again."

"But what is it?"

"Plover, silly."

"I've never heard of plover."

"It's a lapwing, you know, a bird. I'm sure you've heard their shrill. They make a terrible noise when they fly about but an even worse one when they're caught."

He looked at the pitiful excuse for a meal, grasped the tin and attempted to set it down. It skated from the platter and hit his foot. In pain, he grimaced and pulled his foot toward him.

"Oh, isn't it a pity? I suppose now you'll hold out for the good stuff like maybe a little bat or some rat. There are plenty of them."

He coughed and hacked again. "Do you have anything to drink? My throat is parched."

"Thirsty, are you?

She released a shrieking, scream. "Well there isn't any water but there's plenty of blood."

Blood? Doug's stomach rolled within him with a feeling of uneasiness.

"You'll develop a taste," she said, even though she knew it repulsed him to the core. "The life of the flesh is in the blood, you know. We take on the characteristics of whatever blood we drink."

"You mean, I'm going to look like you?"

The woman nudged him with her crooked elbow. "Now why would you want to be gussied up? There aren't any angels running around to look pretty for. Not yet, anyway."

He shuddered at the gruesome options. Why is this person giving me these sickening choices?

"Well then since you don't want to eat, I take it you're ready."

"For what?"

"You just need to follow me."

"What? Wait, where am I? Please help me. I think an accident happened. I don't know where I am. I remember a few things but I need help, please."

"I can't help you dearie, all I do is guide."

"Guide me, to where?"

"Oh, trust me you won't be alone."

"What about my family?" He exclaimed in horror. "What about them? I have two brothers and I need to tell them where I am.

I need to see them."

"See them?" No, I'm afraid they're not going to be able to visit you, not just yet."

Doug's lips tightened across the contorted expression on his face. "Is there some way I can communicate with … "

"Oh, yes, your *precious* brothers."

"I've got to let them know."

"Yes, well maybe you can get one of *them* to send a message."

"Who?"

"Haven't you heard of mediums?"

"You mean fortunetellers? Yeah, I've heard of them but I don't think my brothers have."

She waved her hand back and forth in front of him. "Forget it."

"What do you mean? Were you kidding me? He grasped his hands to his head, hoping to shut out the madness.

"You don't know anything do you? I used to go to mediums and they talked about those who passed. That's the phrase they used, they 'passed.' But they never warned me about this. In fact, they made me think my departed loved ones were fine."

"But … but there has to be something I can do. I've got to get a message to them and warn them!"

"Oh, shut up! I don't want to hear your bellyaching about your family! Besides, even if someone rose from the dead they wouldn't listen. They don't listen to the preaching they hear now, do they?" She came closer to him and said in an eerie tone, "You don't recognize me, do you?"

The question startled him. *How would I possibly know this … thing?*

"You don't know who I am?"

Thoughts raced through his mind. He stammered, "Did, did I live with you?"

"HAAAAGH, that's a good one. Live with me! I don't think so but take a good look because you're living with me now. Pretty soon you'll look a lot like me," she hooted.

His nose wrinkled.

If only he could call Rhonda.

He didn't know what she saw in him. Her crimsoned-colored smile brightened any room. He mentally pictured her long dark hair, oval brown eyes and petite body. Her complexion sported a soft olive tone.

"Why is it you change the subject when we talk about marriage?" She had asked.

"Yeah, well we'll do it someday."

The night they broke up started innocently. Rhonda left for the store. He brought out a bottle of wine, emptied it and half of another. By the time she returned, he sailed along at a good clip.

"I'm home," she called out.

Doug remained quiet.

She carried the groceries in tow and leaned to give him a kiss. "What's that I smell?"

"My cologne."

She slammed the bag on the counter. "Since when does cologne have the same odor as liquor?"

"Since when does ..."

"Don't mimic me."

He stared at her with a glassy stare. "Okay, I won't."

"Yeah, I'm sure. You won't mimic and you won't drink again. At least that's what I've heard for the past few years. You know, I am tired of this. I've had all I can take."

"Sure, sweetie, anything you say."

She put her hand on her hip. "Doug, I mean it. I'm going to leave."

"Go ahead. Leave. You're a big girl and you can do *anything* you want."

She packed her bags that weekend.

His pride got the better of him. He thought *good riddance. No one's going to henpeck me. I can do whatever I want.*

He stood face to face with the ugly, disfigured being.

"I see you bought into the lie," she uttered slowly.

"What lie?"

"About doing whatever you want. Weren't you just thinking

no one could tell you what to do?"

He shook his head.

"Everyone here bought into the lie. The boss," she said in a lowered voice, "lets everyone think when they're up there. 'There aren't any rules and if it feels good and everyone else is doing it, just do it.' He doesn't let them know the end result."

He stared emptily at the pathetic excuse for a person. He didn't want to think about consequences.

She waved a bony hand in front of his face and chased away some smoke.

"That's okay. Too much for you to think about right now isn't it. Well, when you figure out who I am," she said with a long, emaciated hand raised in the air, "let me know. And when you figure out how to get word to your family let me know too. I have a kid up there, an only child, my beautiful daughter. Unfortunately, I didn't teach her what could keep her from landing in here. All I can do is hope she won't make the same mistakes. Maybe she'll listen to someone."

Face to face, he stared into the roadmap -bloodshot eyes.

Her nostrils flared and she lifted her head and sneered. "I hope I don't see her here. That's a good one, huh. Hope."

The word seemed ironic for their situation.

Doug didn't know what to say and thought if he kept the conversation open, it might help. "Who did you say you were?"

"I'm not the Queen of Sheba, but if I were, what difference would it make to you?" she retorted sharply.

. "Please, help me. Please talk to me and tell me what's going on."

"Talk to you? Why? It tires me out and I lose my voice. This is new for me too, you know. I'm not used to this job

"But I don't know what's going on," he pleaded.

"I know, bright eyes but they don't give out medals to newcomers."

"But you don't understand. I don't know where I am."

"You'll find out, sweetie. You'll have plenty of time to figure it out."

Doug ignored the declaration and persisted, "I think I need

to get to a hospital. Can you help me get to an emergency room? I believe St. Catherine's is the closest."

The unpleasant figure didn't respond.

"Don't you understand? I've been in an accident and I should get to a hospital. Can you at least tell me how to arrange that and where I am?"

"How can you not know where you are? What kind of dummy are you?"

"I'm sorry; please don't make fun of me," Doug wrung his hands.

Hoarsely, she replied. "This is the place you've been told about over and over. You've heard about weeping, wailing and gnashing of teeth. They wrote it seven times in the Book."

The phrase sounded familiar. He paused. He looked right and then left. Slowly it dawned on him. "But, but . . . that refers to damnation, doesn't it?'

"Yessss," it hissed.

"Then, this is – hell?"

A shriek cracked like thunder and he knew by its unwarranted pleasure that it was.

His head and shoulders slumped forward. *It's not fair. I never understood. Who is punished because they don't understand? There must be some mistake! I would never have chosen this!*

"Sure you did."

Then he realized he had not spoken audibly. *It must have read my thoughts. But I know I would never have chosen this place. No one in his right mind would.*

"Oh, now you're calling me crazy are you?"

"I didn't mean anything by that, really, I didn't."

"Well I think I should just leave you here and give you time to think about your brothers. They're probably up there saying all kinds of lovely things about you. That's what usually happens."

He trembled at the mention of his brothers. *What if they end up here?* He jerked his head and looked around. *I have to get out of here. I have to warn them!*

"There's no warning them from here."

"But I've got to. I've got to tell them and let them know this is real!"

"Ughhh." A groan emerged from the woman's lips. "Isn't that touching you're such a caring soul. Not to worry, whatever they decide to do they'll decide, just like you."

"But you don't understand. This is all wrong. I didn't choose to come here!"

"You made the choice. If you cared where you were going after you left your body, you wouldn't be here. You're like everyone else. Now it's too late."

"But that's just it, I didn't do anything wrong. Larry's the one."

"Sure, buddy. Well, mister high and mighty I have to go. I'll be back to take care of you later. There's been a disaster and more than we thought were coming, will be here soon. I understand some are CEO's."

Before he could reply, she disappeared into the dense smoke.

He stood helpless with his arms hung at his side. *This can't be happening. It's impossible.* He sat on the rock, pulled his knees toward his chest again, and closed his eyes. "Maybe it'll all go away, somehow."

He opened his eyes again, as sweat ran down his body. He flinched as he remembered what she said about drinking blood.

How many times did I hear about hell? It seems like people talk about the subject all the time, but I never really believed.

liar, liar pants on fire 9

Courtney's legs ached from her knees down. She turned the corner and looked to see if anyone followed her. Relatively sure no one did, she ran as if they had. *Better safe than caught.*

In the middle of the third street, she looked again and finally felt confident she had gotten away. She marched at a fast pace, catching her breath as she went along.

She reached the next block and realized she had reached her old friend's neighborhood. One street up and a couple of houses over and she would be there.

Haley lived in a two-story frame home set back further from the street than the other houses. Courtney went to the door and peeked through the glass on the side. She smoothed her messy hair and rang the bell.

Haley peered through the eyehole and saw Courtney dressed in a short midriff top with her front section bared, and jeans cut across her hips. She wore long earrings and heavy makeup, complete with fake eyelashes. She opened the door. "Hey, what are you doing out here? I haven't seen you in ages."

"Oh, I visited a cousin of mine who lives a couple of blocks from here and I thought about you. So here I am. I'm glad you were here.

"Come on in," Haley muttered, as she breezed past.

Courtney spread her hands out and pranced like a model.

"What do you think?"

"Oh, your clothes. Yes, I noticed them. Where did you change? I know you wouldn't leave your house that way."

"Oh, I wear a big sweatshirt over what I want to wear. Then, when I get out of school, I pull it off and voila. Isn't this cool?"

"I … guess."

Haley noticed Courtney had her dark silky hair cut into bangs. Courtney wore the rest pulled back, looking fashionable in a ponytail.

Haley fiddled with her own dark brown, kinky hair.

"So, you didn't tell me. What do you think of my clothes *and* make-up."

"Yeah, you look kind of like a rock star."

"Well, I don't have your pretty hazel eyes so I have to make up for it somehow. *Make-up,* get it."

Haley pulled her stomach in and answered, "That's cute. So, what's your cousin's name?"

"Oh, you don't know him. He doesn't go to our school. He attends a pub."

"Which public school?"

"Mmmm, I never keep up with the names, you know? I mean they're such a drag. So, this is your house?" she said as she sauntered through the living room.

"Yes, this is it, such as it is. How about some lemonade?"

"Sure, sounds good to me."

Courtney set her bag on the table and looked around. "Hey, I've got something I want to show you." She pulled some CD's from her bag.

"Neat!"

"Yeah, these are some cool CD's."

"Wow. You have a ton of new ones. How can you afford them?"

She shrugged her shoulders and said, "It's no big deal, I mean money. I have a job, and I work, real hard."

"You do? Where do you work?"

"Ummm, I deliver newspapers."

"Wow, that is a lot of work. You've got to get up so early in the morning ..."

"Yeah, well, here, why don't we listen to this one?"

"Looks good to me. Why don't you put it on? The player's right over there."

"Okay."

"I'll get the lemonade."

Courtney turned a CD on and put the rest in her bag. She looked around at Haley's house again.

She gazed at the couch placed across from the fireplace with a chair on each side of the mantel.

A huge mirror hung above the white frame. Art pieces decorated the walls. She walked around and picked up different items. On one of the tables sat a small globe. It caught her eye.

The "snow" globe had a scene of a small hill and a cross at the top of the hill. She turned it upside down and watched the flakes fall gently. She thought about pitching it into her bag.

"That's from our kindergarten Sunday school class, remember?"

Courtney twirled around. "It's kind of pretty," she said as she set it down. "Hey, did you look over our assignment? Is it a hard one?"

"Well," Haley said, "I started to look it over."

They sat on the couch next to each other and Haley crossed her legs, Indian style.

She gulped her drink and said, "That is so great that you have a job, Courtney. I wish I could be more like you."

"You're kidding me, right?"

"No. I mean it."

They opened their Bibles and read while the CD played a song. The chorus sang, "Liar, liar, pants on fire."

"I don't get it," Courtney said after a minute.

"What?"

"You know all this stuff about the wilderness. First of all it irritates me to have to explain something I don't even like to read. Like I said," she continued, "I don't like to read the Bible. You know, they say Jesus was the Son of God and then he's supposed to go to this forsaken place. Why would he want to do that? Then we're supposed to explain why he talked to the devil?"

Haley, half listened but when Courtney mentioned *devil* she reacted and mumbled, "It's not hard."

"What?"

"It's not hard," she said louder.

"So, what's the answer?"

"Well, we're supposed to analyze what took place. The answer is what we find in the reading. Whatever it is that speaks to us."

"Oh, sure," Courtney replied. She read some more.

"And if you look at it from the point of view that he didn't live for his own pleasure, it's clearer."

"What're you talking about?"

"Well, here, for instance," Haley pointed out. "Here, it says he was: 'led up of the spirit into the wilderness to be tempted of the devil'."

"So?" The music blared and Courtney beat her hands against her Bible.

"Well, He didn't just decide to go on a trip but He was taken there and then He was tempted."

"What does that have to do with anything?"

"Well, it goes back to Adam and Eve."

"Oh, Pleeeze!"

"What?"

"Adam and Eve? BORING."

"No it's not."

"Yeah, well what's so exciting about two yahoos eating from a tree?"

Haley could see this might make for a long afternoon and wanted to make it as simple and quick as possible. "That's what I'm trying to explain to you Courtney, it's the same thing."

"What is?"

Just then, they heard a door slam. They stared at one another. "What was that?"

"Haley?"

"Is that you, Mom?"

"It's me," her mother chimed as she poked her head through

the kitchen door. Courtney looked up. "Hello Mrs. Connor."

"Courtney? What a surprise, I haven't seen you in ages."

Courtney smiled weakly and Anna began to empty the grocery bags. She stuck her head back into the room. "Have you been home all afternoon, Haley?"

"Yes, Mom, I have."

"Oh, good. Well, I just went to see Rebecca at the hospital again and went grocery shopping, so I have a few more things to put away."

Courtney waited a moment and whispered to Haley, "Yeah, I heard about Jacob."

"My brother? What about him?"

"Everybody knows, you don't have to pretend."

Haley's cheeks burned. She answered, "I … I don't know what you're talking about."

"Right! Yeah, well I've got to go." Courtney said as she slammed her Bible shut.

Relieved, Haley said, "I'm sorry. I guess I'll finish this tonight."

"Yeah, I will too."

Courtney scrambled for the door with her bag in tow.

"Don't forget your drink."

"Oh, yeah, thanks." She picked up her bag and looked around. "Do you want me to leave the CD?"

"Sure, I don't care."

"Just don't forget where it came from. Bye Mrs. Conner."

Anna peered out from the kitchen. "Bye, Courtney."

Courtney bounded out of Haley's house like a prisoner set free from jail. A beautiful day greeted her and she thought *now I can enjoy the sunshine.* She admired the beautiful blue sky, the pretty houses and neatly cut lawns.

She thought about the CD's she stole today and the way it made her feel. With a smug air, she remembered how she asked her mom for money in the morning.

Her mom had responded, "next month, you'll get an allowance."

What a croc.

Haley dropped the curtain back as she watched Courtney drive off. Her mother entered the living room.

"Haley."

"Yes?"

"Were you with Courtney this afternoon?"

"No, I worked on my homework. Why?"

"Well someone told me they saw Courtney run out of Wallace's Music store and a store employee ran after her."

"She was running?"

"Yes. They said they thought maybe she had stolen something."

"You're kidding!"

"Do you know anything about this?"

"Me? No, Mom, I don't know anything, how would I?"

"What were you talking to Courtney about?"

"Nothing. We were talking about our lesson."

"Oh."

The CD continued to play and Haley hoped her mother wouldn't ask her about it.

"Haley? What about this CD? I haven't heard it before. Is it new?"

Haley held her breath. She didn't know what to say. "Oh, yes. I bought it last week. You gave me some money, remember?"

"Oh, yes. Well, could you turn it down? It's a little loud."

"Sure, Mom."

I'll give it back to Courtney as soon as I can then Mom won't know anything. She turned the music down and went back to her homework. The phone rang.

"Do you want me to get it Mom?"

"No, let it go into voice mail."

"I wish we had caller I.D., then we would at least know who's calling."

"They can leave a message," she called back to Haley.

On the other end of the line, Jacob, Haley's brother, listened to the ringing. He held his lips together tightly as it chimed. When the message machine came on, he slammed the phone into the receiver. *Who needs them anyway?*

At the age of six, Courtney had become sick and stayed in the hospital for about a week.

Her father brought her a coloring book. Unfortunately, she didn't have any crayons.

Daily she looked at the pictures and planned what colors she would use.

One day a nurse told her, "Tomorrow I'll bring you crayons so you can color your pictures." The prospect of finally going to be able to color thrilled her.

The next day her dad came, to take her home.

She didn't want to go. Her mind focused on the promise of brightly hued crayons.

One of the other nurses trashed her coloring book as they packed her things.

"Why did you throw my book away?" Courtney wrangled.

"You are not permitted to take personal belongings out of the hospital because of the type of illness you had."

"But the nurse promised she'd bring me beautiful crayons today."

"She should have never done that."

Through tear-filled eyes, Courtney asked "Did the nurse know I was leaving today?

"Of course she did, it's on your chart. Come on, now. Your father's up front."

Everyone lies. Next month, Mom will have another excuse.

She paraded down the street until she reached the corner. A car pulled alongside her.

"Hey, Courtney."

She didn't recognize the voice. The sun's reflection mirrored brightly and she couldn't see inside. She walked over.

"Hi guys," she said as she realized they were from school. "What're you up to?"

"We're going over to my house. Want to come?"

She didn't give it a second thought and said, "Sure." One of the boys hurdled into the back seat.

"Yeah, let's go have some fun," the driver exclaimed.

Pam hasted down the street, turned the corner and realized he was on Sutton Avenue. He decided not to turn back.

His real name was James. James Jones.

As he passed the open doors, a flood of gospel voices in harmony trickled past him. The music was familiar and for a moment, the melodic sounds brought him back to his childhood.

When he was young, everyone fussed over him. Sunday mornings, James dressed in a white shirt, a vest, black pants and black shiny shoes. He looked like a miniature man.

As boys did, he enjoyed running down the church aisles. When he ran past parishioners, they liked to try to grab him and pinch his cheeks.

He remembered someone once told him, "Young James Jones, you're a fine young man and you're going to be a fine big man when you're older."

A knot rose in his throat.

He recalled the meetings at this house of worship and all the Amen's to the preacher's discourses. The memories overwhelmed him, and he ran until he reached the next corner.

"It's over anyway, James," he muttered under his breath. "Those days are gone and they're never comin' back."

The street glistened from an early rain. Thoughts of his grandmother rushed into his consciousness.

Harriet Jones was a woman who feared God and raised five children of her own. James' unmarried mother, her youngest daughter, died in an automobile accident when he was three months old. Harriet didn't know who his father was and was left with James.

James loved his grandmother and remembered what a wonderful cook she was and how she helped him with his homework as best she could. If she didn't know the answer she would say, "well, don't fret my little pet, we'll find out," and somehow, even if days labored by, she would come back to him and tell him "you know that little problem we were workin' on earlier?"

A smile crossed his lips. *I wonder how many people Mamaw talked to before she found the solution.* She never let him down. He thought she was a saint.

She trusted God and her eyes would sparkle as she talked about the "Holy City, up there, where we're going to spend our eternal days."

At daytime, while she did her various chores, her angelic voice sang beautiful hymns.

"Why don't you sing in the choir?" James had asked her.

"Oh they don't want nobody old like me."

Pam didn't believe her explanation until the day he heard a discussion between two deacons in the hallway.

It was the Saturday before Easter. They were preparing for a large service and Mamaw worked overtime to help make the church spotless. James waited for her while she worked and spiritual songs lifted in worship to her Savior could be heard.

James heard one of the deacons say to another, "Sister Jones sure has a sweet voice, doesn't she? Is she in the choir?"

"That old woman?" he answered. "Nah, they wouldn't take her."

"Are you sure?"

"Yes, I heard it from Brother Johnson the Choir leader."

Neither of the men knew James was there. Crushed, he walked away quietly. He went into the men's room and wept.

As he travelled down the street, the memory of her funeral rushed back. He was only thirteen years old. The well-wishers came and patted him on the back. They said, "She's in a better place, young James."

He didn't care if she was in a 'better place'. He ached to see her familiar face and gracious smile.

Tears rolled down his cheeks and he thought, "Why did you leave me?"

Harriet had contracted tuberculosis and didn't take care of the disease in time. But she wasn't afraid to die. "James, if I stay here I'm happy and if I go I'm happy," she said toward the last.

He didn't feel that way. He wanted her to be here with him. *She had no right to leave me. Those "holy rollers" had no right to be glad she was gone.*

He muttered to himself and spotted a man strolling toward

him. He crossed to the other side.

He looked at the sky sprinkled with brightly lit stars. The night was darker than usual and they appeared brighter and more beautiful than before.

For a brief moment, he thought of heaven. A barren feeling prevailed.

I guess all I can do now is hope I see her again. I know I don't want nothin' to do with any of those people she called 'brothers' or 'sisters.' What Mamaw said about hell sounds like a made up story. Besides, I have time to think about it.

lessons well learned 10

Becky's hands trembled. She couldn't wait to get out of the hospital and only thought about getting out and getting high.

She felt silly as a nurse pushed her through the hall while she sat in the wheel chair. "I'm not in invalid you know," she grumbled.

"Hospital rules."

They reached the large double glass doors and the nurse asked, "Is your ride here?"

"Oh, yeah, sure," she replied. *Ride*? The only person she knew with a car was Pam and she had already left him about five messages.

Before the nurse came to a stop, she jumped out of the chair. "This is fine."

"Suit yourself," She replied curtly and steered the chair back inside.

The grey brick hospital sat on the edge of the city, close to the pier, a few blocks south of downtown.

Bright daylight caused Becky to squint. She sniffed and wiped her nose continually. She didn't know how she would connect with Pam or one of the others. *Where am I going to get money?*

She fumbled through her pocket and produced a few quarters. The words *IN GOD WE TRUST* were barely visible.

I'll call Pam again. He may have a job for me. She shuddered at the thought of what she would have to do. Pam had various jobs for her, but not legal ones.

She wouldn't admit how it repulsed her more before. All she let herself think about was her need to find Pam.

The crowds hustled down the street, relieved as they searched for a quick noonday repast. Except for Jacob, who strutted with his eyes fixed on the bounding figures before him.

He bumped into people and muttered an expressionless, "Excuse me."

The arrangements for the wedding were set. They chose the date, found a minister and reserved a small reception area. He reserved a room for his parents at a hotel, at his expense, so they could enjoy the weekend together.

His dad's letter, which stated they couldn't attend, came yesterday. *Why didn't they tell me in person? Or, at least call. What will my friends think?*

With his hand on the door of the restaurant, he hesitated. He reached into his pocket and felt the crumpled letter. His face flushed.

As he peered through the glass door of the café, he saw a friend in a booth, alone. He collected himself, took a deep breath and entered.

Engrossed in her latest novel, Sheila partook of her meal in short bursts. She wore very little make up and had her brown hair trimmed short.

Jacob approached, and she glanced once and then took another quick look.

He slid into the booth and mumbled, "Hi."

"What's wrong?"

He hesitated a moment. "How did you know something's wrong?"

"It's written on your face, Jacob."

"Well, you won't believe it."

"What?"

"My parents . . . they're . . . they're not coming to my wedding."

"What do you mean? I've known your folks for a long time and they don't seem like the kind of people that would snub their own son."

He clenched his hands into fists. A flush of red permeated his countenance. He stared straight ahead and didn't respond.

"I'm sorry, Jacob." She reached across the table, patted his hand and then retracted it in haste.

"Thanks."

"This must be a blow to you."

"Yes it is. I had hopes …."

"I wish I could think of something to help you but all I can say is … I am sorry."

"I should have known better. I guess it's the . . . the finality of it." He sat with his eyes fixed on his fists.

"Jacob, I know it makes you feel bad but if they've chosen not to come, well, as far as I can see, that's their loss. You've made your choice. You don't need a committee to make a decision. And you're the one who's going to have to live with the person you've chosen."

He shook his head but didn't look up.

She continued. "Don't worry about it. You're a grown man. You're almost thirty, an adult, right?"

"They don't understand. Kent and I aren't hurting anyone," he said as if he hadn't heard.

"I agree, you're old enough to make up your own mind. Is their acceptance that important?

He slammed his fist on the table and she jumped. "I bet my so-called mother is behind this."

Sheila didn't get a chance to respond before Michael, a work colleague of hers, approached the booth. "Hey guys, how are you?" He stood with his hands in his pockets, looked at Jacob and then at Sheila.

"Fine" they replied in unison.

Michael's lower lip puckered. He peered back and forth at them again. He hadn't seen Sheila since he left the company a couple of months before.

He stood silently for several moments and then placed his hands on the table, leaned forward, and spoke softly into Sheila's ear. "What are you and Jacob doing here together?"

Her face colored and she didn't know what to say. "Jacob … Jacob came in for a cup of coffee."

"Really," Michael said coolly. He straightened his stance and looked down on Jacob.

"Yes," Sheila continued, "We were discussing his wedding."

"His wedding? Oh, wow, no kidding?" He stood back in amazement. "I had no idea."

Jacob's dark eyes glared.

The silence thickened and then Michael whistled a short 'whew' through his teeth. "Well, I guess I better go."

He turned and said with a concentrated grin, "See you later, sweetie." Then he marched way.

They watched as he exited, whistling.

"I can't believe him," she muttered. "I wish he wasn't so arrogant."

Jacob shook his head. "I can't believe him either. I think he has a crush on you. He acted jealous don't you think? Can you imagine he thought you and I had something going?"

The comment stung. "Where were we?" she snapped.

"My parents."

"Oh, yes, your dad."

"What did you say you told him?"

"It's not important what I said to him. He gives me this 'holier than thou' stuff. Dad and I have usually had a great relationship and we talk all the time but he was unsympathetic. It makes me angry. We're not harming anyone and there's absolutely nothing wrong with our being together."

"Maybe you're letting this get to you more than it should," she said softly.

"I don't think so." He barked.

She saw the look in his eyes and wished she could slide in next to him and comfort him but knew she couldn't. "Maybe you need to learn to live without their acceptance."

"Acceptance? Do you know what they said? Well, it wasn't really 'they' because my dad wrote the letter. He said I wanted people to agree with me and the most important thing was whether God accepted me. He said I was intent on changing the natural laws.

He doesn't understand anything."

She remained quiet as he poured out his anger.

"Yes," he rambled, "he wrote and said, in black and white, 'it's not whether we accept you but whether God accepts you.' Even though churches accept it, I know by the tone in their letter that they don't think it's right. You know, I'm just going to forget it. I don't care."

She looked down. "Sounds like a good idea."

But he didn't stop. "He didn't even have the decency to call and talk to me. I bet they're not even a bit concerned. They're probably at some meeting having a great time and my step mother is probably who put my dad up to it."

She didn't know what else to say. "Maybe you have to try to see their point of view."

"They're bigoted, narrow-minded people. The only thing they see is their side. All they talk about is 'God' this and 'God' that. I don't care if they won't come to my wedding."

He rose and hurried out of the restaurant. A Bible verse he learned as a child softly played in his mind. *"All we like sheep have gone astray, we have turned everyone to his own way."* He remembered the paper sheep he colored and cut out. He brought them home to his dad and birth mother.

I can't think about this anymore. I'll go crazy trying to figure out what they stuffed in my brain about heaven and hell and who cares if there is a hell, anyway?

Haley sauntered down the halls with her loaded backpack weighing on her.

Why do I always have such a hard time finding my locker?

Finally, she spotted it, and said aloud, "There it is."

From behind, she heard, "there what is?"

She turned and spotted Courtney. "My … my locker."

Courtney leaned her body against the locker next to Haley's. "What did you think of the CD?"

Haley fumbled with the lock and wished she would go away. But she answered weakly, "Oh, yeah, I liked it."

"You know, Haley, I thought about us getting together after

school today."

"Really, what for?"

"Oh, I have an idea."

"About what?"

"Well, you know I told you I had a job delivering papers in the morning."

"Yes," Haley answered cautiously. She wondered if Courtney would tell her the truth.

"Well, I don't have it anymore. So, I thought about another way I could earn some money. I know you probably have everything given to you so you don't have to worry."

She looked away.

"Don't feel bad about it Haley," Courtney babbled. "It's great your parents buy you everything you need. I just thought you might like to be a little independent and make some money of your own."

"I am independent," she answered as she slammed her locker closed. She walked away and left Courtney. However, the denial didn't faze Courtney. She pushed her weight off the locker and caught up to Haley.

"I think you're self-reliant Haley, don't get me wrong. I didn't mean you're spineless. I just thought it would be neat for you to be able to contribute."

Haley stopped and looked at Courtney. "How are you going to earn money? What kind of a job is it?

"It's, well, it's different than most jobs. It's fund raising," she announced.

"For who?"

"For us, silly."

"I don't know what you mean."

"Well, you know how the school raises money by selling coupon books."

"Yes."

"Well, I have this great idea! We can go to the neighborhoods close to school and tell them we're selling magazines! Then we take the money and keep it."

Her mouth dropped open.

Courtney nudged her and said, "What are you shocked about? We can do it after school and we can go together so we'll be safe."

Just then, Frankie Norton and Jeremy Fellows, two of the most popular boys in school came alongside Courtney. Their faces lit with big smiles, they winked, and greeted Courtney. They hovered a moment and turned to Haley. "Oh, hi there," they added.

As they walked away, Courtney responded with a melodious, "Hi."

The fact these seniors addressed Haley thrilled her. Two of the most handsome, admired boys in the school, the top of their class both scholastically and athletically, spoke to her. She couldn't believe it as she watched them leave.

Courtney smiled and nudged Haley again. "Com'n, what do you say?"

Haley realized she had Courtney to deal with. "I don't know, Courtney, I just don't know."

"Listen, this is so easy, it would be like making a one-minute microwave dinner."

Thoughts ran through Haley's mind. Everyone seemed to like Courtney, especially the "jocks." If she hung around with her, it would boost her own popularity. She thought a moment and heard herself answer, "No, I don't want to."

"What? Are you crazy? Don't you want to get yourself some new music and clothes and stuff?"

Haley remembered the CD Courtney left at her house. She tried to think of how she would tell her she heard she stole it.

Courtney pressed Haley again. "Haley, don't you want to be able to buy things for yourself? Oh, yeah, I forgot your parents will get you whatever you want."

"No, I don't want to get involved," she said and brushed past her. Her gait quickened and she sped away.

In class, she slid into her seat and thought *why does life have to be so complicated all of a sudden?*

Then she remembered Courtney's CD in her locker.

She thought about going back to get it but that would make her late and their teacher, Miss Blake had already arrived. *I'll have to do it soon. I don't even want that in my locker.*

Isabel Blake wore her jet-black hair straight back on top of her head.

Dressed in librarian-styled clothes, she wore a long sleeved, high-necked cream-colored blouse, a dark mid calf skirt and square-heeled dark shoes.

Nevertheless, even if she dressed matronly her quick wit prevailed most of the time.

She watched as students filed into the classroom, humming a tune to herself under her breath.

Haley sat in the center of the room. Courtney, slouched nonchalantly in a perpetually rested pose, sat a row over and one person behind Haley. If Haley were to look over her right shoulder, she would see Courtney's legs crossed in the aisle.

"Good morning students. How are we doing this morning?" She stood at the front of the class, turned to the blackboard and began to write.

"Good."

"Fine."

"Wish I could be somewhere else," someone remarked.

"Well," she turned once again and faced her students. With a bright smile and added, "we have a wonderful lesson today and we're going to have an interactive morning so just chip in whenever you feel like it."

Most of the class let loose a groan.

She enjoyed these sessions. She felt the students could glean more than, if they listened to a lecture. There were times she learned new things and saw a different perspective because of the questions the students raised.

"Let's open our Bibles to Matthew four."

"What's that teach?" one of the students asked.

"Matthew four, beginning with verse one; its right on the board behind me."

For the most part, pages busily rustled. A few sat unmotivated with their chin in their hand.

Haley turned to the chapter and looked closely at the scripture in front of her, the ones she studied with Courtney.

"Who would like to paraphrase?" She scrutinized the students but no one raised his or her hand.

"Well, if you don't volunteer, you know I'll call on you," she said cheerfully. She leaned back on her desk and crossed her ankles. Her gaze went from one side of the room to the other.

"Dylan?"

Dylan glanced at their teacher. "Yes, Ma'am" he answered with a respectful drawl.

"Why don't you start?"

Dylan's dark brown eyes flashed. With a precise and crisp manner, he thumbed his way to the first page of the chapter. He had read his assignment so he felt good about it. "Well, Ma'am, it says Jesus was led, he fasted and he was tempted. It seems to me he was obedient and did what he was supposed to do. That's all I got to say." He closed his Bible.

The class snickered at his summation. She raised her eyebrows until the scoffs hushed. "Thank you, Dylan, for the accurate and clear-cut summation."

"Can someone else add to Dylan's observation?" She spoke, enunciating her words slowly as she glanced across the room in search for the next person to call.

Quiet slipped across the student body. Isabel Blake's eyes swept over the rows until they met another one of her favorite students.

"Jennifer," she called out. "You're my talker."

Jennifer looked up. It didn't bother her when Miss Blake called on her to share. That may be why Miss Blake turned to her so often. "Dylan had a good summation," she replied with a smile. "Jesus was led and he fasted and was tempted but the other thing I thought about was how hard it would be to go forty days without food. It had to be a severe temptation because he must have been really hungry."

"Good point," Miss Blake replied. "I like hearing different viewpoints. Thank you."

She looked around and then asked, "Someone else? Courtney?"

Courtney sat up to attention when she heard her name. Quick

on her toes she replied, "Oh, I agree with Jennifer, Miss Blake. In fact, when Haley and I studied yesterday, that's exactly what we saw."

Isabel's eyebrows rose at the news. She turned her attention to Haley.

"Haley?"

Haley appeared immersed in her Bible and didn't respond.

"Haley?" Miss Blake said again.

She looked up and replied, "Yes Ma'am?"

"Can you share with us what you and Courtney studied yesterday?"

She looked down. She didn't know what to say. She didn't like being put on the spot. She looked up again and stared ahead for a moment. Then she started slowly. "Well, we saw that about the fasting and all. We did see that."

"Is that all?"

"No," Haley answered as she straightened in her chair, "there's the part about not living by bread alone that intrigued me."

"And why was that?"

Her face reddened a little. "Well, when I looked at this last night I saw a parallel between when Jesus was in the wilderness and when Adam and Eve were in the Garden – and even the Israelites in the wilderness.

Miss Blake nodded her head but wondered how this all related. Intrigued, she said, "Yes, go on."

"Well," Haley continued, "When He was tempted about turning stone into bread He responded about not living by bread alone.

"I see. And how does that relate to the Garden of Eden?"

Haley fidgeted with the pages. She glanced up again and took a deep breath. "God commanded Eve, through Adam, not to eat of a particular tree. The trees were there as bread for them, except for one."

"Go on."

"Well, God gave them the commandment and instead of listening, she followed her own desires. She looked at the tree and yearned for it. It says in Genesis it was 'a tree to be desired to make one wise.' She gave in to her desire, where Jesus didn't."

"So do you think disobedience played a part?

"Yes, but the most important point, as I saw it, is she followed her own passion and didn't put the commandment, or word, first. Her faithfulness failed."

"In other words she did what she wanted to do."

"Yes, I guess you can say that."

"And what about the Israelites?"

"They were in the wilderness forty years and were tested so God would know their heart, to see if they would keep his commandments or I guess you can say to see if they would keep his word and be faithful. In this case, he provided bread daily but told them this happened so they would know man doesn't live by bread alone."

"And how does that pertain to the Garden of Eden or the Wilderness?"

"In each of the cases, the vital quality of keeping God first and not having any other Gods before them is premium."

Isabel Blake's features lit up like a theater marquee, as if someone served a choice piece of meat. "Yes, I see what you mean. So, Adam and Eve failed and chose not to live by every word and instead did what they wanted. In addition, the Father didn't try to withhold anything from them. Knowledge of evil is awful. We could have done without calamity or distress or trouble or wickedness."

Haley shook her head as Isabel grabbed a hold of it and paced up and down in front of the classroom. She got more excited and said, "That reminds me of the book of James! He said people are drawn aside by their own desire."

Haley sat in her chair and nodded her head.

"Haley, what I believe you're saying is, our own desires, when they're not lined up with the word of God, is what causes us to go astray. Remaining with Him is a choice on our part once we know Him, right? God didn't make man a robot but instead gave humanity a will. Eve could have given back the gift of free will she received by submitting and declaring, nevertheless not as I will, but thy will be done like Jesus did in His garden – Gethsemane." She whipped around and pointed to Haley, "Is that correct?" she blurted.

Haley stared ahead with a blank expression. Isabel continued. "Well, let's just let that soak in for a few minutes. "Thank you for sharing with us Haley. Now, I'd like Jeffrey to expound on the subject. Jeffrey?"

Jeffrey, the class clown, hardly ever paid attention to who said what. He looked up, opened his eyes wide and lifted his eyebrows. With a quizzical look he said "Who me?" He had an accent and talked with a lilt. The class erupted with giggles and chuckles. It wasn't what he said but how he said it.

""Yes, Jeffrey, I'm speaking to you, We don't have another Jeffrey in the class," Isabel replied unamused. But a disruption had begun and she regretted calling on him. *If I let go now, I'll play right into Jeffrey's hands.*

"Jeffrey, I think you're an intelligent person. I think you lack a small amount of desire to apply yourself and you're not alone. I've seen many kids come through with the same problem. Now, can you look at your Bible and relate to me what you think the passage is about?"

He grinned and rolled his head from side to side in an exaggerated manner. Then he lifted his head and answered, "I'm sorry Mizzzz Izzy but it just so happens I dooon't have my Bible with me."

The "o" when he pronounced the word "don't" sounded nasal and he drew it out on purpose. He sounded like a donkey.

The class roared.

"Jeffrey, it's not polite to make fun of people's names."

"Oh, yes, I mean Mizzzz Izzz-a-bel," and smacked his tongue between his lips. Saliva spattered out of his mouth as he made a show of his enunciation.

His eyes twinkled with a mischievous glint and then he said, "By the way, why don't you ask Courtney again about this stuff? Actually, Courtney and me were doing the studying yesterday afternoon at my house. Courtney and I got into it if you know what I mean."

"Courtney and I," she corrected.

"Oh, were you there too? I don't remember you being there."

Hysteria broke out.

Isabel's face flushed as she felt control of the class slip from her to Jeffrey. She was close to losing control of herself. Finally, the students quieted down. In a firm tone, Miss Blake spouted, "Mr. Ramirez," with an emphasis on "Mr."

He straightened his posture in his chair and sat rigid, with his hands folded on the desk, like a first grade school boy. Now he rolled his eyes from side to side. Some of those around him covered their mouth with their hands in an attempt to refrain from laughing.

She continued, "Do we need to take a walk to the Principal's office?"

Jeffrey loved the attention and answered, "Well, Ma'am," he said respectfully, "I don't need to but if you feel you must, please feel free."

That lit her fuse. She turned, set her Bible on her desk, and motioned for him to get up. "Let's go, young man."

He smirked, slid out from his desk and sauntered to the front. She called out, "Jennifer, you're in charge. I'll be right back."

Her temples throbbed and as she opened the door, she came face to face with a man. He stood with his hand perched in the air, ready to knock.

"Who are you?"

"I'm sorry," he gushed as he flashed an agreeable gracious smile. "I don't mean to interrupt."

"You haven't answered my question, yet."

"Oh, I thought you were advised I would be doing a short lecture in your class today."

"What kind of lecture?"

"Well, just a short talk we're doing to familiarize ..." His voice dropped off and he pulled his jacket lapel back.

Her eyes engaged a shiny badge.

"I'm sorry, I should have introduced myself. I'm Detective Bailey. Kent Bailey."

"Oh," she replied. "Well, no, they didn't notify me at all about this but please come in. I'm sorry; I didn't get your first name."

Isabel pulled at the stray strands of hair at the back of her neck, noticing his curly blond hair and light eyes. He had a small goatee and mustache. She backed into the classroom as he entered.

"Thank you," he replied, stepping into the room.

The classroom of youngsters remained reserved.

A short interval of time passed, enough to become uncomfortable. Detective Bailey's' eyes gazed from one side of the classroom to the other, and then to Isabel. "The name is Kent Bailey," he said, addressing the class and Miss Blake.

"Kent," she repeated softly. She offered her hand and felt his firm grasp. "I'm happy to meet you."

"I'm happy to make your acquaintance also."

"Well," she said, "I'm sorry but I have to leave right now. You're welcome to address the class. I shouldn't be long."

Detective Bailey stood in front of a classroom of young men and women. His authority exuded through the clothes he wore, a blue suit, beige shirt and a brown and blue tie. Quite GQ.

"Students," he bean, with a nod, "I'm here today because we want you all to have notice about what has been happening."

This was the first time someone from the Police Department had come to this school. Detective Bailey noticed for the most part they seemed curious about what he had to say. He cleared his throat and continued, "There've been several murders lately, all young women. Is everyone aware of that?"

They sat quietly and didn't give any indication oneway or the other.

"Good, I mean, I'm glad we don't have to start at the first level," he continued. "We're approaching students of your age level to inform and notify you so there will be extra awareness exercised by youngsters, such as yourselves.

A silence fell among them after he mentioned "youngsters." Kent looked fixedly at them. He rocked back and forth on his heels as he stood with his hands crossed over his chest. "As I said, we want students to be aware and careful. Four young ladies were found," he paused, "well, let's just say their condition ... But, we also want to make everyone aware it can happen to young men." He waved his hand at several of the students.

With only a few words, he delivered his message. Usually, he worked with investigation and communicated with his peers on a day-to-day basis. One-sided conversations were not his style.

"Unfortunately, up until now we don't have any clues as to who is responsible but we do believe the perpetrator is one person and therefore we're dealing with a possible serial killer."

Quiet loomed. Their unresponsiveness surprised him but he didn't know what else to say to them. He continued, "So please keep a look-out for anything you consider suspicious. Are there any questions?"

No one moved.

"Fine. Thank you for your attention." Detective Bailey took determined steps to the door. Without glancing back, he left.

He sauntered down the hall, and spotted Miss Blake. She rushed toward him with a lustrous smile.

"Mr. Bailey?"

"Oh, yes, and you're Miss Blake, correct?"

"Yes. Are you through so soon?"

"Yes. I'm just here to bring special attention to the four killings that occurred recently."

"Oh, I see. I had heard but I didn't know about the individual talks to the school." She stretched her hand forward again to shake his. "Thank you for coming."

The bell rang and students poured into the halls. Haley brushed past Detective Bailey and Miss Blake. She hurried to meet her boyfriend, Matthew. They usually met between these classes. She craned her neck eager to catch a glimpse of him. Then she saw him at their usual spot.

She approached him and he murmured, "Hi, you." His eyes followed her intently as she came nearer and his dimples deepened in a smile.

"Hi," she said softly. She leaned forward and gave him a hug.

He brushed her hair back. "Are you having a bad day? You look a little upset."

"Oh, yeah, just a little something that happened before class today, concerning Courtney."

"Courtney? Since when do you hang out with Courtney?"

"Well, she came over my house yesterday and then today she acted as if we were the best of friends and I don't know it just upset me."

Matthew took Haley by the hand as they walked down the hall. "Don't let it get to you, whatever it is. Hey, I thought we could meet after school today and go over to my house, what do you say?"

Haley stopped short. They had this conversation before. She and Matthew were different from some of the other kids when it came to sex. They decided to wait until they were married. They had decided not to be alone together, so that they wouldn't be tempted.

"No. No, it isn't like that," he remarked. He had a big smile on his face. "Mom will be home because she has time off from work and I'd like her to get to know you a little better."

Relieved, she let out a small laugh. "Sure, I'd love to. I'll see you at the car?"

"Yeah, see you there." He gave her a gentle kiss on the cheek and Haley kissed him back. They glanced at each other longingly and then pulled away. They mouthed *Goodbye* to one another and went their way.

futile 11

Doug sat, with shoulders hunched and head cradled in his arms. *Larry's free isn't he?*

He raised his chin, shook his head from side to side and resolved to think about good things. *I'll think about High School. Those were the happiest times of my life.*

Football, his beloved sport flooded his mind. He envisioned himself as he ran on the field, pulled his arm back and let the ball loose in the air. He watched it spiral through the air. A joyous wave overcame him as he visualized it sail into the hands of the receiver in the end zone. *Touchdown.*

The fresh smell of newly mowed autumn grass after an early morning dew evoked visions of a sun-shimmered green field. He raised his head, took a deep breath and could almost smell the aroma of dirt and wet turf. He basked in the glory of the picturesque image.

Cheerleaders leaped and waved pom-poms on the sidelines. The mass of students responded enthusiastically to their appeal to root for their team. Doug reveled in the recollection. He saw himself on the field on a bright and sunny day as crowds cheered.

The experience lasted until a moment of reality rammed his consciousness, like the Titanic hitting an iceberg.

The sun! I'll never see the sun again! He sat, dazed.

A mournful wail wafted into the air as his agony escaped from within. His chest heaved with strained breath and a deep remorse overwhelmed him. *Why did I ever think about those wonderful times? Why?*

"Grass," he said aloud. "Green grass, I'll never see it again." Panic mounted. "I'll never see anything that's vibrant and alive!"

His hands covered his face in an attempt to hold back the tears. He sank his head into his arms and heaved large, remorseful sobs.

Through his tormented wails, he heard a familiar raspy voice in the darkness. "I see you're still here and miserable." She coughed, hacked, and then said, "But where would you go?"

A grief-stricken pained look clouded his face.

"What's the matter, sonny, don't you feel well?"

"What do you care about how I feel?"

The woman shrugged. "I don't. But you're making a lot of noise. In fact, you're causing more of a stir than they do in heaven."

Doug's bloodshot eyes widened. "So, there's a heaven? What's it like."

Her face became devoid and empty. "I'm told it's peaceful and quiet. Very quiet. I don't think they make any noise there." She stood next to him. "What's the matter, don't you feel well anymore?"

He had his pride. He rubbed his hands across his face to wipe away the moisture. "I feel fine. It's hot here."

"Oh, I see you don't think I'm entertaining," she continued, "but maybe someday you'll get a kick out of demoralizing someone else since there isn't any other kind of amusement. I know I feel much better when I make someone else feel worse." Her throat sounded hoarse as she rasped the gravelly words. Sometimes he guessed at what she said. He hated to talk to her but he also hated being alone.

She hacked and coughed some more and then shouted, "My throat!"

The sudden plea caught him off guard.

She continued to cry out, "My throat, can't you see there's something wrong?" Than a strange hiss emanated as she cackled and coughed.

Doug didn't move. Instead, he said coolly, "Don't you care about anyone but yourself?"

"If I did care about myself I wouldn't be here," she managed to snap back flippantly. "The sad thing is that you realize a lot of things once you are here." A long guttural noise followed as she cleared her larynx. Then a wad sprang out of her mouth. Doug winced at the black lump.

"Ah, that's better," she said, clearly. "I see the wrong choices I made. Up there they call that hindsight but up there they have a chance to change. Here, I'm miserable because I think to myself, 'I wish I hadn't done this, or I wish I did that.' It makes me crazy."

As she spoke, her head rolled back and forth and her eyes enlarged with a frantic appearance. "And you miss all the beauty up there," she continued with raised hands and grand gestures. "The splendor of the world and daily enjoyment of whatever you want. Isn't it a pity? No more baseball games, golf – or football?"

He cringed and turned his face away.

She babbled on. "I know how you feel. You can't hide it from me. I even know about situations that will happen in the future."

"The future? How can you know that?"

"Oh, yes," she continued, in a soapbox stance. Her hands rotated as if around an imaginary crystal ball. "I know about things that are going to happen. I only wish I had then."

"Who are you?"

"You don't recognize me do you?"

If I did, I wouldn't ask. He shook his head and perspiration spattered into the darkness.

"You wouldn't ask," she retaliated. "Don't be so smart."

"How do you know what I'm thinking?"

She ignored his question and said in a mournful, sympathetic tone, "Well, I don't care if you don't."

During her life, the paparazzi followed her everywhere. She had beautiful clothes and lived a lifestyle that few could afford. *Stunning* could have been her middle name and she had everything she wanted. All the clothes, houses, and boyfriends she ever wanted were hers. People said her talent amazed them and they ate out of her hand. She missed the notoriety and easy life immensely.

When she would arrive at a Premiere and step out of the limousine, her long beautiful legs commanded attention.

She had beautiful chestnut brown hair, styled in a coiffure piled high on top, with curls flowing down one side. Her impeccable make-up and vibrant lush red lips were her fashion statement.

She wore lavish jewels and designer see-through sequined spectacles that were embarrassingly expensive.

Many envied her beauty and everyone wanted to associate with her and her boyfriend, whoever he was at the time.

There were moments that she longed for the fame so much, her heart ached. However, she remembered how empty and vain it was. *I took care of the physical and ignored the spiritual,* she would think remorsefully.

Angrily she yelled aloud, "I didn't listen to the important question, 'what shall it profit a man, if he shall gain the whole world, and lose his own soul?' That was me!"

Increasingly grotesque features were the cruel result as she bantered back and forth. With no way to turn back and no way to stop the downhill slide, it became the epitome of futile.

Doug retorted, "So are you going to tell me about the future or stand there and moan?"

"Ooooh, aren't we snippy? Sure, I'll tell you but not because of your manners."

She clamped her lips together for about five seconds, put her finger to her mouth and hissed.

Doug nodded his head and responded in a low voice, "a secret?"

In a scraped whisper she said, "I know about the big battle."

"Battle? What're you talking about?"

"Yesssss," she hissed, "a big battle." She walked to the other side of him on her toes and whispered in his ear, "I think the time is close."

"For what?"

A wry smile crossed her contorted face. "You don't know anything do you?"

"Not while you're playing this guessing game. What are you talking about?"

"Oh, so you think it's a guessing game. My guess is, it's time for you to move."

"Move? What does that have to do with a battle?"

"Only that things are changing."

116

"I thought you said it ended here for me. What're you talking about?"

Suddenly, a moan arose inside him and he groaned involuntarily.

"Oh, no, sweetie, there's more for you than this."

Puzzled, Doug wanted to ask what she meant but before he could open his mouth, she said, "This little rock you've become attached to isn't for you. When we get to your destination, remember, it only gets worse from there."

"What do you mean?" Doug replied with a thin sound to his voice.

"Shhhhh, she sizzled. "There's worse and then there's a lot worse. It's horrible that we missed it and weren't here before."

"When? For what?"

"I heard about it but I didn't see it. It must have been something."

His face reddened and he screamed at the top of his voice. "What in the world are you talking about?"

"Don't get so worked up," she yelled back. She continued. "Like I said, it was something. They said a great big light came down."

He tried to imagine brilliance in the midst of the blackness surrounding him and echoed, "A light?"

"Yes," she hissed. "The light came down ..." She pressed her face closer to his. "...and He preached."

"Who? What're you talking about?"

"The king's son, Arnion," she answered with a slight lisp. "They said He died and the next thing they knew He was here. I wish I had been here to see it, I really do."

"What did he do?"

A starry-eyed expressed crossed her face. "He gave a talk to the spirits that were in this prison."

The news had a strange effect on Doug. He felt more forlorn than ever and more despondent.

"And then, he took some of them with him."

Doug's expression resembled someone watching a fast-paced ping-pong game.

She motioned to him to come closer. "It's time."

"Time for what?"

"Time for you to *follow* me."

The moment the words came from her mouth, they shot off like a rocket and soared through air. Doug unwillingly tracked directly behind her, speeding through pitch-black darkness, except for the glint of a few shiny objects.

They ventured further and the dim surroundings gave way to a thick haze. The lighter it became, the more the noise level rose, until it became raucous.

They stopped and Doug bounded onto his feet.

"There you go."

He looked around. A large porthole appeared through a small clearing in the haze. He walked to it and looked in.

A large pit made of an ebony material lay below. It resembled rock, but he had never seen rock that looked that bleak. He strained to see what lay below.

It appeared like a gigantic mass, but it moved.

"What's ...? What's down there?"

With a quizzical smile, she said, "This is where you get off."

He leaned forward. Perspiration streamed down his face and he wiped it away with his sticky hands.

Then he gained insight as to what the mass was.

At the bottom of the cavernous pit, an enormous number of beings stood, tightly packed against one another.

They pushed and shoved as fiery flames flared on top of the rocks around them.

Bats hung from small crevices and ravens and vultures screeched eerie sounds as they flew above.

With hauntingly sorrowful looks, the beings shouted obscenities at each other.

He placed his hands over his ears. He had used curse words in his lifetime but he had never heard such profanity. It was bedlam.

In disbelief, he looked at the woman. "There . . . there must be some terrible mistake."

"HAAAAAAAAGH," she cried. "And, remember, this isn't the worst of it."

Doug panicked. "What do you mean?"

"This isn't Tartaroo."

A blaze shot up behind her when she mentioned, "Tartaroo." She jumped and virtually landed into Doug's lap.

"Aaaah" Doug yelled. "Why did that fire erupt?"

"Because I mentioned ....you know. But that isn't as bad as when the Ruler of the Realm speaks. When he speaks, the souls below panic. They shove each other so hard the pressure splits the rocks and the earth moves."

A surge flowed over the top of his head. Then he thought about what she had mentioned. "What's . . . what's, you know, what you said before?"

She put her finger to her mouth, frightened and answered, "It's the deepest part of Hades."

"But what about the battle you mentioned? Is someone going to come and rescue us?"

Her eyes widened and she appeared like a woman who had gone mad. "Rescue us? No, that already happened remember? We weren't here. No, after the last battle then we'll all be moved."

Where? Where are we going?"

"As the French would say, 'Tombre de la poële dans la braise, or out of the frying pan into the fire."

"Frying pan?" His voice weakened as he repeated the phrase. He looked through the hole again. The throng underneath had not abated their rant.

"I've heard that expression," he said. He feared the multitude below was the frying pan.

"That's right, buddy boy, you're going from this hole to another that will be more horrifying. It'll be a lake but not one of water. It's a lake of fire."

He looked through the hole once more at the chaotic pandemonium below.

"But it can't get any worse. And I don't feel well. I'm hungry!" He yelled.

"My advice is to enjoy the good times while you have them."

Good times? Doug thought she had lost her mind. The veins on his neck enlarged and he felt as if his head would burst. "No! It can't get any worse!" He shouted; his head pounded from all the noise and he yelled, "You don't understand!"

"Yes, I do," she said in a tone he hadn't heard before.

The change took him by surprise and he stopped for a moment and wondered *is she being sympathetic?*

"I don't want to see this happen to my family. This is atrocious and everything in my being wants to warn them. My brother Evan, he's the youngest. And Kent."

"Kent Bailey?" she asked in a whisk of a second.

"Yes. Our last name's Bailey. If you knew them, you would understand. They're both nice guys but I know they're not religious."

"Isn't that too bad but religion doesn't have anything to do with it. The fact is there're religious creatures here. It just kills you.

"But if you knew Kent and Evan you'd see. They're my flesh and blood. There are extenuating circumstances."

"Tell me about it Dearie," she prodded.

"Well my brothers were older than I. By the time I entered Junior High, they both had graduated. Not only were they older but they weren't like me at all."

"Oh, isn't that too bad."

Doug ignored her feigned sympathy.

"Well, Kent locked into a career as a detective and Evan followed close behind, except he became an attorney. Our parents were proud of them. Unfortunately, I know now that I perceived this incorrectly. I felt inferior in contrast to their achievement."

"So sad."

"You're not hearing what I'm saying," Doug pleaded.

"If you felt second-rate, why does it matter to you where they end up?"

"Are you kidding? This forsaken hole isn't for anyone."

"Yes, you're right."

Her acceptance dazed him for a moment. *Will she relent and let him go?*

She drummed her fingers against her cheek. "No worries. I enjoyed your story for a while but this is just about my favorite part of my job. ENJOY."

She placed her misshapen hands against his back and pushed

him sternly through the hole.

Her strength surprised him. His legs flung over his head and he somersaulted through the air. After a long, harrowed fall, he landed prostrate on top of the crowd.

A multitude of hands caught him and passed his body over their heads.

They chanted, NO MORE ROOM ... NO MORE ROOM.

open wide 12

The six young angels broke out in a verbal melee and Jonathan pounded the podium with his gavel.

They quieted down, one by one, until Gordan piped up and said, "That's the view of the review for now."

In the midst of the disorder, the guest stood quickly. "If you will all excuse me."

They searched each other's faces, quizzically. What could he want?

"I believe I have a call from my ... my administrator."

Jonathan glared at the guest. "This place is one of freedom. You're free to go as you wish."

"I'll be back before you resume," he said and hobbled past the surprised group.

Lev didn't move as Skotoo brushed by him. A lump came to his throat as he watched the visitor struggle as he walked with a crooked gait.

Abigail spouted, "He's such an ugly black thing."

Her declaration released a pandemonium of voices from the rest.

"Here, here," Jonathan shouted above the ruckus. "Attention, squadron, your attention is needed without more ado."

Nathan addressed the others. "Look, we don't know why this entity came, but we need to be composed and work with this the best we can."

"I think there's something seriously wrong with the fellow," Gordan responded.

"Wrong?" Shay quipped. "He's definitely daft. Most definitely."

"It's obvious, he hasn't a pittance of purity," Elizabeth offered as she considered her nail grooming.

Lev remained the only one who didn't comment.

Inaudible to mortal ears, the black visitor heard cries that pierced the cavernous, black tunnels.

Hopeless, futile groans and shattering screams went unheeded, heard only by those who made their bed in the dark forsaken tomb. Their helplessness added to their woeful, sorrowful shrieks.

He had grown indifferent to the howls.

Nevertheless, fear gripped him as he rushed haphazardly through the long dark passageway.

His terror intensified the closer he came. Thoughts bombarded him. *Does he want me for a different assignment so soon?*

He reached the door of the auditorium and a thought beset him. *What if it's because I did something wrong?* He paused a moment. *I don't dare think about this. If I appear distraught, it will give him even more reason to be upset.*

As second in command, he didn't take anything for granted. He worked hard and long to reach this prestigious level but he knew he could lose his stature in a quirky millisecond.

His previous briefing included the usual script on how to disrupt the opponent. He had similar missions before and felt comfortable with this one. *Maybe that's it, I was too confident.*

He arrived, stood and waited for the summons. He yearned to wring his hands, but refrained.

Dreary smoke swirled making Nachash barely visible. In the ancient scrolls, they referred to him as the old serpent, a title he loathed.

However, he detested the monarchy of the Ruler of the Realm and His son, Arnion, most.

In the beginning, he lived in the Ruler of the Realm's kingdom. His desire to become king drove him from the purview of the court. The ruler cast him away and he lost everything.

Now his existence thrived only to settle the score.

Nachash's purposed to guide myriads to desire to be their own ruler and separate themselves from the noble kings.

Every thought drove him into deeper desolation and as it did, his outer skin of thick red scales, intensified in color.

A blaze of fire discharged from his nose and mouth. Centuries had passed since his inception but he chose to shed his former perfect nature.

He rarely exhibited his past beauty of precious stones. Sardius, a deep red colored gem, topaz, diamond, golden lustrous beryl, onyx, sapphire, emerald, red garnet and gold wrapped about his form.

Bitterness caused his luster to dim. At times, he mustered the image of an angel, the luminosity a shadow of his prior exquisiteness.

The summoned visitor stood until it became abysmally quiet. Somehow, he garnered the strength to peek through the slit of one eye.

Smoke settled to the lower portions of the ground. Skotoo's other eye popped open.

No one else was there. Skotoo could not remember a time when the dragon's circle didn't include scores of beings that wanted to befriend him. It seemed they had scattered to their own corner out of the range of Nachash's previous rage.

"ENTER!" The commander roared.

He shuffled forward with a stiff gait, moving one foot in front of the other, peering cautiously at the throne.

His neck craned back as he peered high above him. Nachash sat, puffing large scorching breaths of flames.

Pitiful wards from the dark realm had gnawed the huge black rock with their teeth for years until Nachash found it acceptable, at least to a degree.

He demanded a pyramid-shaped throne, with steps to a flattened apex, where he situated his throne. They dutifully dressed it with brilliant gems as he decreed, but the heat and smoke blackened the brilliant gems over the thousands of years.

He stood before his leader and watched as his seven heads tossed wildly.

A crown perched atop each of Nachash's heads somehow remained. They symbolized his rule over that kingdom. Ten horns sat upon his shoulders.

The beastly form roared a loud reverberating sound.

He sniveled, "Did you send for me, your highness?"

"Would you be here if I didn't?"

"No, I would not, sir. I only ask since I was in the midst of a review when I received your call."

"I called you because of your incompetence."

His narrow-slit eyes widened. "Sir? May I ask what I've done?"

"Not you!"

He shook and looked around. "Then, then … why am I here, sir?"

"The new recruit, you know the has-been, movie star."

He searched his memory. Then, he recalled. She had recently begun as an escort. "Yes … I know exactly who you mean."

"She's worse than an idiot."

"I agree. Yes sir. Yes, you're absolutely right."

"Don't patronize me," the dragon bellowed.

His lips puckered tightly. "Of course not," he muttered. "But what can I do about it now? I'm in the midst of this …"

"Idiot! I know where you are. You don't have to tell me. I want you to return to your assignment and think about how to deal with this woman. When you get back here, I want this incompetence eradicated, do you understand? If there's incompetence beneath, it makes me look ineffectual.

"It will be taken care of expressly when I return."

"Now get out of my sight and get back to work."

He bowed. His body shuttered as he bent over in a long, honoring bow. He scooted away and out of his superior's presence.

What an ordeal. I'm fortunate to be chosen to bring destruction to others. What would I do if I merely existed for eons in nothing but suffering? Now, back to my lovelies. I have to do well and ingratiate myself back into Nachash's grace.

"Good grief," Austin said aloud.

The morning seemed as if it started well until he found the article.

"Listen to this. Police identified the body of a young woman in Oakshire County yesterday. Detectives believe a connection may exist to the disappearance and murder of a victim found two weeks ago. There are two other murders that also may be connected."

His mechanical-sounding voice echoed into the air. He glanced to see if his wife paid him any attention.

Anna stood at the sink with her back to him so he couldn't tell. He held his coffee in his hand, savoring the heat and fresh aroma.

He continued. "Identification is being held pending notification of next of kin."

"It's incredible these awful things happen," Anna proclaimed. "It's chilling. I mean, did these young girls make a decision for Christ? What a difference that would make if they did.

She looked back at Austin. He sat seemingly engrossed in his newspaper. She turned and continued wash strawberries, set them in a bowl and poured cream on top.

"How do you read all of that stuff while you eat? Doesn't it give you indigestion?"

"All what stuff?" He answered with an aloof tone. "How am I supposed to know what's happening in the world if I don't read about it? We quit watching television."

"That was your decision to stop, although I totally agree with you."

At the mention of television, his eyes swooped open. He wasn't irritated so much with Anna as he was with the subject. "It's a fiasco," he said. "First, they corrupt movies with sex and violence and then television portrays morality as if it doesn't exist."

"Isn't that why you call it 'hellivision'?"

"You're absolutely right. The few times I've tried to watch something I get disgusted because of all the sex and violence. When they first invented it, you didn't even hear a curse word. Now, I can't even watch the news because commercials are filled with sexual innuendos."

"You're preaching to the choir," she replied. Then she added, "But it works doesn't it?"

"What?"

"The media thing whether it's television, movies or the theater. They feed people images of men and women sleeping with each other without being married and before you know, no one cares about what they're doing."

"Well, I wouldn't say no one."

"You know what I mean. Most people thought it was wrong years ago. They thought it was wrong to have a child out of wedlock awful. But society has been desensitized."

"I know. Kids today receive such a distorted view. They parade every subject under the sun before them and they're told to believe that all of it is acceptable. They're being brainwashed. They don't understand if everyone in the world does something wrong it doesn't make it right. It's amazing, and when you try to tell someone it's wrong, they've been told this so long they don't believe you."

"That's where the Lord comes in."

"I know. It's not our job, it's His."

He read for a while and noticed Anna had become very quiet.

"What's wrong?" He asked.

"Nothing, I was just thinking about Jacob."

He set the paper down. "I don't understand him. He knows the truth. We didn't allow him to go to R-rated movies or anything. Now he lives his life as if he had never been taught anything."

"At least he was brought up with the right instruction. Train up a child in the way he should go, right? Just think how many people are brought up without that."

"Yes, but even if they haven't been raised as a Christian, the beauty of the Spirit working in their life is that they can come to know Him. When their spiritual eyes are opened they would never want to do anything that would sadden Him."

"I guess that means his spiritual eyes are closed," Anna said softly.

"They must be." It hurt Austin to know his child was out of the fold. "Even though he knows better," he continued, "he wasn't bombarded with all of the stuff that's on television these days. It's hard for me to understand why he turned away."

She thought for a moment and then said, "I guess we're forgetting something."

"What?"

"Well, we're all born with a sin nature. If Jacob didn't give his life totally to the Lord then his old nature has taken over again."

Austin paused. He had never thought about it that way. "Yes," he said slowly. "We all have the ability to sin. Like this article about this young girl. The murderer certainly had a choice right to the end."

Anna let out a deep sigh. "I wish you wouldn't read that stuff."

"Like I said, I need to know what's going on." He lifted his newspaper in front of his face.

"There won't be any in heaven," she replied over her shoulder.

He looked up and caught her quick smile and the gleam in her eyes.

"I haven't seen that look for awhile," he said.

She blushed. "It's amazing, we were talking and I when I said 'heaven,' a slight breath of God swept over me. I got a warm feeling all over. Won't it be wonderful?"

Before he could answer, Haley entered the kitchen. "Morning," she said.

Anna smiled. "*Good* morning."

Haley portioned the strawberries onto a plate and sat down at the table. After only a couple of bites, she walked over to the sink. While no one looked, she scooped the rest down the drain.

"I'm going to be late this afternoon, Mom," she said in a half-muffled tone.

"Oh? Why?"

"I'll be meeting a friend."

"Oh, are you seeing Matthew?

"No, I saw him yesterday. He has to work today."

"When did you see him?"

"Oh, I forgot to tell you. We went to his house. Don't worry his Mom was home. She's nice. Matthew said he wanted her to get to know me."

Anna and Austin glanced at each other with an approving nod.

A single parent, Matthew's mother, LeAnn, remained divorced for several years. She attended the same church as the Connors' and Haley and Matthew went to Sunday school together. As children, they liked to be together. Unsurprising, their friendship bloomed into something more.

"So who did you say you're meeting today?" Anna asked.

"Not anyone you know, just someone I met. We're going to go have a pop after school and go over some homework and then I'll be home. I'll just be about an hour or two."

"You're not seeing Courtney, are you?" she asked.

"No, Mom, I told you. It's just someone at school."

"What's her name and phone number?"

Haley took a deep breath. "Her name is Jessica and I don't have her number. Besides, we're going to the little café on the corner and you won't be able to reach me there anyway. I don't have a cell phone, remember?"

"Okay Hon, but you know I don't want you to get mixed up with Courtney. I think she's trouble. Don't forget to pick up the photos."

Haley grasped her bag, and dutifully kissed them on the cheek as she muttered, "Love you."

She thought about the CD in her locker at school. *I'll give it back to Courtney today after school. I wish I didn't have to sneak around to do this but once I give it to her, it'll all be over.*

what a tangled web we weave 13

Jonathan cleared his throat and announced, "Students, our guest has returned."

Abigail sat and flipped her hand through her hair, seemingly agitated. The others shifted into their chairs.

The visitor entered and repositioned himself at the front next to Jonathan's podium.

Nathan spoke. "Jonathan, I have some questions before we go on if I may."

Jonathan nodded.

"Although we've discussed several factors with our guest, we don't know his name. Nor do we know how he received an invitation. Are we correct to assume he is a fallen angel? If so, aren't they held in chains in darkness until the Day of Judgment?"

Jonathan didn't want to get into a discourse in regard to those held in the underworld and answered, "Yes, Nathan, you're right I haven't introduced our guest. I have been remiss. Please forgive me.

He turned his back to the class and wrote on the board. S-k-o-t-o-o. "Let me introduce you all to ... to ... Skotoo."

"Skotoo?" Nathan reiterated in a high-pitched timbre. Nathan would never laugh at someone's name, but this seemed strangely comical.

His breath shot forth in small patters in his effort to contain his amusement.

"Yes, Nathan, it's pronounced Scoot-oo-oo"

The others covered their smirks with their hands.

"Scoot-oo-oo?" Gordan repeated. "Maybe we should call him Scooter."

It may have been nerves, but they couldn't hold their delight any longer. First a giggle spurted, followed with a gaggle of laughter.

Skotoo's narrowly slit eyes widened as much as they could and his jaw dropped open.

The group held their mouth, their stomach and even turned around as they rolled in hilarity.

Nathan collected his outburst first. He hoped to help the group recover, and in a lower tone of voice he commented, "We shouldn't laugh about this you guys."

Gordan realized the seriousness of Nathan's statement and added quickly, "He's right, you guys, it isn't funny. You don't know what his name means."

Elizabeth peeked over her hand, which she had placed on her face. "Well, studious Gordan, what does it mean?"

"You would think it meant *obscure* ..."

"You mean you don't know?" she chided. Her remark spurred the group to snicker even more.

Gordan held his hands up to calm them and said, "No. I mean yes, I do know. You see the word *obscure* is from Skotos, which is similar to Skotoo. But his name means to obscure or blind – one that is full of darkness."

Darkness. The grim reminder settled over them. One by one, they understood that this wasn't for their entertainment. An almost tangible silence hung like a heavy veil.

The gloomy description sank in and Gordan continued. "His name represents the epitome of eternal damnation, the exact opposite of what we know. We have light and joy while the dark kingdom has only dreariness and sorrow. This so called 'Scooter,' as you've nicknamed him is from the pit itself."

They sobered as the information soaked deeply into them. Then they heard a strange sound.

"Hee ... hee ... hee." The sound resonated as it squeaked

through the drawn curvatures of his mouth.

Lev spoke. "I'm glad we've finally become calm. I don't like this anymore than you do but to simplify matters, I suggest we refer to our guest simply as 'Scot'."

The group agreed.

Skotoo's eyebrows lifted at the new occurrence of receiving a substitute name.

Nathan saw his chance to get back on track. He said, "As I requested earlier, Jonathan, how is it that . . . that 'Scot' is here and has freedom to come to our instruction class?"

"Skotoo ... that is, Scot, is ... well, he's here on a mission."

"What kind of mission?"

Jonathan took a deep breath and exhaled a long, low breath. "I'm not eager to discuss this. You see Scot is sent out, much as you are sent out but in a completely different manner of course. Nevertheless he is sent out."

"Who sends him?" Nathan asked. "How close is he to the evil one?"

Jonathan gazed at Skotoo.

A queer smirk swelled across Skotoo's countenance. Both ends of his mouth turned up in a semi-circle and it appeared as if someone drew the grin in a haphazard way. Clearly, he wasn't used to this type of facial exercise.

"He's very close to the evil one," Jonathan continued, "You might say he's his right-hand-man."

The angelees were amazed that one so vile and wicked would be here to begin with but the fact that he was the evil one's ambassador astonished them.

"He's the right-hand-man to the evil one?" Abigail repeated, frightened.

"Well, you heard what his name means," Shay countered.

Astonished, Elizabeth added, "This is terrible! What good can it do?"

Abigail concurred. "I don't see how we can learn anything from that side of the world."

Gordan and Lev remained pensive.

Nathan attempted to soothe the opposition. He repeated,

"Don't worry, don't worry," in as calm a voice as he could muster.

The commotion amused Skotoo. He chuckled and wheezed with a "hee, hee, hee," sound, similar to an old squeezed music box but without a melodious tone.

Lev stood up and said, "Now that we're calm, we need to concentrate. We're here for our review, which you all know is important. Don't you remember we're to receive the power to fly at the end of this lesson? Let's stop fluttering around and get back on course."

"He's got my dander up'" Shay piped. He had not forgotten that Scot and he were from the same star, a fact he could hardly believe. It irritated him immensely.

"We need to think about this with our hearts as well as our heads," Lev interjected again and sat down.

The group seemed focused again. With that, Nathan took the lead. "Well, Jonathan, before our outbreak you addressed our visitor's mission."

Jonathan sighed deeply and looked at his beautiful, innocent, band of angelees. Youthful faces, with countenances that glowed exquisitely, looked expectantly to him. Their cherubic looks reminded Jonathan they were mere babes compared to angelic beings that existed for eons. He perceived that even when challenged with adversity, their beauty would remain unsurpassable.

He knew Skotoo's plan to entice one, or all, away from their loyalty to the Ruler of the Realm. He wished he could alert his wards.

In a low, muffled tone he said, "He's here to present a proposition."

"What does that mean?" Abigail asked.

"A proposition. You know, a scheme or plan," Gordan responded.

"That's not all, Gordan." Shay answered. "There's more to it than that. Our past lessons showed us that 'The devil, as a roaring lion, walks about, seeking whom he can devour.' Figure it out. I think our friend Scot here has his mouth wide open."

Abigail responded, "Can he devour us?

The question hung like a balloon in the air, unanswered.

Abigail continued. "Does Arnion know he's here?"

❖

Arnion, translated, meant *Lamb*.

Elizabeth envisioned the heir to the Ruler of the Realm's throne.

They called him Amnos before he died. Yes, he died before he adapted his new persona.

His name indicated his nature and the character of his sacrifice. After his death, his name changed to Arnion, which represented not only his sacrifice but also His acquired power, majesty, and honor. How did he die and yet remain alive? That was another story.

The old dragon manifested himself as a tempter and approached Him. "If you are the Son of the Mighty One, command that these stones be made bread." The request exhibited the characteristic of enticement that the dragon possessed.

Stone turned to bread was a feat the Son, or Amnos could easily perform in demonstration of His power. Amnos answered, "It is written, Man shall not live by bread alone, but by every word that proceeds out of the mouth of God."

The old dragon took Him into the holy city and set Him at the top of the temple, the figurative footstool of the Ruler of the Realm of the Magnificent City. He proclaimed to Amnos, "If you are the Son of the Mighty One, cast yourself down, for it is written, He will give His angels charge over you, and they will bear You up in their hands, lest You strike your foot against stone."

Amnos stood at the pinnacle of the temple, built with the learned craft of costly stones extracted from the quarry.

Long-handled picks were cut above, below and on the sides of the building material. They drilled small holes in rows and drove wooden wedges into the holes. They poured water on the wedges, which caused them to swell, which split the stone and freed it from embedment.

At the height of one hundred and eighty-seven feet, wind buffeted wildly against Amnos.

He replied, "It is written again, you shall not tempt, test thoroughly, or try exceedingly the Lord your God."

The dragon took him to a high mountain and showed Him many kingdoms of the world. They consisted of lands, peoples and gold, silver and precious jewels. Again, he maligned the imperial monarchy and said, "These things, all taken together, I will give You, if You will prostrate Yourself before me and do homage and worship me."

Amnos would have nothing to do with him. "Begone, Satan! For it has been written you shall worship the Lord your God, and Him alone shall you serve."

He addressed him as *Satan* and proclaimed that he was the archenemy of good. To grant honor to this fiend was unthinkable. In all of the attacks, the Son upheld His deity and prevailed.

Elizabeth drank in the revelation of Arnion and then cried out, "oh, my!"

❖

Shay continued. "*May* devour, Abigail. *May* not *can*. That means it doesn't have to definitely happen."

"I've something I have to tell you all," Elizabeth spouted.

"We really must continue" Jonathan declared, interrupting their conversation. They had arrived at the most intense part of their review. He knew Skotoo had authority to attempt to delude one or all of the angelees. The king granted the trial of Job's endurance by the evil one. Their allegiance would soon be evident. Jonathan wasn't worried but hadn't angels fallen before?

He had a duty to inform his little ones.

He squared his shoulders, mustered all he had and announced in a loud voice, "This is a test."

Bewildered, they turned to one another. They had no idea what he meant.

Lev said, "We've never had a test before, Jonathan. Is it possible you've mixed us with another group?"

"No, Lev, I know exactly whom I'm addressing. This … this is the Teleiotes Squadron, which will be engaged in a special mission."

Gordan's hand darted into the air.

"Yes, Gordan?"

"Could you clarify the definition of Teleiotes?"

"Well, its pronounced teliotace not teleiotes."

"Oh thank you sir," Gordan replied. "From what I understand,

Teleiotes means 'completeness' or 'perfection'. Is that correct?"

"Yes, that's correct."

"Duh," Shay interjected. "We should have known that."

Jonathan smirked and continued. "The magnitude of your undertaking as this select group mandated that it be kept from you until now."

"But sir, there have been other squadrons by that name before haven't there?" Gordan continued.

"Yes, but a final group has never been appointed."

"Oh," Gordan said and his voice trailed off. The group tried to discern what this meant and a murmur arose among them once again.

"Does it mean that the group is perfect?" was one comment. "What's this perfection about?" Someone else asked.

"This is what you'll discover as we conclude this class. We are required to conclude our review, which will not be the end of your education because you have much preparation to partake yet. But first we must continue and conclude this examination."

Abigail rose to her feet. "So, what you're saying is that Scot is part of the test?

"Yes, Abigail, he is."

Her heart sank and she didn't know if she should ask the next question or not. Then again, she knew she had to. "Does that mean one of us has to leave and won't be here for the rest of eternity?"

Radiance itself seemed to cease in the midst of this beautiful, lavender-skied afternoon. Jonathan gazed at their confused, trusting faces.

They all held their breath, the quiet revealing Skotoo's wheeze.

Jonathan broke the silence. "No. That's not what it means."

Skotoo shot a look over to Jonathan. "You hope it doesn't," he said sharply.

"I believe it doesn't. It doesn't mean that absolutely one or more will fall but we all must be aware there are pitfalls and we need to be on the lookout."

Again, stillness pervaded. If an object had fallen, it would have resounded loudly.

Nathan took the lead again. "Well, logically, it seems we shouldn't have to face this."

"Oh? And why do you say that?" Jonathan asked.

"We're ministering spirits, sent forth to them who shall be heirs of salvation, isn't that right? Am I also correct that since we go to those who will inherit salvation, we don't need to obtain salvation for ourselves?"

"Up to a point."

"There you go, up to a point, again!" Skotoo lambasted. "You and your points!"

"If Skotoo will allow me …

"Scot. We decided to call me Scot, remember?"

"Yes, as I said, if Skotoo will allow me, what Nathan has brought up is partially true."

They were on the edge of their chairs.

"Forgive me, Jonathan, if I've spoken incorrectly," Nathan blurted. "I only meant to ask a question."

"It's all right, Nathan. What you've verbalized is your sincere observation and there is no ill persuasion in it. You are correct. You are ministering spirits who care for the salvation of mortals and you cannot receive in the same way. Your spirit is different from theirs, as you contain the same atoms found inside stars. However, you are capable of choice for good or evil as mortals are the proof being those angels of long ago who chose to either stay or go with Nachash."

Audible gasps were heard as each of them exhaled in succession.

"Then, you mean it could happen again?" Gordan said.

Elizabeth stammered, "But … Jonathan," "Na… Na…"

"Spit it out, Liz," Gordan offered.

"Well, Nachash's heart was lifted up because of his beauty and all he possessed. I don't think that pertains to any of us."

"It wasn't only his conceit, Elizabeth," Nathan said. "Yes, his beauty was an obstacle but at his core he believed he would exalt his throne above the Ruler of the Realm and that he would sit upon the mount of the congregation, in the place of control. That caused his downfall."

Elizabeth countered once again. "But, I don't believe anyone here has that attitude."

"Perhaps not," Jonathan responded. "But mortals, whom you protect, wrestle against these principalities. We all have to be aware of deceitfulness and trickery and defend against spiritual wickedness in high places."

Skotoo's chair squeaked as he shifted his weight, uneasy. He scowled with displeasure at their enlightenment.

Jonathan continued. "So, Job received a test and did not sin with his lips against the Ruler of the Realm. A test doesn't mean a failure. A test simply reveals character and knowledge. Job did not try to exalt himself although he accused the Ruler about seventy-four times. The important thing is that ultimately he repented."

"But we don't have anything that can be taken away from us as Job did," Abigail pleaded.

"You have your will, Abigail. The axis of your sincerest motive is, that's where the matter lies. Whether you regard Him," he said pointing toward the Ruler's throne.

"Regard Him in what sense?"

"Well, for instance ... as in the Garden."

At the word, "Garden," Elizabeth blurted, "Wait! I have to tell you all. Remember when we talked about the devil and how he walked about to see who he may devour?"

Unfortunately, no one paid attention and Abigail continued, "You mean when Eve was deceived?"

"Yes. Yes. When Eve was deceived," Jonathan answered.

A voice from behind interrupted the discussion.

"You mean when we *think* Eve was deceived."

The alienated tone sounded unfamiliar.

Jonathan looked to see who had spoken. He thought at first Skotoo had uttered the words, but the declaration came from the back of the atrium.

His eyes fixed on the angelee standing alone.

mended fences 14

Detectives Sealy and Owens reported to the briefing room. Captain Hodges hadn't arrived yet but the rest of the detectives did. Normally there would be four maybe, and then they would fill each other in later. This time, the staff of eight filled the room.

John Sealy winced and placed his hand on his sternum. "My stomach burns. I don't know if it's something I ate or the job."

Owens rested leisurely in the wooden seat of the classroom-style desk. His dog-tired eyes surveyed the room. He wiped his brow with a paper towel, crumpled it and set it on top of the desk. "I thought I would be out of here early," he said with a sigh.

"That's right, I forgot you're usually one who gets updated by one of the other guys."

Hank Owens shrugged. He threw his pen on the desk, aiming for the wadded paper. "I guess I can use the overtime."

The men glanced up as Captain Hodges arrived. Gray haired and mustached, he appeared rumpled in his gray suit.

His belly, which he had accumulated from thirty-nine years of home-cooked meals, may have contributed to the look. He cleared his throat. "Gentlemen."

About half of them paid attention. He cleared his throat again and repeated, "Gentlemen," a little louder. They seemed to be in a talkative mood.

He turned up the pitch once again. "As you were informed, I

have new information which I believe will lead us right to the serial killer."

The men sat and leaned forward. Captain Hodges now possessed their attention.

Hodges surveyed the detective's faces. "Thank you all for being so prompt. I apologize for not being here right on the dot but I wanted to get these copies made for you."

He held sheets of paper in his hand and passed them out to the front of the rows. They shuffled them quickly down each row until each man had one.

Sealy eagerly read and reread the few lines. He looked sideways at his partner. "I don't think I get it."

Owens scrutinized the statistics. He shrugged. "I don't either."

Hodges continued. "On this sheet of paper, you'll see names of several businesses, all of which have one thing in common." He looked over his group and saw tired eyes look back at him. "All of the stores listed on this sheet develop photos. Here you have a name of a grocery store, a prescription store, a large discount warehouse, and so on."

The men sat with blank stares as the captain droned through the presentation. A few coughs every now and then broke the silence.

"Even though these are not all photo shops, per se, they all offer developing."

Owens stomach became more agitated by the moment. He began to think he should have stayed home.

With a copy in his hand, Hodges walked to the chalkboard and wrote the victims' names.

Tess Coleman
Emma Bates
Betty Glen
Catherine Crest.

The crime scenes flashed before Sealy and he cringed as Hodges scratched their names on the board.

Hodges looked back at the men, turned to the board, and continued to write. This time he wrote the names of four businesses.

He drew a circle on the side of the board with an arrow

from the circle to each of the stores. He turned back to the group of detectives who sat in silence.

"This is where we believe there's a connection." In the middle of the circle, he wrote "Home's Photo Processing."

Like hound dogs on the trail of a scent, Owens and Sealy sat straighter in their chair.

Hodges continued. "This processor services all of these stores."

Across the room, heads nodded.

"Two of the victims can be tied to these stores. They each had film processed before the murders and we believe the killer became associated with them in this manner. He knew what they looked like, their address and their phone number. That's how he picked them out. We also know that two of the girls attended St. Mary's but that's such a generality we don't know where it will lead. You know, I'm not committing to this lead as absolute. Remember, it's a lead."

The hair on Sealy's arms stood on end. He looked at Owens.

The Captain continued, "We have a lot of work to do. As you know, all of these girls were teens and because of that, there can be other connections. However, this is the strongest lead we have. We need to run a check on all employees of Home's. Owens, you and Sealy take care of that."

The men nodded.

"We'll need a stake-out at the plant. That'll be, Lucero and Fisher for the first shift. Taylor and Macy, you two take the second shift. Let's see …" He looked around for those he would call for the third. "Kent. You and Johnson cover the third. And remember, we're not making any announcements to anyone. Is that understood?"

They were used to cautions about the confidentiality of information. As always, they agreed.

"When we get a solid suspect, then and only then, we'll move. Now go on, get back to your shifts or get home and get some rest."

The men walked out.

Johnson nudged Bailey. "Great lead, huh."

Owens and Sealy went up to the Captain. "Captain, you know we have teenage girls at home," Owens said, "but even if we didn't, we would want this guy off the streets. It's a sad day when kids aren't safe."

"Nobody's safe, Owens."

They spoke with Hodges a few more minutes. The conversation made them feel good, like a pep talk from a coach. Only this wasn't a game. It was life.

"Don't worry, guys," Hodges reassured them. They shook their heads in agreement. They knew they had to work fast to keep these youngsters safe.

"We've got to alert these kids. This is a nasty one," Owens said.

Sealy's face revealed a bitter expression. "I hope he burns in hell."

John Sealy's job took a toll on his marriage. Divorced with two teenage daughters, these recent discoveries were even harder. On the force for twenty-three years, he loved his job in a way but in so many other ways, he hated it. The fulfillment when they caught someone helped to make up for hours of frustration.

John would give a person twenty dollars if they asked for ten. Off-duty, he hung out at "The Hound," a local pub. Most of his friends hung out there, using it as therapy. If anyone ever suggested this to John, he would have said, "You're the crazy one."

His partner, Hank Owens, or "Hank the Lank," as some called him, demonstrate more conservative attitude, less giving than his friend. His height gave him an air of distinction. His friends told him they would never had guessed he was a Detective and Millie, his wife, always said he should have been a movie star. Hank would laugh. He was flattered but in his mind, he thought, *no way.*

Hank and John worked together for about ten years and read each other like newsprint on a tabloid.

Then there was Kent Bailey. He could pick up victim's clothes and bag it for evidence with little or no emotion. When it came to his curiosity, the computer assisted him in following data like a Sleuth Hound on a trail. He scrutinized information from every angle at least a couple of more times than the others did.

Sealy brushed past Kent. "Like I said, I hope he burns in hell."

144

Shay looked back, then Nathan, Abigail, Elizabeth and Gordan. Lev stood partially in light and partly in shadow, separate from everyone else. His tone sounded defiant, an attitude Jonathan had never seen demonstrated by him before.

Nathan spoke first. "Jonathan, if it's alright with you, I'd like to call a consultation."

Jonathan hesitated, and then replied, "Yes ... yes, whatever you think is right, Nathan."

He motioned to the others. They formed a huddle with their arms around each other's shoulders.

"We need to regroup to see how to handle this," Nathan exclaimed.

Shay's head bobbed to the left and to the right. "What do you mean?"

"What I mean," he said as he peered at Lev, "is we need to figure out if this is ... apostasy. If it is, Lev may be in a disastrous condition. He may not be able to ..."

Before he finished his sentence, Gordan interrupted, "All he said was 'when we *think* Eve was deceived.' He didn't make a deliberate statement except for 'when we think.' Aren't we allowed to think?"

"Gordan, don't you see? Lev questioned a fact written in the Holy Writings. Skotoo planted doubt in Lev's mind and has caused him to suspect the events did not happen the way they did. He's undermined Lev's faith. He might as well have detonated a bomb in comparison to what this may do to him. We can't let that doubt remain. How can Lev convince anyone else about faith if he isn't convinced himself?"

As they spoke, the circle tightened. Abigail, squeezed between Nathan and Gordan, wiggled and said, "Take it easy, you guys."

"Yes, take it easy," Elizabeth reiterated.

"I'm on your side Nathan," added Shay. "This Scot 'thing' isn't going to come in here and convince me any differently."

"All right, all right," Nathan said as he lowered his tone. "Let's calm down."

Gordan peered at Lev and yearned for him. "Why are you acting as if he's not one of us? Look at him standing there. I don't think it's right. I think we need to give him a chance."

"I didn't say he's out," Nathan snapped, "but we need to agree on how we're going to handle this. I believe there's been a breach in the fence and we need to mend it."

"I know who's to blame. It's that Skotoo's fault," Shay added.

"We're not here to charge or accuse, we're here to fix."

"And what if we don't?" Elizabeth said.

"If we don't, we could lose Lev. And even worse, we could all fall."

Nathan's words caused the angelee's mouths to drop.

"What . . . what do you mean, we all could fall?" Shay asked.

Nathan looked back a quick second, then returned to the huddle. He whispered, "Because of Lev."

Their eyes shot back and forth between them. Their minds raced to absorb the connotation of Nathan's statement. The allegation overwhelmed them and their ability to focus became clouded. This possibility never occurred to them.

"Skotoo knows that Lev is the most emotional one among us," Nathan continued, "and that he has the greatest sense of sensitivity and affection. He received an enormous amount of the deepest emotion in the Universe, love. I 'm not saying we don't possess love but Lev received more of this infilling when he was formed. Skotoo knows this and wants to use the tender heartedness he has for others against him. When you think about it, what probably happened was Lev sympathized with Eve in such a deep manner that he overlooked the facts. He may have even sympathized with Skotoo."

"In other words, Lev is prone to being too empathetic?" Elizabeth queried.

"Yes, and without Lev, we're nothing. If Skotoo gets to him, he can get to the rest of us. We're to complete this journey together and our assignment is much too important. We have to fight for him and fight for ourselves. Not only would our mission be aborted but our very existence with the king hangs in the balance!"

"Oh, my," Elizabeth exclaimed through short pants of breath.

146

Abigail's eyes misted. *How dreadful it would be not to be part of this wondrous world.* Immeasurable joy permeated those who partook in this existence.

She glimpsed at Jonathan's pained expression, which affirmed the statement.

Moments passed without a word from anyone in the group. They pensively considered how to surmount this mammoth hurdle.

Then Abigail announced, "Well, we know where the doubt came in, so I guess we need to go back to that point."

"Yes, we need to go back and press in!" Elizabeth added.

"Sounds like a plan." Their affirmation spread around the circle until it came to Gordan.

"Are you with us Gordan?" Nathan asked warily. He didn't want to lose him either. They needed to be in complete accordance.

"Yes. Of course, I'm with you. Whatever we all agree on is okay with me. I just didn't want Lev to feel alienated and alone."

Nathan took a deep breath and said, "Okay, let's move."

If they were on earth, there might have been a "hut" when they broke out of the huddle. They walked back to their places. They displayed a strong look of resolve on their faces.

Nathan and Gordan left their original place and walked back to where Lev stood. They positioned themselves one on each side and with their arm around him, walked him to the front. He was reluctant at first but then went along as he ambled in a seemingly dreamy state.

Skotoo seethed as he followed their every move. He had hoped they wouldn't have anything to do with Lev. Nevertheless, he worked hard up to now. *I'm not about to give up now.* "So, all is covered with brotherly love," he snipped.

Nathan had barely lowered himself in his chair, when he sprang up again. "It seems we have more review to cover," he said as he nodded in Jonathan's direction. "If that's okay with you, Jonathan."

"Oh, it's fine, fine with me," Jonathan replied. "If you want to review again, certainly go right ahead. I'm all for you … I mean I'm all for it."

Nathan walked up to Lev and stood next to him. He placed

his hand on Lev's shoulder. "Lev, don't feel like you're not a part of us, because you are. We had to have a discussion between us to know how to continue."

Lev nodded. He had a faraway look in his eyes. He turned to his left and stared at Nathan, as if somewhere and unable to get back. "I'm a little bewildered, Nate. I don't understand. What's happening?"

Nathan held his head up and announced in a loud voice, "I have an announcement. We feel our discussions on the Garden should be reviewed."

"Reviewed? Skotoo snapped. "What is it with all of you? We've gone over, and over, and over this. Frankly, I'm tired of the reviews!"

"You don't have to participate if you don't want to," Nathan replied, "but we've decided to go back."

"Not participate?" Skotoo answered. "No, no, no, of course I'll participate, even though it seems totally redundant."

Nathan breathed in deeply. *If only I can get Lev to recognize the truth.* "We should discuss what happened with Eve."

"Yes," Lev said mechanically, "that's what you said we would do."

"Lev, earlier, you made the remark 'when we *think* Eve was deceived.' Do you remember?"

"Yes, I do."

"Why did you say that?"

"Why? Because it's what I thought."

Skotoo's face revealed a screwed-up smile again. "That's most likely due to my superb articulation." *One for my side is about to come up, soon.*

Shay knelt with his back to Skotoo. "Lev, You know I wouldn't steer you wrong."

"Yes, I do. But, I don't know … I'm kind of confused about why this is so important."

Shay leaned in closer. "Well, buddy, it's important because of the names written all over the goofy guy behind me that's why." He motioned to Skotoo who remained in his chair with a ridiculous smile plastered on his face.

Lev leaned to the side peering over Shay's shoulder. As he looked at Skotoo, he responded, "yes, when he first came in he was absolutely repulsive but he doesn't look so bad now."

As if a shot when off into the air, Jonathan and the rest of the crew reacted to his volleying words.

Abigail stepped forward first. She knelt next to Shay. "Lev, I want you to look at me."

He glanced at her, his eyes half-closed in a state of distant confusion.

"Lev, think about the discussion we had earlier."

"All right." He responded with a slow drawl.

"Concentrate Lev. Think about when we discussed the lie that was told to Eve."

"Yes, well, that's where I think I got a little mixed up."

Her heart skipped. This may be the beginning of the road back. *At least he said he was 'mixed up.'*

She continued. "Lev, you were the first one to talk to Skotoo and he called you 'astute,' remember? He sided with you right away, which made you feel important and appealed to you. He talked at length about the serpent and said he was soft spoken and how he wanted merely to be friends with Adam and Eve, remember?"

Lev looked down. "I guess I do. I didn't know what he had to say was that crucial."

crafty temptations 15

Jacob dropped the receiver into the cradle and stared at the phone. *A lover's quarrel? Or maybe wedding jitters?*

Kent's bitter words resounded in his ears. "Are you ashamed of me?" He had lashed out.

"I can't help it if my parents don't want to attend," Jacob replied. "You know, you're driving a wedge between you, me and my father."

"Well, who means more to you, me or your father?"

He's always pushing me, he thought as he stood by the window. *What difference does it make? Dad doesn't want to attend. Kent's angry. Everything is going wrong.*

He stood and gazed out the window. The light inside his apartment glared on the sheet of glass and blocked his view.

There's no reason to live, is there? The bizarre thought crept in faintly. His brow furrowed and he turned and rambled around the living room. He sat down and put his head in his hands. *There's nothing I can do.*

Maybe I need something to eat. The contents of the refrigerator were bleak and he angrily slammed the door shut.

He glimpsed at his expensive, carefully chosen furniture.

What's wrong with me? I have everything I need. Things couldn't be better. But, then they're just things.

An accusing whisper echoed back. *What has that to do with*

relationships? That's what's important. Look at you and your Dad. And what about Kent?

The thoughts sobered him. His greatest ambition of attaining happiness, reaching for the brass ring, might be past his reach. It seemed, as he stretched forward with all his might, his finger skimmed ever so slightly past his prized objective.

What do I have to live for? I've tried to satisfy other people all my life and where has it gotten me? Why did Kent and I have to argue?

The questions lingered and after a brief moment, he thought, *This is not my fault, it's Dad's.* He practically spun around with the revelation and his craze-filled depression took flight. *That's right. It's his fault. If I let him know how despondent he's made me, he'll probably change his mind.*

He pressed the numbers with deliberate intent. *We'll see what he has to say about this. I'll give him an ultimatum. Either he comes or it's sayonara.*

❖

Haley rushed out of school that afternoon anxious to find Courtney.

Clumsily, she ran down the street with her books in tow. She remembered Courtney lived on the other side of Newport Avenue and walked as fast as she could. She spotted her as she ambled along at a comfortable pace.

"COURTNEY!"

Courtney looked up and saw the angst-ridden look on Haley's flushed face. "What are you doing?" She asked cautiously.

Haley labored to breathe as she shuffled as fast as she could toward her school friend. Humidity had frizzed her hair and she sputtered, "I wanted to get your CD back to you."

She fumbled through her bag, pushed, pulled and poked until she found the prized CD.

Ceremoniously, she handed it to Courtney and declared, "Here. Here's your CD."

"Thanks," Courtney replied in a chilled tone.

Haley shrugged her shoulders and muttered, "Whatever."

She walked away but before she got too far, Courtney came

up behind her.

"Have you given it any more thought?"

"What?"

"You know the game I told you about."

Haley gave her a quizzical look.

"Yeah, the one about when we go to people's houses."

"Oh," Haley said. "Well, I didn't think of it as a game."

Courtney let out a deep infectious laugh.

Her unsolicited delight endeared her to Haley and for a brief moment, she forgot Courtney's shortcomings.

Courtney continued. "It's kind of like – we'd be making a movie. We go and tell a story, like actors. It's no big deal. Look at it as receiving a contribution. People enjoy giving to charity."

"Yes, but we're not."

"But they don't know that. It wouldn't hurt anything and you'd be helping me out."

"What do you mean?"

"Well, remember I told you I had a job? I don't have it anymore," she said cheerfully. "Even if we just do a few houses, it would help."

It irritated Haley that Courtney talked about a non-existent job. She replied crossly, "I don't think so."

"It's easy for you, Haley. You have everything you need but I have to scratch and scrounge for whatever I get."

Haley walked away.

"Okay, I'll tell you the truth," Courtney blurted, frustrated.

"The truth about what?"

"I don't have a job and I hate what I did."

"What."

"Well I took those CD's from a music store and I'm sorry."

"Oh."

"See if you help me I won't be tempted to do anything like that again. Please?

Haley struggled with her plea. She didn't know what to say.

Com'n," Courtney nudged her and pleaded with a lost puppy-dog look.

Haley hesitated. Finally, she answered, "I don't think so."

"Why not?"

"Because it scares me. I don't think I can do it."

"You know you're able to do a lot more than you think you can."

The strategy didn't affect Haley. Courtney tried another tactic. "I thought we were like sisters."

"You did?"

"Yeah, we're a lot alike. We haven't really hung out together since we were kids but I think that from now on we can be really good friends."

"But, I'm not sure I can do it," Haley said. "What if someone tells my parents?"

"Who's going to tell? These people don't know us. You *can* do it. You know what they say, 'can't lives on won't street.' It'll be a snap. I'm telling you, it'll be easy."

"If it's so easy why don't you just do it alone?"

"Cause, it's more believable if there're two of us. Come on," Courtney entreated woefully.

Haley remained pensive as they walked down the street. They stopped and Haley caught a glimpse of a ranch style, stucco, home.

"Let's just try it on this house," Courtney announced.

Haley gazed at the house with the neatly trimmed lawn. *Maybe no one will be home and then she'll leave me alone.* "All right, come on."

They leisurely walked up the driveway, came to the front door and rang the bell.

Time seemed to loiter and perspiration beaded on Haley's upper lip.

Good no one's home, she thought but then all at once the door flew open. Her heart leapt to her throat and she thought the woman at the door would be able to hear it thunder inside her chest.

A silver-gray haired woman with granny type glasses met them. Haley thought she looked like Mrs. Claus.

Haley stood in front of this precious-looking woman and wanted to bolt from the porch. She thought, *what do I say?* Nevertheless, she heard herself confidently pose a question, "Hi.

How are you today?"

"Very well, thank you," the woman replied.

"Good. That's good." Haley responded rapidly. She shot a glance at Courtney who stood alongside her, dumbstruck.

"Well," Haley continued, "we're here today from the high school."

The five-foot woman didn't reveal any expression.

"From the school over there," she said as she pointed up the street. "We're having a fundraiser."

"Oh?" the woman replied, with in innocent tone.

"Yes. We're selling magazine … magazine subscriptions," she stammered.

"Well, I don't take any subscriptions," she said melodically and began to close the door.

"Oh, but Ma'am," Haley said abruptly, "we only have until today to finish our quota."

She held the door half-open.

Haley flashed a coquettish smile. The words poured out easily.

"You see, we were just given a few days to meet our quota. My friend … Alice and I just have a few more sales and we're *almost* there." She stretched the word *almost* out and held her fingers up about an inch apart while she cocked her head to one side like a little puppy.

The woman gazed at both of them but remained quiet.

"They're only five dollars each Ma'am," Haley said as she stretched her hand toward the door.

She put her hands in her pockets, fumbled around and then said, "Let me see if I have some change." She turned and went inside the house.

Courtney flashed a huge smile and jumped up and down. "I think we have one," she said without moving her lips in a ventriloquist fashion.

The woman returned beaming. "Here, Dearie, I do have enough to help you out for a couple. Where do I sign?"

Courtney thrust a piece of paper that looked official into the woman's hand. "Right here Ma'am," she said delighted.

The woman wrote her name carefully on the sign-up sheet and checked off the two subscriptions she wanted. "When will I begin to receive these?" she asked.

Haley and Courtney blurted out at the same time, "Two weeks."

"Two weeks. My goodness, that's a lot sooner than I would have expected."

"Yes," Haley replied. "Well, we have an excellent fundraising program. Thank you so much." Hastily, she took the money from the woman and turned to walk away.

"Oh, Miss," the woman called out.

Haley turned around. "Uh, yes?"

"You never did tell me your name."

"My name? Oh, I'm … Beth."

"Beth. Okay, Beth and Alice, wasn't it?"

"Yes."

"Well, my name is Corinne."

"Yes. Don't forget, we're … she caught herself before she blurted out their real names. We're Beth and Alice. That's right we're Beth and Alice." Haley stepped backwards away from the door. "It was nice meeting you."

"Well thank you both. I'll be looking forward to my periodicals."

"Periodicals? Oh, yes, the magazines. Yes, well, we'll see you later."

They scurried away as fast as they could and when they got about half a block away, Courtney burst into raucous laughter. "See! I told you there wasn't anything to it."

"Oh, right. You know you never even said anything."

"Yes I did. I told her where she could sign."

But Haley felt terrible. The woman trusted her and she lied and took her money.

"Just think!" Courtney said triumphantly. "Think of all the things we'll be able to buy. I can get some new tops, some more make-up …"

"Courtney!"

She stopped in the street, oblivious up to that point. "What?"

"All you said was sign here!"

"Well, that was something wasn't it? Besides, I helped you with moral support didn't I?"

"Yeah, well, it's not like I've done anything moral."

"So what? What difference does it make? She doesn't know who we are. And if she ever says, 'I know you,' you can tell her it's just a case of mistaken identity." She threw her head back and cackled. "Ten bucks in ten minutes. Now that's what I call a great job!"

Her excitement prevented her from noticing a car pulling up alongside them.

Haley looked over. A man drove the car, but she couldn't make out the passenger.

He lowered the window and motioned to them.

Courtney and Haley's eyes met and they both began to march away. The man drove a few lengths ahead of them, stopped and got out of the car.

He stood on the sidewalk, with his hands on his hips, barricading their path.

Haley walked to one side of him but stopped when she brushed against him.

"Good afternoon, ladies," he said with a broad white smile.

"Don't talk to him," Courtney muttered under her breath. She forced her way past him and left Haley behind clutching her books in a semi-frozen state.

He gestured, as if tipping an imaginary hat. "The name's Pam. What are you up to today?"

She looked past him and caught sight of Courtney half way down the block. The rush of adrenaline caused her heart to beat rapidly. It pounded in her chest, like oceans waves on the shore.

She attempted to maintain composure as fear mounted. *I have to think of a way to get past him.* Her eyes met his. "Excuse me." Her voice sounded muffled to her ears.

"Sure I will, but I have a question before I do that," he replied.

Her mind reeled as she tried to think of what he could possibly ask her. She stood stoically, afraid if she said anything else her voice would tremble and give her away.

"I wondered if you would like to make some quick money."

Haley's mind raced. She had just made some quick money. *Is God punishing me?* She backed away and shook her head vigorously from side to side.

"You're sure about that?"

In that moment, Haley realized the full meaning of his question. Her cheeks flared with a burning glow.

He grinned and stepped sideways, gesturing with his hand. "Well, maybe someday, young lady."

She jetted past him despite her weak knees and hiked the block as fast as she could. She caught sight of Courtney at the end of the street.

"Courtney."

Courtney stopped and waited for Haley to catch up.

Haley reached her and shouted, "Why did you leave me alone?"

"I was going to get help."

They walked the rest of the way and Courtney said everything she could think of to pacify Haley. Repeatedly, she said, "I'm sorry. You know I wouldn't leave you. Honest, I was going for help. We're buddies! Do you want to come over?"

Haley ignored her excuses and declared, "I can't come over. I have to get home."

In a quick turnaround, Courtney shrugged her shoulders and said, "Okay, I'll see you later."

Haley watched Courtney fade from view. The more diminished her frame became the worse Haley felt.

Becky threw her head back and laughed with gusto. She almost choked. "Did you see their faces?" she squawked.

❖

Pam sat with his arms folded in front of his chest. "I shouldn't have done that. I don't know why I let you talk me into it."

"Yeah, well may be it'll scare them enough to keep their little caboodles close to home. Sometimes I wish someone had done that for me."

"You made your own choices and you know it," he retorted.

Her pity party attempt didn't move him.

She shot an angry glance at him. "You don't know what you're talking about!"

"Whatever."

"Yeah, you can be cool about it 'cause you're a guy."

"What does that mean?"

"Women are vulnerable."

"So, who put the pea in your mattress, princess?"

She took several short puffs of her cigarette. "I guess you haven't heard about Tess."

He fixed his eyes on Becky. "What about Tess?" .

"They just found her."

"What do you mean?"

She twisted her body toward him. Her throat tightened and an ice-cold expression came across her face.

"What?"

"They found her body."

Pam stared straight ahead.

Becky didn't know if she should continue, but went on anyway. "I read about it in the hospital. It sounded gruesome. Tess didn't look like a street person. I could half understand if somebody thought she was trash and treated her like this. But Tess always looked like she'd been places, you know what I mean?"

"She was just a kid."

"She was my age."

"That's what I mean, you're still a kid.

Pam remained dazed. He had known Tess since they were kids. He loved to tease her and he'd fight her over the water fountain at church. But he always considered her part of the family.

"Wow, I wonder where she is," Pam mumbled. "When my grandmother died, I didn't give hell a second thought. But there's no one to tell me she's in a better place."

"Yeah, well who knows if hell even exists?" Becky replied.

out of control 16

Abigail's face paled. "Lev, I want you to see how he got to you. He appealed to your sense of self but he also appealed to your sympathy. He wanted you to feel important about yourself and he wanted you to feel sorry for the serpent. He made it sound as if the serpent tried to be a friend but the serpent doesn't deserve sympathy because he's not only a liar but a murderer too. Don't you see, Lev, its like when a person goes to trial and the defense attorney causes the jury to focus on the defendant's weakness It's a 'poor me' portrayal."

Lev appeared even more at a loss but tried to take in what Abigail said.

Gordan came behind Abigail and knelt down next to her. "Listen to her Lev, she makes sense. You know Arnion, or Jesus as the world knows him, inhabited the wilderness when the evil one spoke to him. Arnion protected himself with the word."

As the others cajoled Lev, Elizabeth couldn't help think about the Garden. She remembered their history class about the *Temptation* seal found among ancient Babylonian tablets. The seal depicted a tree in the center with a man on the right and a woman on the left. A snake stood over her, as if whispering to her. An ancient Babylonian inscription found on another tablet stated, "Near Eridu was a garden, in which was a mysterious Sacred Tree, a Tree of Life, planted by the gods, whose roots were deep, while its branches reached to heaven, protected by guardian spirits, and no man enters." Another seal, found on earth, depicted an uncovered man and woman, downcast and bent over. They walked, followed by a serpent. She recited the judgment that the Ruler of the Realm gave to Adam. "In the sweat of thy face shalt thou eat bread."

A mere dozen miles south of Ur in a land called Eridu the cunning, crafty Nachash approached the woman. He knew destruction would come if he could persuade them to defy the command. Envious of their position, he slyly asked a question that would not arouse suspicion.

They succumbed to his intertwined shenanigan and scales of innocence dropped from their eyes revealing their unclothed state. They sewed leaves together to cover themselves.

"That's it! You guys, that's it," she exclaimed in a frantic state. "Remember when we talked about the devil going about like a roaring lion?"

"What does that have to do with me?" Lev asked.

"Well," Elizabeth answered, "the devil tried to devour the Son in the wilderness, like Gordan said, but he wasn't able to because of the word!"

"That's what I said, Elizabeth."

"Yes. But as I tried to tell you earlier, that's how the Son got the victory. He spoke a specific word to the devil. He said, 'Man shall not live by bread alone, but by every word that proceeds out of the mouth of God'. The Son, when He took on the form of a man, could have declared Himself equal to the Ruler of the Realm but He didn't choose to do that. Instead, He submitted Himself to the word and declared that as a man he would not live by bread but by the word."

Gordan smiled and clasped Nathan's hand. "Elizabeth's got something here."

She continued. "Yes, and when Adam and Eve were in the Garden, the fruit in the garden was their bread but they weren't to live by that bread alone – don't you see? God gave them the word but they were unfaithful to the word, the exact opposite of Arnion and they chose themselves to be god."

"It was a test," Abigail added.

"A lot like the test the first kingdom endured," Shay responded.

"What was that?"

"They were about to enter the land given to them after being in their wilderness for forty years. The Ruler of the Realm said he tested them to prove their inner being, their heart. He spoke the same words to them. He said, 'man does not live by bread only, but by every word that proceeds out of the king's mouth'. Whew. This is confusing to *me* now," Shay confessed.

"It doesn't have to be," Elizabeth continued. "We've been to the history lessons. The first realm didn't believe …" Her voice trailed off.

History was clear. Unbelief kept the tribes from entering the land when the Ruler of the Realm released them from bondage. They doubted his direction.

Perhaps these examples will help Lev to see his error, Elizabeth anticipated.

But Lev persisted. "I don't understand. What does that have to do with what I said about Eve?"

Elizabeth happily responded, "Well, first, let's look at the facts. The king would never lie! If He said Adam and Eve were tempted and did wrong, then they did and if He said that the serpent lied to Eve, then the serpent did. And second, we are all given the choice to either live by every word of the Mighty One and align ourselves with him or reject him and live for ourselves."

Cobwebs that had embedded Lev's thoughts slowly began to break away. He acted as if he started to understand.

Nathan joined the others. Now all of Lev's colleagues encircled him.

"Lev, take a good look at Skotoo," Nathan said. "I didn't understand before but I see it now. Look at the words written on him. The first one means *liar*. That relates to his master, the one who began all this with a lie. Why do you think it is written in the king's writings that 'all liars, their part [is] in the lake which burns with fire and brimstone which is the second death'?"

Lev glanced at Skotoo quickly and then looked back at Nathan.

"That's the first word. Look at the rest of the words: m*urderer, thief,* and *destroyer*. Why do you think these terms are on him? Because the old dragon through his *lie, stole* eternal life and that made him a *destroyer* and *murderer.* The entire vocabulary put together expresses the character of the one who sent him."

Lev looked at Skotoo once again and for a moment hated the sin that he saw. When revealed, it wasn't "pleasant to the eyes" as Eve regarded the tree but ugly and destructive.

Lev stood with a fixed gaze and his mouth opened in amazement.

"Lev?" Nathan said.

He didn't respond but started intently, as if hypnotized.

"Lev?" Nathan said again, "Are you listening?"

Nathan spun around to see what caused this dazed stupor. "Good grief!" He exclaimed.

Doug lay prone on top of the angry hordes of people. Their hands pulled and snatched his body as they passed him over their heads. He heard angry cursing among the throng.

They were livid and some bellowed, "He's not going to invade my space. Get him out of here."

Emptiness mixed with bewilderment filled his being. He wished he were dead. Then he remembered he was.

At last, they shoved him between a narrow slit in between them. He looked from side to side. All he could see were the heads of those jammed around him. He was stuck.

The heat stifled him as they pushed and shoved each other. He tried to push back but didn't get anywhere. The mass moved in their own direction and he had no choice but to move with them. Driven along, he tried to squirm through them but they pressed him back.

An ear-piercing scream wailed above the clamor. He saw two figures with their mouths wide open, shrieking. His gaze fixed on them for a moment. Their screams intensified and he screeched back. Then he realized the creatures next to him were his mother and father; a family reunion he never expected to experience.

Now I understand this din. People must recognize one another. He turned his face away. *Why didn't I listen? Meredith tried to tell me.*

Meredith seemed a chronically happy person. He thought her the perfect example of joy.

She also worked at the bank with Doug and Larry. Larry liked her small frame and waist length brown hair and Doug admired her after Larry attempted to come on to her.

On a couple of occasions Meredith told Doug she knew she would go to heaven and that she had been saved from the terrible torment of hell. He scoffed but she remained confident.

He asked her how she knew and she answered because she believed in the Son and in His word and that caused her to know the truth and because she knew the truth, she was set free.

He thought if he received Jesus, people would regard him as weak and that he would lose his freedom. Now he realized he would have gained it instead.

Free, he thought, *what I wouldn't give to be free now. If only I could go back but there's no way to turn back.*

He looked for his mom and dad. Somehow, they were pushed away and he didn't see them. *Dear God, please don't let me see my brothers here too!*

Then a raspy craggy voice spoke. "I see you're still going on about it."

Standing next to him was the woman who pushed him through the hole. "How did you get here?"

"Unfortunately I'm not able to run errands all the time, yet. Once the master sees what a great job I do, I won't have to serve my time here at all. Since I'm here, I thought I would check up on you. I felt *so* bad about having to escort you and all. You just have no idea how it hurt my conscience."

He retorted, "I don't think you have a conscience."

She cackled. "Whatever you say to me has been said before. You're getting what you deserve."

"But, I didn't do anything bad," he whimpered.

"You weren't a saint or an angel were you? And even if you

were, there are angels that'll be thrown into the lake of fire."

"Angels? How could that happen?"

"They thought they could take over heaven with their Master but they couldn't and they were cast out with that old serpent."

"Where are they now?" He asked, even though he half believed what she said.

"Wouldn't you like to know? I bet you think if you knew where they were that they could help you. But they can't," she snapped.

"I'm telling you, there's some kind of mistake. I've never done anything to deserve this."

"HAAAAAGH," she whooped. "Don't tell me you never did anything wrong. Did you ever tell a lie?"

He thought, *yes, I lied. What if I did? What's the big deal about lying?*

"What about stealing? Did you ever steal anything?"

The vision of Larry flooded his mind. *But it wasn't my fault.*

"Oh, sure. Like I said, we've all earned and wormed our way in. And what about women. Did you sleep with any?"

"No. I mean, yes, I did, but not that many. You know there were many diseases going around. But what's wrong with sleeping with women? It's better than a man sleeping with a man."

"Haaagh. You think? Actually, it's the same."

She smacked her lips together and continued, "Lying, stealing, having sex. So you didn't want to catch anything. Well, you caught hell, didn't you? You threw yourself in with the lot."

"You never did tell me where the fallen angels are," he replied weakly.

"Some of them are up there," she said as she pointed into the air.

Doug looked up. "On earth?"

"Yes, up there in the world. They exercise control over those who haven't made an alliance with the Creator."

Doug grew wearier the more he learned. He looked around and noticed how sick everyone looked.

"What's wrong with everyone?" he said in a hoarse voice.

"Oh, I see your eyes have enlarged. What a pity."

"My eyes. What do you mean?"

"Just look at me. Do you like what you see?" She leaned toward him and said, "Not particularly lovely is it? My looks meant so much to me at one time."

"Am I going to look sick like them?" he stammered.

"HAAAAGH," she replied. "What did you expect? This is the opposite of heaven in every way."

Sobered, he didn't answer.

"It doesn't matter; you don't have any control over it anyway. It's ironic that the ones who end up here are the ones who wanted total charge over their life up there."

I've lost control over everything and I'm an eternal prisoner. I'll never have what I want. It's hopeless. He lamented, *Meredith, why didn't I listen to you?* "I could have helped my family," he agonized aloud.

A strange sound echoed out. It didn't sound like a scream or a yell but like a yowling cackle.

"What was that?"

"They're getting riled up. They smell a kill."

"A kill?"

"Yesssss, I know that Skotoo is at work again and he's the best we have. He has quite a few feathers in his cap, so to speak. It may be someone he's worked on for a long time or someone who has followed the other Father."

"What other Father?"

"Well, there's our father here and there's a Father in heaven, he's the Holy One."

Doug thought he had heard it all but he hadn't heard this.

"What's the matter, buddy boy?"

"I feel so humiliated and disgraced. I'm disgusted with myself."

"You don't know what disgrace is," she barked back. "The real stigma will be when they make the marks on those up there. That's when it'll be bad. Listen. Listen to them yelp like coyotes at a kill. Somebody important must be going to break down. That's when they make that weird sound." Her eyes glistened. "Maybe it's a politician, or a back-slidden Christian. Who knows who's next?"

A cry from deep within his inner being tore into the atmosphere. Then again and again. It wouldn't stop. It could have been the frustration from the smell, heat and darkness, or his sorrow. *With all my might, I wish I wasn't here.*

"Too late," she said.

"Too late," he echoed.

Crushed from every side, a myriad of hours passed. The perpetual noise persisted when Doug heard someone yell above the din, "You never get used to it." He endeavored to see where it came from, but couldn't tell.

"Why don't they ever stop?" He yelled at the top of his voice grasping at a straw of sanity.

"Millions and billions of reasons," he heard. "Take you, for instance, and multiply it by the enormous amount of people that are here. And this is only the tip of the iceberg."

The thought of "ice" made Doug long for a cool drink. "The tip?" He shouted back.

"Yes, just think about how many caverns there are like this one that are filled up with hordes of souls."

The involuntary groans arose from within him again. He couldn't perceive the thought of numerous caverns filled with sorrowful beings. Just knowing his hostage situation and the fact that he would have to endure an eternity of darkness and sorrow was enough of a trial. "But, if we all did what the devil wanted us to do why should he punish us more?" He called out to this newfound "friend."

"It's the nature of the beast, I guess. We're self-serving – we only care about what we want and we ended up serving the underworld. We weren't concerned about where we would end up. But even though we did his bidding, he hates us. He hates everyone and everything and there's a universal law in place. What goes around comes around. The only ones who escape this damnation are those who've repented."

A spark of hope sprang through Doug. "You mean you can repent?"

"Not now. You have up until the time of your death. Murderers and rapists who repented before they died were saved from this."

"They didn't end up here?" His voice became throaty as he tried to communicate, but the fact that people escaped sounded incredulous to him.

"That's right. They made a 'turn-around' as they say. Born again. They made a complete about face.

"What about the people who got away with it? You know, they had a trial and were declared not guilty."

"Getting sanctioned by human judges doesn't mean anything. If you die in your guilt you end up here." The voice became faint.

"Are you sure there isn't a way we can ask forgiveness now?"

"You can say you're sorry all you want but it won't do any good. If it did, don't you think everyone here would have done it by now? This place would be empty. I'm telling you there's nothing we can do now."

The last words were hard to perceive but Doug knew. *There's nothing we can do now.*

Tears rolled down his cheeks. If only he had acknowledged and declared the truth in time.

The chant, "no more room," mushroomed. He knew there were others coming.

In his peripheral vision, he saw something come toward him. He put his hands up to keep it from getting in next to him.

As the man passed by, he wailed, "I didn't do anything wrong,"

Doug's heart skipped a beat.

Larry.

"It's Larry," he screamed at the top of his lungs. But Larry didn't hear him.

His face wet with tears and perspiration, his jowls drew down as he winced in despair. Nothing mattered. Another soul was lost to the underworld.

When would it ever end?

decisions 17

Nathan turned about-face. Next to him stood an exquisite angel with long golden hair, attired in white. It emanated a brilliant light as its large wings glistened radiantly.

The angelees gawked at the vision. "Where's Skotoo? Where did he go?" They questioned.

Jonathan stood close to the apparition and answered forlornly, "This is Skotoo."

Skotoo's smile gleamed radiantly. He looked magnificent. With outstretched arms, he fluttered above them. As he encircled the room, their eyes remained fastened on him and their necks craned, so as to not lose sight. Skotoo lowered himself gracefully and rested at the front of the class.

"Jeepers," Gordan murmured. "Isn't he remarkable? I've always wanted to look like that."

Abigail and Elizabeth smiled and ambled slowly around Skotoo, one on his left and the other on his right. They had seen many angels but none as stunning except, perhaps, Gabriel.

Nathan stood with arms to his side feeling insignificant and powerless.

They quickly forgot their visitor's previous appearance.

They "oohed" and "aahed," except for one.

Shay knelt in front of Lev. "Lev, listen to me. Skotoo doesn't look like this. This is something he's concocted."

His plea went unheeded by the novice group. But, he

continued to talk. "You've got to listen, Lev."

He turned and caught sight of Jonathan as he left the room.

Jonathan flew above the garden, oblivious to his destination. *These are children. At least, for the number of years angels exist, they are. Never in all my days have I seen Skotoo pull such a dirty, low trick.*

He circled the mighty wall and traversed toward the center of the City.

He found himself at the palace of the Ruler of the Realm, by the outer gate, along the pathway. With hands clenched behind his back, he pondered *there must be an answer.*

As he reached a turn in the path, he discovered a man sitting on a portion of the wall.

"Good afternoon," the gentleman offered.

"Good afternoon," Jonathan replied automatically. He started to walk by and the man said, "I see you have something on your mind today."

"I'm … I'm upset, actually."

"Maybe I can offer some assistance."

Jonathan stopped short from declining the offer. He eyed the man, who he supposed worked tending the grounds, and then decided to stop. He hopped on the wall next to him and released a heavy sigh.

"It can't be as bad as all that. Not here, in the Magnificent City."

"You have no idea."

"Then why don't you tell me."

"I'm … I'm an instructor here in the City. I report directly to the Ruler," he added as he waved his hand toward the palace.

"Yes. I thought you might be."

"I have a class of six young angelees who are in my charge. They're wonderful young angels. Their mission is one of utmost importance and a test by an important entity from the underworld is part of their preparation In fact, he's approached them at this moment."

The man looked up and Jonathan gazed intently into his clear blue eyes. The steady gaze gave him confidence to continue.

"They're completely mesmerized by the image my adversary created, except for one."

"Then there's hope."

Hope. The word hung in the atmosphere.

The man turned his face downward and continued to weave.

"What are you doing?" Jonathan said.

"I'm braiding these leaves."

"Yes, but why?"

"It reminds me that a three-fold cord, when braided, is not easily broken."

"The ancient writings speak of this," Jonathan answered.

The man nodded his head but remained quiet.

Pensive, Jonathan thought. *A three-fold cord. Shay and I are two.*

"It's a pity it takes three to plait a braid. Tell me, was no one else involved in your group of pupils?"

Jonathan mulled the question over. The students comprised one cord. Jonathan made another. *There is a third.* "Gabriel," he responded.

"The high angel, Gabriel?"

"The very one. He visited us before this wicked ambassador came on the scene."

"What did he do?"

"Let's see. He spoke with us and said he had come to impart wisdom, give understanding in their achievements and strength in trials."

The stranger said nothing but continued to perfect the braid, which neared completion.

Jonathan bounced off the wall. "That's it!"

A contented smile crossed the stranger's lips.

Jonathan's face beamed. "I don't know how to thank you," he blurted and traipsed away.

"No need. That is what we're here for, to help one another."

"I have to get back. Tell me, what is your name?"

"It's not important. What's important is you know what you must do."

"Yes," he shouted and sprang into the air. "Thank you again," he called out. His words of gratitude flickered like stardust upon the kind, gentle laborer.

In a trance-like state, five of the angelees remained staring at Skotoo.

Shay continued to entreat them. "You guys don't look at him. He isn't for real."

"This group is bright and astute," Skotoo purred in an altered voice. "They can see with their own eyes what's before them."

Skotoo walked toward Lev. The other angelees eyes grew wider as he neared them but Skotoo seemed to be interested in one in particular.

"Lev."

"Yes, Skotoo," he whispered back.

"You could be as beautiful as I am. I can offer you so much more than you have here."

"You can?" His answer sounded robotic.

"For instance, look at this."

Skotoo waved his hand and before Lev's eyes, a golden oval window appeared. The center appeared dark blue with white cloud formations. Lev blinked a couple of times. The vision didn't disappear. "What's ... what's that?"

"It's earth, Lev, or the world as it's called."

Lev peered inquisitively into the window. He had always wanted to know more about earth. The scene inside the framed aperture drew him closer, as if magnetized.

Before his eyes appeared seashore. He watched the ocean surf pound against sandy white beaches. Strong waves crashed against rocks and spilled silently onto the smooth grained coast. A smile crossed his lips.

Another scene appeared. Rugged peaks on mighty mountains blissfully covered with white snow jutted against the skyline. "Wow," he uttered to his colleagues. They stood beside him with their arms crossed.

He returned to the portal. The illustration flashed before his eyes quickly, as if he were flying. Brilliantly lit cities with tall buildings that reached into the sky emerged. Darkness surrounded a myriad of lights spread across thousands of acres. Small, flickering lights moved in columns.

"What are those?" He pointed to the tiny illuminated dots.

"Cars," Skotoo countered. "Humans occupy them."

"Humans live in those tiny spaces?"

"Well they don't live in them. They use them to go from one place to another.

Lev leaned to examine the view on the side of the oval. An illuminated bridge spanned across a large river. *Where could that be?*

Clouds flashed by quickly and Lev looked upon a magnificent waterfall that cascaded with a great rush of water. He pointed once again.

"That's Niagara," Skotoo retorted in a bored tone.

Lev sensed the power of the rushing waters. He came closer to the arch at the bottom of the falls and witnessed the powerful surge. He couldn't stop smiling. The scenes beckoned to him from within the gilded case.

Skotoo leaned close. "Did the Ruler of the Realm say that you could not leave this City? Come with me, Lev, and I'll give you power over all of these empires," he murmured.

Lev gazed intently at the world before him and as he stared into the windowpane he answered, "The king has not denied passage to us from our city. I can roam the world with freedom when I receive flight to my wings. I don't understand what the difference would be."

"Yes, it's true you can go to and fro over the earth, but to whom, Lev?"

"Well, I don't know. We'll go on assignments. I guess they'll be important."

"Do you think so? Let me tell you. With me, you'll go to those who have power over heads of state, celebrities and famous people of every type. I have so much to give you Lev. Some of those we'll call on rule the earth. The difference is you'll have direct input as to the behavior of kings and dictators, not just do things for them. They're so accustomed to doing their own will they don't even have to give permission."

Elizabeth, Abigail, Nathan and Gordan's trance deepened

with each of Skotoo's words.

Their group stood together on one side and Shay remained on the other side of the room. *Where is Jonathan? How can he leave at this crucial time?* He felt the force within him wane. His opponent's feats appeared gigantic in comparison to his own. He heard a small still voice within him stir. *"What about David?"*

Shay paced and rubbed his chin with his fingers. *The least expected received the summons for this lopsided challenge. But didn't David kill a lion and a bear? Yes, but that exhibited his lack of fear and possession of trust.*

Masses had gathered in the amphitheater to hear from the Ruler of the Realm's servant, David, the King of Israel.

David's foe, the champion Goliath, stood about thirteen feet tall. The call to conquer him came to David, the youngest and probably smallest, of Jesse's eight sons. The king chose David because of his heart, not his appearance.

Goliath tormented the army of Israel daily. He defied them morning and evening for 40 days and dared them to choose a man to fight against him. Tradition called for a representative of each nation to battle, with the belief that their God would give them the victory. A loss affected the entire nation.

Men fled when they heard Goliath's challenge, for no one had the nerve. He wore a helmet of brass and a coat of mail that weighed about one hundred and sixty pounds. His spear weighed about twenty-three.

I don't have armor but neither did David. .

Shay thought of how David *ran* toward his opponent. *I have to take the situation by the horns. Even if I feel alone, I'm not. David had a helper.*

He stopped in mid stride. "I've got something to say, Skotoo."

The scene resembled Jack facing the giant in the beanstalk. Shay, the smallest in stature, stood firmly in front of the formidable, skilled Skotoo.

Amused at first by his defiance, Skotoo answered tauntingly, "Yes?"

"You appealed to Lev to give him power over people in high places. Well, people in high places may be brought down low." He stood resolutely as he spoke, legs outspread in stance with his arms crossed, ready to do battle.

His demeanor surprised Skotoo. In fact, the retort displeased past the border of irritation. He hoped because of their common roots, Shay would at least be in the group of those he recruited. He didn't want any distractions at this point of the game. Skotoo replied, "Don't let Shay divert you, Lev, he's young and doesn't know what he's saying."

"But, I do know Skotoo." Righteous anger reflected in the young angel's voice.

Like a pesky fly, Skotoo tried to shoo him away. "You're the smallest and most diminutive of all and you want to instruct ME?"

"My stature has nothing to do with what's at hand, Skotoo. I know you; something inside me knows you all too well. I don't know why but in my innermost being, I know you. I wish there was some way I could explain what you're all about to Lev and the others but they'll have to comprehend your corruptness and hideousness on their own. You've covered it over with glitter and glamour but they will see, Skotoo, they will."

Skotoo's eyes widened a little and he raised his eyebrows. His opponent may be a little more formidable than he originally thought. He hadn't expected opposition once he transformed himself. Then he let out a short curt chuckle. "Oh," he said, unconcerned, "you're quite an adversary aren't you Shay?"

"Don't try to flatter me Skotoo."

"Tell me Shay, what you think about …" His mind searched for something to distract him … "about Job?"

"I think Job has nothing to do with this, Skotoo. You see you didn't grasp the fact that I know you. You're cunning, conniving and devious. Sure, you look beautiful right now and you have charm, which you turn on and off when you want to. But truth only passes your lips when you mix it with lies, which makes it half-truth. You act vulnerable and dependent so others will feel like they're helping you. Like I said, you look beautiful now on the outside but inside you're deceptive like the serpent that ruined the Garden of Eden. I don't know where or when you went wrong Skotoo but because your existence is ruined, you want to ruin everyone else's. For centuries, your goal has been to rob, kill and destroy, just like your father. Misery does love company, doesn't it? Your problem, Skotoo, is that you've gotten away with it for so long you don't think it will ever end. But it will."

Skotoo flipped his hand indifferently as if he didn't have a care in the world and turned his attention to Lev. He had a "hook" in him and didn't want to lose it.

"I expect, Master Lev that you're ready to partake of all the wonders of the earth and all I have to offer?

Lev's eyes had a glazed appearance and he sat, staring at the floor. Finally, he spoke.

The question fired like a volley out of a canon.

"What would happen if I want to have a 'trial' with Skotoo?"

no secrets 18

The sound of metal banging on metal resounded throughout the school's hallway. Students jostled past Haley rushing to their next class. Haley searched earnestly for Courtney's bright, made-up face.

Finally, she saw her standing with Ellie next to the water fountain.

They held their hands over their mouths as they squelched a snicker. Haley sauntered up to them.

They looked at each other and giggled some more. A twinge of jealousy sprang through her.

With a taut lip and narrowed eyes, she approached them.

"Hey, Haley," Courtney said as she tried to regain her composure.

"Hi. How are you?"

"Fine," she answered. She giggled again and poked Ellie "What's so funny?"

"Oh, you wouldn't get it," Ellie answered.

Courtney chuckled again and said, "Tell her El."

Ellie's eyebrows lifted a bit. "You want me to?"

"Yeah."

"Tell me what?" Haley asked.

A strange smirk crossed Ellie's face. She took a stance right in front of Haley, came close to her, and said, "Okay, I'll tell her."

She looked at Haley and announced, "We just found a hole."

"A hole?"

"Yeah, you wouldn't believe where it is. It looks right into the boys' locker room."

Courtney and Ellie squealed with delight.

"It's kind of like playing peek-a-boo only you never say boo," Ellie responded with a snort.

Haley watched them revel in their so-called discovery. "That's disgusting," she managed to mutter.

They laughed even harder.

"What's wrong with that? Are you some kind of a prude?" Ellie exclaimed.

"No, I'm not. There's nothing wrong with little kids that are naked or being naked when you're married."

They looked at each other and exploded with laughter again. Tears came to their eyes as they cackled at Haley's expense.

"What's wrong with you guys?"

"Well you're naked when you get out of the shower in gym, aren't you?" Courtney said.

"No, I wear a towel when I get out. I don't go around in public naked so why should I in there."

"Why? What's your problem? Don't you have a nice body? What are you, too round?"

"No, she's square." Ellie chimed.

Haley's felt her face reddening.

"It doesn't have anything to do with the shape of my body. I just know better."

The remark went over their heads at first and then Courtney turned. "Are you calling us stupid?"

"When did she call us stupid?" Ellie asked dumbfounded.

"A minute ago. She said she 'knew better'."

Ellie's brown eyes flared with anger. "Did you just say we didn't know any better and that we're stupid?" Ellie razzed Haley as she pointed in her face.

Haley's eyes widened. "What I said was I just know better."

"Better than what?"

"It's … it's common sense you know, knowledge, like in the

Garden."

"Oh no," Courtney moaned, "Here comes the lecture."

"It's not a lecture. You're ignoring the fact that we're born with a sense of right and wrong and you want to do *whatever*." Haley turned to go to her locker. She wanted to get as far away from them as she could. They followed.

"Oh, so you think that's disgusting. You probably think it's disgusting for two girls to kiss," Ellie goaded.

The thought of what Ellie alluded to flashed through Haley's mind and she wished Courtney had never come over to her house and that she had never talked to her. She didn't answer.

"You think you're so high and mighty don't you?" Courtney goaded. "You think you're perfect but you're just a prig."

With that, the girls stopped following her.

Relieved, she tucked her books under her arm but Courtney turned back and came up behind her.

In a loud, tone she called out, "Don't think you're so smart. We do have a little secret between us, don't we?"

Haley stopped in her tracks. She turned around with a slow deliberate motion. "You wouldn't," she said in disbelief.

"Maybe I would and maybe I wouldn't. I guess you'll find out," Courtney countered and walked away. She walked a few steps, turned and strode back to where Haley stood.

She whispered in her ear, "You're not goody-two-shoes after all. You think you're so holy and your brother's a fag!"

Haley's eyes widened and her face flushed. She wanted to run home or anywhere else, that would get her away from Courtney.

How she arrived at her classroom was a blur, but somehow she found herself at her desk. *I hate them and I wish we had never met.*

Detectives Sealy and Owens attacked the employment records for Home's Photo Processing. Vigorously, they poured through them a second time. Evidently, they missed a connection because they didn't come up with any leads.

"There's got to be a link," Sealy said frustrated. Owens didn't look away from his computer. He continued to input names and look for records that corresponded. He searched for addresses and previous places of employment for all of the workers.

Near the end of the shift, Bailey entered. He quipped, "What's up guys?"

Neither of the men looked up. Disgruntled, they thought if they stared at the records longer that it would somehow make sense.

"Want another set of eyes?"

Owens stopped. "Sure. See what you can find."

Surprisingly, Kent didn't go to his computer, but pulled a chair up next to Owens. "What have you got so far?" Sealy came over and joined them.

"Well, these three guys have popped up. All three have a record."

"I can tell you right now that the one on the bottom is in jail."

"We ran a search on him and he didn't come up."

"That's because he was picked up under an alias but I know the guys face."

"Good. That gives us these two."

The men stared at the names. Maybe by osmosis, the answer would appear.

"Maybe we're looking at it from the wrong angle," Kent said.

"What do you mean?" Sealy and Owens responded at the same time.

"Jinx! You owe me a coke." Sealy blurted.

"Whatever." Owens answered, too tired to argue.

Kent continued. "Maybe we need to look for the next victim."

Deadpan expressions revealed their exhaustion.

"You know the latest pictures of females who attend Carson High."

The lights went on for both men at the same time. "Yeah. We can run a grid of the school's boundary."

Sealy jumped back to his computer. Within minutes, he had the coordinates.

"Here, plug these in."

Owens crosschecked them with the list of customers.

Sealy bit his nails. "We've got to come up with something.

We've just got to."

❖

Austin returned to his office.

"Dr. Connors, you look pale," Destanee blurted as he walked past her.

"I'm fine."

"Are you sure," she questioned and stood to her feet.

"Yes, and I'm sorry, I didn't mean to …"

"No problem, Dr. Connors. I hope it's all right, I was just leaving."

"Yes, yes," he replied. "It's past your quitting time. I'll lock up."

His nurse quietly slipped out the back door as Austin trudged to his office.

He slipped into his black leather chair. Thoughts of Maddie returned, at least the woman who reminded him of Maddie.

God, I don't know how long I can do this. There's so much going on. There's Jacob, his wedding and Becky. Haley's the only one that seems straight.

And that woman. He lifted his eyes and surveyed his office. Medical books propped in a row on the shelves to his left, photos of his wife and children on his desk. He covered his face with his hands.

I'm tired Lord and … I don't want to think about this woman.

He placed his hands over his eyes and with elbows on his desk, he rested. *I can't do this. I just can't keep fighting these battles.*

❖

Becky reached Pam's apartment and felt for the hidden key. *Good, right where it's supposed to be.*

She opened the door, entered, and slammed it behind her as if followed by a posse.

Becky enjoyed her escape to what she considered her oasis. The tidy surroundings reminded her of home. Pam had a beige velour loveseat and chair nestled in a cozy conversational grouping.

Driven by the thought of a hot shower, she looked for clean clothes. She relished the soap's fragrance and scrubbed until her skin reddened.

She threw on clothes that belonged to another of Pam's friends and noticed the fit was snug.

She went to the kitchen. A clean plate, cup and fork rested in the dish rack next to the sink. She surveyed a dirty plate with dried pasta sauce and a half-cup of coffee. *I wonder who left that mess. I know Pam wouldn't.*

She searched for something edible but the offerings were meager.

After she washed a glass, she filled it to the brim with water and grabbed a box of crackers. *This will help.*

Becky gulped the crackers down to the least insignificant crumbs at the bottom of the box and guzzled a glass of water.

A curious thought crept in. Her mother had loved to eat crackers and drink water when she was pregnant with her.

She put her hand to her stomach and felt a soft protrusion. She tried to recall when her last cycle transpired, but couldn't.

Rummaging through the cupboards yielded a few more morsels of old snack bars. At least it was something. As she devoured the last bit of rations, she forgot all about her concern.

Restlessness overcame her, and she decided to go back out to the streets. Once downstairs, she rushed out through the back door into the alley.

Pam entered the front seconds after Becky's exit. Two by two, he sprinted up the stairs.

He opened the door and a few scattered effects. Any other time he would have been upset and would have straightened it with a passion. This time it was different.

He strolled to the nightstand and opened the drawer slowly. The revolver lay as if it expected him to show up some day.

His hand grasped the cold barrel and he withdrew it from the drawer. The weight of it seemed heavy. Then he laid it on the surface of the stand.

That wasn't what he sought. The unobtrusive book underneath it was his goal.

Tenderly he slipped it out, set it in his lap and sat on the edge of the bed.

He opened the book slowly and flipped through the pages.

The last time he saw it, his grandmother had passed.

Warmth filled his inner being. What a simple thing. He didn't understand why he had fought this for so long.

Filled with remorse about Tess' death, Pam had left the house a couple of days before.

He found himself in front of his old church. He approached the steps and found the janitor as he cleaned the glass on the front door.

With a smile, the man said to Pam, "Good morning. How are you doing today?"

Pam nodded but didn't answer.

The man turned back to his work. "It's a beautiful day, isn't it?"

"What are you so happy about?" He said irritated.

"I'm happy because I know where I am and I know where I'm going."

"You sound like my grandmother."

"I know what you mean. A lot of us sound the same. It's beautiful that God can put this knowledge in a person, don't you think?"

Instantly, the man knew by Pam's demeanor that Pam didn't know, at least he didn't know right now.

"I'll tell you what."

Pam looked lazily at the diligent worker. "What?"

"I'm getting ready to break for breakfast. If you'd like, we can go together."

Pam thought he didn't have anything to lose. "Sure," he said. That's when it happened. At breakfast.

Pam sat across from this simple soul. The man was about thirty years older than Pam. His strong hands displayed the years of work they were involved in as he joyfully went about his breakfast.

"So, tell me about yourself," his newly found friend coaxed. His hair had begun to gray, except for his mustache, which was completely white.

Pam sat with his legs sprawled in front of him unconcerned about their age difference and color of their skin. "I've been around."

The janitor chuckled. "I know what that means. I've been

around too. Let me tell you something," he said, wiping his mouth, "I think this was a God-incidence."

That was a new one for Pam. It was his turn to chuckle now.

"I've run into people a lot at the church but I'm drawn to you. I think there's a dynamic reason you came by today."

With a raised brow, Pam soaked in the words. "What kind of reason?"

"There doesn't have to be a kind of reason. How do you feel about God?"

"I've had my conversations with Him in the past. He knows my name."

"You've got that right! He does know your name and He's calling it today. Did you know that today is the day of salvation?"

Pam had been away a long time but knew the plan of salvation. This time, he didn't resist. He shook his head and nourished his body as the man fed his soul.

"I love how simple it is," the man continued.

"Simple doesn't always equate to easy," Pam replied.

"You're right. It wasn't easy for our Lord to die on the cross but the comprehension should be simple."

"I get you."

"It's all about love, man. It's about His love for us and then we can love others that way too."

Their discussion lasted about forty minutes. The man told him he didn't have anything to lose – and everything to gain.

Pam decided he was right.

Anna called her sister's house but no one answered. The radio, tuned to her favorite program, emitted tones of a soft ballad, one that Anna particularly liked. But it didn't take her mind off Haley.

She looked impatiently out the front window. *It's not like her to be late. Maybe I should start dinner. That might take my mind off everything else.*

She went to the kitchen and realized she hadn't defrosted anything yet. With a sigh, she decided to go to the grocery store, a couple of blocks away. She set the alarm and left hurriedly.

She drove back and observed her daughter a short distance from the house as she stood next to a car. Haley leaned into the window and picked at her disheveled hair while she talked to the driver.

Relieved, she honked and pulled into their driveway.

"Who was that?" Anna said.

"Oh, that's Jeffrey and his friend. They're a couple of guys from class."

"Did they give you a ride home?"

"No, I just talked to them. Why?"

"I'm ... careful. With everything going on these days, you can't be too cautious."

"I know. We had a detective come to our class. Aren't you the one who says we should trust?"

"I trust people but that doesn't mean I'm not going to be careful."

Darkness began to fall. The garage light's radiance was dim. They approached the door and as Anna lifted her hand to the alarm control a voice said, "Be quiet and no one will get hurt."

Anna flinched as she looked over her shoulder. A man stood behind her. She felt something sharp in her back. Without thinking, she opened the door.

"WARNING. WARNING. YOU HAVE VIOLATED AN ENTRY. LEAVE IMMEDIATELY."

Her body stiffened and the man shoved her and Haley into the house. "Are you trying to be funny? He yelled.

Her hands quivered at first and then her body quivered. She blurted weakly, "I didn't mean to."

The phone rang immediately. Anna stared at it and looked back at the man. "I have to answer or they'll think something's wrong."

He grabbed Haley around the neck, pulling her close to him as he rushed to the phone. He held Haley against him with his arm, using the wall for leverage.

"There's no ID number. Pick it up, but if you let them know anything's going on, she's dead," he said gruffly.

Anna walked to the phone. "Hello?"

The voice on the other end sounded professional. "This is Alamo Alarm with a well check. Who am I speaking to?"

She responded hesitantly, "This is Anna Connor."

"What is your password?"

"*Father*. My password's *Father*," she answered. She heard the words coming from her mouth but it seemed as if they were in slow motion.

The man with the crazed look tightened his grip

"I …I opened the door into the house without taking the alarm off."

She placed the phone back and stared at the unwanted guest. "Please, don't hurt her. I gave the alarm people the password."

In time for dinner? 19

Perfect. Skotoo's plan worked. The only thing he had to do was to get Lev out of the Magnificent City.

Shay exploded. "You can't mean you really want a trial period!" Lev's face remained expressionless.

Shay turned to his friends. Elizabeth, Abigail, you know this isn't right."

Abigail pursed her lips. With a slight shrug to her shoulders she said, "He's mature enough to make his own decisions."

Elizabeth nodded. "Yes, that's true. He's old enough."

Shay looked at Gordan who stood smugly next to Nathan. "Don't look at me if you want someone to agree with you. I for one believe we should run our own lives and not do as everyone says. Independence is supreme."

"And so is obedience."

"Who is he being disobedient to?"

Shay couldn't believe what he heard. "So, you think it's all right for Lev to leave with this brute?"

"He should be able to do whatever he wants. We're not under bondage here."

Before Shay could utter another word, Nathan continued. "Gordan's right, Shay. And you, especially you, can't go around instructing us. You're not the mentor of this group."

"But you are Nathan. You should be telling him."

Skotoo smacked his lips together with a large grin. "I have a proposition, Shay," he exclaimed.

"I'm sure you do."

"This should settle the disagreement once and for all."

"What bright idea do you have now?"

"I thought, since we're from the same star, that you and I should take a trip together."

"Oh, no. I'm not going anywhere with you."

"Don't worry. I'm not taking you to earth. That's Lev's gift. I believe that if you'll accompany me to our birthplace, you'll understand. This would be a perfect opportunity for you to see where you came from."

Shay paused. His face squiggled as he thought about the offer. He wished Jonathan were there. "How long will this take?"

"We'll be back in time for dinner."

A glimmer sparked in Shay's eyes at the mention of food. *That's right we were going to cook Minglings. But that seems like eons ago.*

Gordan, Nathan, Elizabeth and Abigail gathered around him.

"You don't have to go if you don't want to," Gordan offered. "It's your decision."

Shay's lip squirmed. *I have to make the right decision.*

"Perhaps it will help Lev," Elizabeth offered.

"I think it's the strong thing to do," Nathan added.

His eyes flickered to the right and then to the left. He paused and then said, "All right, I'll go with him."

He turned squarely and faced the dazzling vision. "If you promise that you'll bring me back by dinner time."

"I promise. You'll be here before the bell rings."

"And Lev and the others stay here. Agreed?"

Skotoo eyed the apprehensive group. "No problem. They can stay until we return."

They left the atrium. Shay mounted and felt Skotoo's bony body with his knees. His heart raced like the mixing blades of an electric beater. *I can't believe I'm doing this.*

Soaring through the atmosphere with wind-tousled hair, Shay glanced over his shoulder. The Magnificent City shriveled from his view. He had a gut-wrenching sensation in the pit of his stomach. *I wish I'd never left.*

The unusual duo glided effortlessly through space. Shay wished he could catch sight of the vista past Skotoo's wings but his size prevented him.

"There's our bright leading light," Skotoo announced proudly.

They approached a large object that glowed, bigger than earth's orbit. Shay's mouth opened in awe. The unexpected mammoth rays engulfed him as it glared his eyes until they closed.

"What's it called?" He shouted at Skotoo as if the mass would affect his ability to hear.

"Our beautiful star is named Migmah." It had been centuries since he had been there, but nonetheless Skotoo felt a twinge for his motherland.

They landed on the edge of a crater of great magnitude, about two hundred yards in diameter. Though the planet appeared strangely desolate, Shay experienced a surge of arrival as he slid from Skotoo's back onto the soil beneath his feet.

"It's good to be home, isn't it?" Skotoo gushed.

The star, though dismal looking, had a welcoming quality. But Shay had to be careful that he didn't lose sight of their motive for being there.

"Now what?" He quipped.

"What? You can't mean you don't want to investigate and see our roots?"

Shay turned and scanned the panoramic view. The horizon appeared dusty with silver specks sprinkled across the landscape.

"Where is everyone?"

Skotoo's head bobbled back and forth, as he surveyed the large expanse. He didn't even think about the others. "I don't know. I surmise they have migrated to other places as we have."

Great. I've always wanted to know about my beginnings and here I am on this hulky bulk, alone with my not-so-favorite person – or should I say, thing. "What a waste of time. Why did you feel we should come here? There's nothing and no one around. It's barren." He kicked the ground and small spider like insects scurried along the ground. *Not exactly, desolate. There are creepy-crawly things.* Disheartened, he walked away and slapped his arms against his sides.

"It may look desolate, but I can fix that. What would you like to see?"

Shay turned.

"What's your favorite way to pass time? Your favorite games?"

With a furrowed brow, he scrutinized what may happen next. "Why? What would transpire if I told you?"

"I can make all your dreams come true."

Not that I really want this for myself but let's just see what the kink can do. "Hmmm, well, I love train stations."

"Large or miniature?"

"Both."

"You shall have it."

Skotoo turned north. He waved his hands with the gesture of a musical conductor and grandly continued until the area filled with smoke.

Shay sauntered next to Skotoo, looked into his face in the midst of it, and saw his eyes transfixed in a lunatic fashion. A chill ran down his spine. Skotoo turned and smiled. "Master Shay, your heart's desires at your fingertips."

Shay looked away from the mad inventor.

The terrain bustled with people as far as he could see. Some prepared busily for their departures while others arrived.

"Paper," a newspaper carrier yelled.

"Excuse me," said another, "I'm going to Astron thirty six. Can you tell me if this is the right direction?"

The vista enthralled Shay and he toddled onto the busy scene like a movie fan visiting a film set. *Amazing.*

He felt the ground rumble and heard a strange sound behind him. *A train must be coming.*

He rushed with the rest of the crowd toward the well-worn tracks and gazed down the corridor. Then the whistle blew.

Wow. I love that sound.

A complete replica, it reminded him of their studies of earth.

"Popcorn, peanuts," cried a vendor. The heavenly scent nearly got past him before he stopped him. The vendor heartily gave him bags of the commodity. *This is better than I thought.*

Skotoo stealthily slipped next to him. "There's something else here, Shay."

They sauntered toward a beverage shop, called *Apate's Beverages.*

"What's in here?"

"Go on. I told you there was more."

Shay pulled on the heavy door and entered the establishment. The customers lingered longingly while they sipped their favorite potion. Another whistle blew. He lifted his chin and gazed toward the back of the establishment. A miniature train set complete with houses, trees, towns and little people stood on exhibition. *This is what I saw in the film about earth.*

Since his formation as an angel, for some unexplainable reason, Shay loved miniature models. The inanimate objects, detailed and crafted, charmed him.

Warily, he moved nearer to the model. A train chugged rhythmically as it crossed through the station, over the bridge and toward a tunnel.

He glimpsed into a shop in the miniature town. Tiny replicas of beautifully dressed porcelain dolls lined the shelves. *Wow, wouldn't a little girl love these?*

I wonder what will happen if I touch something? Gingerly, he lifted a small bridge. Nothing happened. No one objected or asked, "What are you doing?" He realized it was his alone to enjoy. Evidently, he didn't have to share with anyone. *Cool.* Shay fiddled with the various buildings at first and then moved the depot. He lined the vehicles on the road in order. *This is fun, like being king of your own country. After all, aren't I entitled to some fun?* The railroad cars, complete with caboose, gave him hours of amusement.

Gosh, Lev would have loved this set up.

Lev. Saintly outer space, I forgot about Lev.

Shay rushed outside the shop. The crowds traversed back and forth, busily. He peeked into some of the shops that lined the station. "Skotoo, where are you?"

He pushed through the crowds, as he continued to call Skotoo's name. His angelic vision enabled him to see miles around but he could not find his companion.

He felt a tug at his shoulder and whirled around.

"Skotoo!"

"Did you miss me?"

"Where were you? You must have known I was looking for you."

"Not to fear, my little brother. I never left."

"I'm not your little brother and we have to get back."

"Do you have an engagement?"

"I have to get back to Lev. I haven't seen anything that's changed my mind."

"That's because you haven't seen everything."

Shay was leery. He wanted to dismiss the notion but instead, he questioned, "What haven't I seen?"

"The superior game of the ages. The Panorama Bowl."

Cucamonga. The Panorama Bowl. "Where is it?"

In what seemed a millisecond, Skotoo transported them to an arena with a crowd of thousands of cheering, wild fans. The roar was sensational.

"This is for real, isn't it?"

"Of course, it's real my young friend. This is for your entertainment. Your seat is right here, down in the front, on the fifty yard line."

Awesome. Shay sat down, his face glowing with elation. The thrill almost equaled the din churned by the multitude.

The game began.

The Zimmah's lined up on the left side of the field dressed in slick black and silver uniforms. Their helmets sported fiery red flames, which flickered against a shiny black background.

On the right were the Basar's with Gold headgear that wielded a silver lightning bolt. Dressed in bright gold and white they appeared to be the weaker side but Shay had a hunch they were the better team.

The players stood in formation, clad in their pads and cleats. They balanced themselves against their opponents. At the sound of "hut," the field became a flurry of heaving muscled bodies. The Zimmahs jostled against the Basars, valiantly. Shay's hands flew to his mouth. He didn't normally chew his nails, but found some comfort with his fingers in his mouth.

The skirmishes lasted a long time. Back and forth they went. Neither side seemed to gain any ground. *Wow, this is the real stuff. I wish Gordan and Nathan were here.*

Immediately he sprang to his feet. *Sacred astronomical objects, I've done it this time!.*

Shay yelled Skotoo's name at the top of his voice. His call became drowned in the crowd's bellowed roar.

He ran down the field toward the end goal. *How do I get out of here?* The stadium seemed to be seamless, with no way out. He heard the multitude roaring in the background.

He turned and started back to where he started. On the side, he noticed a tunnel-like entrance. *That must be the locker rooms.*

He sprinted into the entry that had high walls of stone on each side. The sound of his feet beating on the hard surface beneath him corresponded with his heartbeat. *I should have never listened to that impostor.* As he reached the exit, the door flew opened. Skotoo stood in front of him.

"Were you looking for me?" He purred, pleased.

Shay wanted to wrestle him to the floor but restrained from the foolish concept.

"Did you enjoy the game?"

"Your game's over, buddy. I think it's time to take me home."

"You are home my little brother."

"I told you before, I'm not any kin to you."

"Be careful now, you may hurt my feelings."

Shay didn't want to be unkind but knew he had to be firm.

"Look, Skotoo. You asked me to take this trip so that I could 'understand.' Well, I understand, all right. That game, didn't you get what that was about?"

Skotoo shifted his weight from side to side. "It's the Panorama Bowl, the famous celestial football game. The final play of the season."

"The teams, Skotoo, the teams. What they represent is clear.

This is about you and me, evil versus good.

Skotoo's air remained stoic. "So, blood isn't thicker than water."

"If we were ever related, Skotoo, you broke those bonds by the choice you made."

Skotoo raised an eyebrow.

"Choice is what forms angels," Shay continued.

Silence deepened between the two forms as they stood as if in contested battle.

"It looks like you win, little one. You've expressed your desire not to join me."

"That's the way it is, Skotoo."

A few moments passed. Shay didn't know what else to say and as he proceeded to ask Skotoo to take him back, something strange occurred.

"Skotoo?"

"As I said, Shay, you had the desire not to join me."

Shay watched as Skotoo visually disintegrated before his eyes.

"Skotoo!"

The dark angel was gone. Shay heard a roar from the crowd inside the stadium. Someone had made a touchdown.

He fell to his knees. Tufts of grass pricked him as he knelt where Skotoo appeared last. *He's gone. He vanished before my eyes and I'm out in who knows where. What am I going to do?*

Shay gazed skyward. The blackened space around him, void of bright light, depicted the bleakness of the situation. *At least I'm not alone. I can go back to the game and see if someone can help me get back to the Magnificent City.*

He turned. To his amazement, the door disappeared. The exit didn't exist. *"What is this?"*

Shay felt numb as he ran across the desert-like ground. Dust scattered from his heels. With no one in sight, he ran until his breathing became so labored he had to stop. *This can't be happening. Someone has to be here.*

He trod along hoping to find the train station. Miles later he realized the power of an illusion. He was alone.

Okay. I have to think about what someone else may do in my situation.

The hike through the empty terrain seemed endless. Without water, his tongue felt fuzzy and heavy. Shay laid his head down. *I don't understand why there's no one to help me. I've always been around to assist others.*

A significant period of time passed. Shay raised himself to a sitting position and looked across the barren land. Nothing had changed. He found a substantial rock, folded his arm under his head and with his head on his arm against the rock, fell into a deep sleep.

good to be back 20

The man's size didn't frighten Anna as much as his gaunt, steely-eyed stare. He didn't let up on his hold around Haley's neck. Her pale image frightened Anna, but she stood sternly, determined not to let the man know her terror.

The man nervously pulled on the bill of his cap. It tipped, revealing a shiny baldhead.

He licked his lips and said in a sinister tone, "This isn't going to take long."

Suddenly the phone rang.

All eyes darted toward the jangling receiver.

"Don't touch it," he snapped.

She did not intend to attempt to touch the handset.

The answering machine clicked on. Jacob's voice sounded strained as he left his message.

> "Dad, I want to talk to you about my wedding and want you to understand how I feel. Kent and I are getting married, and if you choose not to attend, the consequences will be on your head."

A pause followed and then he continued.

> "This is difficult for me, Dad. If you can't be part of our lives then we won't have any part of yours."

A click ended the communication.

Anna paled even more as she sorted through his words.

The man shifted his weight and the phone rang again. He nodded his head. Anna knew she couldn't answer. This time, the voice of a young girl left a crisp message.

"Haley, this is Courtney, you know, your 'friend' Courtney. I wanted to tell you that you're no better than anyone else is. You're involved in this just as much as I am and everyone's going to hear about it. There's no way I'm keeping this a secret."

The machine clicked off again.

Mother and Daughter stared at one another.

Anna saw a pleading look from her frightened daughter. Then, as if scripted, a loud knock rattled the front door.

"Mrs. Connor?" A man's voice called from outside.

With a snarl, the intruder motioned to Anna to answer.

"Yes, who is it?"

"Pizza delivery, Ma'am."

Anna shook her head, indicating her absence of knowledge.

"Where's your bedroom," he whispered hoarsely.

Anna motioned toward the hall, feebly.

The man pulled tightly on his chokehold and walked backwards down the hall, dragging Haley with him.

Haley's eyes bared a panicked look.

He stood in front of the bedroom door and pointed to Anna to answer as he pushed Haley inside.

The door closed behind them.

Austin's office darkened as he sat with his head buried in his hands. *How do I pray to you Lord? I've got to get this woman out of my mind.*

Temptation is like a bird flying over your head, he heard within him.

His hands dropped from his face and he looked up.

That's right. Pastor has said temptation isn't sin, but that temptation is like a bird flying over your head. Sin comes if you let the bird build a nest and harbor the thought. I didn't do that.

His eyes brightened. *I'm okay. I haven't set my wishes or desires on this woman. It surprised me, to say the least, but I haven't done anything wrong.*

His back straightened in his chair and he switched the light on his desk. His Bible sat on the corner. He reached, picked it up and began to read. "Yea, though I walk through the valley of the shadow of death, I will fear no evil."

The rap at Anna's door continued. The young man continued to call, "Pizza."

She swung the door open and found a teen smiling eagerly, holding a large square box. Anna didn't know what to make of it.

"Here you go Ma'am," he remarked as he handed her a piece of paper with the hot box.

Anna looked and saw the note. It read:

"If you are under duress, shake your head in affirmation and hand the note back. If not, just say so."

Anna thought she would faint. Her eyes began to tear and she shook her head vigorously while she handed the note to the boy.

"That'll be fifteen dollars."

She grabbed her purse, thrust a twenty in his hand, and almost forgot to take the box. "Thank you," she said audibly.

She closed the door.

"He's gone," she yelled aloud.

The man walked down the hall with Haley. He eyed the pizza. "It might not be a bad idea to grab a little grub." He pushed Haley toward her mother. "Don't get any funny notions."

Anna and Haley stood clutching one another as they watched him lift the lid with great care.

Poof!

A wisp of green smoke blasted into the man's face. Instantly, he grabbed his eyes and choked.

In a split second, Anna and Haley bolted out the front door into the arms of several police officers and detectives.

"He's in there," Anna shouted.

The officers ran in and grappled with the man, twisting his arms behind him until they bound him with cuffs.

Anna watched as he twisted from side to side, like a roped calf hauled to market.

"It's over now," Detective Owens said with a sigh.

"Yes, and I'm so glad."

"We'll have a few questions, if you don't mind."

"Not at all."

The routine lasted close to a half-hour. The officers finished and left quietly through the garage.

Anna and Haley reentered the kitchen. "Thank God," she said softly.

Haley gazed at her mother. "Should we call Dad now?"

Anna took the phone and dialed Austin's office. She reached him almost immediately. You may want to sit down."

"Why? Has something happened to Jacob?"

"No, Jacob's okay. it's … something else."

"What is it?"

"Well, I think it would be better if you came home. Yes, it will be easier to talk to you when you're here."

"I'm on my way and … I love you."

Anna's face colored. "Oh, I love you too." She switched the talk button to off.

The light on the message machine blinked. Anna and Haley stood in the kitchen and stared at the red reminder.

Haley picked her books up and walked across the kitchen. She set them down again. Neither one spoke.

Finally, Haley broke the silence. "You didn't tell him about Jacob."

Anna moved to the table where family photos lay.

"Looks like my project will take awhile longer."

She picked up a stack and shuffled through, piling them onto the table one by one. "I remember when Jacob was little. Your dad and I had just met and I thought Jacob was one of the smartest children I had seen. He never gave us any trouble with grades and he wanted to play in all of the sports. He was a model …"

"Mom."

She looked up and said, "What's wrong with remembering?"

"As long as it doesn't cloud the present, I guess nothing."

Out of the mouth of babes, Anna thought. Mackinsey had told her there were times she felt she could be blown away with a feather.

"What's the big deal about Jacob anyway?"

"Haley!"

"I mean we hardly ever see him anyway. I know it's wrong to have sex outside of marriage but as Jacob said, they want to make it a union.

"The problem is, it's man trying to tell God what's right instead of accepting what God has told him."

"But, he's not talking to God he's talking to Dad and us."

"That doesn't matter. One of these days he'll have to account to God."

After a moment, Haley replied, "But how do we know for sure that it's wrong?"

Anna prayed silently. She and Haley normally didn't get into these discussions and with every fiber of her being, she knew what she wanted to say but she wanted to say it with the right spirit.

She spoke with an even, controlled tone and said, "God's word says he that sows to his own flesh, shall reap corruption from the flesh; but he that sows to the Spirit, from the Spirit shall reap eternal life:"

Haley shrugged her shoulders.

"Don't you see, Hon? When someone sows something they put it into the ground and whatever they put in grows doesn't it?"

Her eyes blanked over as she stared ahead.

"We can't live to satisfy our own sinful desires because we'll harvest the consequences of separation from God. Plain and simple, we're not to live for ourselves and plain and simple, we don't want to be separated from our Eternal Father because He's good and loves us."

Haley didn't act as if what her mother said had any impact and simply said, "Okay," and started to walk out of the kitchen.

"Haley."

She stopped and waited but didn't turn around.

"What did Courtney mean?"

Haley turned and faced her mother. "She didn't mean anything Mom and I have to do my homework. Do we have to talk about this right now?"

"Yes," she replied softly.

"Why don't we talk about it when Dad comes home?"

"Because I don't want to wait."

Haley crossed her arms and looked at her feet. Her body swayed back and forth.

"Haley?"

She breathed a heavy sigh and said, "I didn't do anything wrong Mom."

"I distinctly remember telling you not to hang around with Courtney and I distinctly remember you told me that you weren't."

"It's not what you think it is Mom and it's such a long explanation. Can we wait until Dad comes home? Please?"

"I never thought you'd lie to me Haley."

"I'd like to talk about this later. Besides, if what you said about Jacob is true, then this isn't as bad."

"What?"

"Jacob. If what you say about him is so bad, what Courtney and I did isn't nearly that bad."

Anna couldn't believe her ears.

"Are you trying to slide by … by comparing yourself to Jacob? That's not it, Haley," Anna said sternly. "It doesn't matter what kind of wrong you do, a wrong is … wrong. Actually, I guess it does matter because the greater the sin the greater the punishment. But if you lie and cheat and steal you're going to end up in the same place as someone who, well, someone who commits adultery, whether it's homosexual or heterosexual."

Haley stood with her hands crossed and folded against her body. "Well I don't see it that way. What about Becky? Are you saying I'm as terrible as she is?"

"Listen here, young lady. I'll never say what Becky's doing is okay. The drugs that she's involved in could take her life at anytime and if she were to die in a drugged state I'm afraid I don't know if she would spend her eternity with the Lord or not. However, the day she repents, the slate is clean. She may have the effects on her body from the consequences of the drugs but forgiveness is hers from that time forward. She wouldn't carry her sin into eternity. She would be a brand new person."

Anna watched her daughter look up to the ceiling as she spoke. Evidently, she didn't want to have this discussion right now. She continued. "I don't want you to walk away thinking you or I or anyone else is better than the other person. We're all sinners and we all need to repent."

At that moment, the phone rang. Haley picked it up quickly before it went to voice mail.

"Haley?"

"Yes," she answered.

"This is Matthew."

Why does everything happen at once?

"Listen, Haley," he began, "I won't beat around the bush. I heard something at school today that disturbed me."

Her heart skipped a beat. "You did? What?"

"It was about you and Courtney."

"Well, I don't know …"

"Haley," he interrupted, "Courtney said that you guys ripped somebody off by selling bogus magazine subscriptions."

"I … I don't want to talk about it right now."

"Is it true?"

She didn't respond.

"Haley?"

Haley held the phone.

"I guess your silence must mean it's true I don't think we need to see each other anymore."

"Matthew."

A dial tone resounded in her ear.

"I guess I'll talk to you later," she said, as if talking to Matthew. She returned the receiver, defying the tears.

"What was that about?"

"Oh, Matthew. Everything's okay," she said. Inside, she felt as if something had swallowed her up.

"Well," Anna continued unaware of what had happened, "sin is sin and there are consequences. I hope I'm getting through to you."

Haley looked down at the floor.

The phone rang again. "Honestly!" Anna exclaimed. "We'll

discuss this later," she announced.

"Anna?"

"Oh, Mackinsey, hi, how are you doing?"

"Great! How're you?"

"Well, I guess I'm fine but ..."

"What's wrong?"

Anna turned to see if Haley could hear their conversation and saw that she had left. She turned back, cupped the phone in her hand and whispered, "We've been through so much today. A man forced himself into the house."

"A man did what? What happened? Are you okay?"

"We're fine. Austin's on his way but there were a couple of messages left while we were going through this nightmare."

"Oh?"

"One was from Jacob and the other from Courtney."

"Courtney? Isn't she the little gal we were talking about the other day?"

"That's the one. She left a strange message for Haley and I can't seem to find out what it's all about."

"Oh, don't worry, it doesn't sound too serious. What's up with Jacob?"

She hesitated a moment and couldn't remember if she had even told her. "He's upset." She replied.

"About what?"

"Well, I don't know if I told you ..."

Haley stood in the hall and listened to her mother's whispered conversation. She thought *what am I going to tell my Dad.*

She heard her mother say, "Yes. I know some churches ordain them and that they say God loves you the way you are. He loves you but hates your sin."

Apparently, her aunt said something and then she heard her mother reply, "Thanks, but the best thing you can do is pray for him, Okay?"

Haley slipped quietly down the hall. *Pray for him? What good did they think that would do?*

She thought about her situation and remembered Courtney and Ellie's as derision in the hall and Matthew's tone of voice when he said, "I guess we're done talking."

"I can't lose him," she cried and threw herself on her bed with her head in her arms. Tears flowed down her cheeks as she cried as quietly as she could. Then she became angry and a twinge of bitterness crept. She thought *I'm old enough to pick my own friends and do whatever I want.*

But as she lay there, she wished she had never had anything to do with Courtney.

A long time passed by and her thoughts turned to Jesus. *I feel so bad because I let you down*, she thought. *I didn't even see it coming.*

Tears welled up in her eyes from the shame of taking money but especially for the lies she told. *Lord, I'm sorry.*

She remembered what her Mom said about Becky.

If Becky can repent, why can't I? Quieted, she heard the words, "Come unto me, all ye that labor and are heavy laden, and I will give you rest."

She took a deep breath and something lifted. She felt peaceful and calm. She lay there for a few minutes and thought about Courtney. She knew she had to forgive her and prayed to the Lord quietly. *I'm sorry for saying I hate Courtney.*

She got up, went in, washed her face, and went back to the kitchen where her mother had just hung up the phone.

"I have something to tell you."

"I have something to tell you too," her mother answered. They stood and looked at each other for a minute and then hugged. As Anna embraced her daughter, she whispered in her ear, "I have wonderful news. Becky's friend, Pam called your Aunt and told her he came back to the Lord."

"He?"

"Yes, I'll explain that later."

"That's great! What happened?"

"Mackinsey said that Pam was shook up because his friend died."

"Pam? A friend of his?"

"Yes, Pam's real name is James. It's a long story. Anyway, the thing is Mackinsey's worried because Pam helped take care of

Becky out on the street."

      They hugged.

      "You're all right now, hon."

      "Yes, I am Mom."

lessons from the past 21

"I don't like it. I don't like it a bit," Nathan mumbled as he marched in front of the podium. "First Jonathan's gone then Skotoo and now Shay. Who's leaving next?"

"I know the prospect of another one of us disappearing is depressing, but let's look at the bright side," Abigail chimed. "Just because Jonathan isn't here doesn't mean something has bad happened to him."

"Absolutely," Nathan concurred, picking up his gait.

Lev sat at the rear of the room, lethargic and unresponsive.

For a lack of anything else to say, Elizabeth spouted, "Let's play a game."

Nathan made a face.

"Or, let's not," she added. She turned and looked despondently at Lev. Then, her eyes sparkled and a wide smile crossed her lips. "Jonathan!"

"Forgive me, children. "I've been busily meditating what your next step should be."

The group swarmed around him. "Jonathan," Abigail began, "you don't know what's happened."

She left off her sentence and Gordan picked up. "Skotoo left with Shay."

Then Nathan chimed in. "I've thought of nothing else since. Shay wanted to convince us and talked for some time."

"That's a good thing," Jonathan replied.

"You don't understand," Nathan pleaded with his hands raised. "We didn't listen. In fact, we convinced him to leave with Skotoo and … they haven't returned."

"Who hasn't returned?"

The angelees swung around.

Skotoo glided toward the band of angels.

"Where did you sneak up from and where is he?" Nathan demanded.

"He?"

"You know who I mean."

"Yes, of course, our little friend. He's back on his star."

"He didn't want to come back with you?" Gordan asked.

"Is there something wrong with him?" Abigail added.

Elizabeth didn't say a word.

"Really, there's nothing to worry about. Shay and I enjoyed our excursion immensely. We arrived, and Shay liked it so much, he didn't want to leave. The last I saw of him, he was at a Panoroma Bowl Game, having the time of his life. As I said, there's nothing to worry about."

Skotoo smiled as he spoke with a reassuring tone.

The squadron mumbled to one another, "beat's me," and "who would have ever thought?"

But he didn't convince Jonathan. "Skotoo, did you say he decided to stay behind?"

"As I said, he loved the planet and was having the time of his life."

❖

Shay awoke groggily. He laid a few minutes longer, wrapped snuggly in his wings. *I guess I have to face this dilemma some time.* He arose and brushed himself off with a brisk sweep as the dusty ground seemed determined to cling to him.

He examined the barren landscape. *It doesn't look like there's anything to eat out here.*

The thought brought a smile to his face. *If Gordan or the others knew I was looking for something to eat they'd say, "Can't you think of anything else beside food?"*

The amusement didn't help. He felt a burgeoning desire for food. *Well, I'm not going to find anything standing around here.*

He trudged across the vast emptiness marked with craters that pocked the terrain. *There has to be a morsel of some type of ration around.* Shay remembered the little critters he saw when he and Skotoo first arrived. *They're here and they can't exist on air alone. At least, I don't think they can.*

He sojourned for what seemed to be hours. *Now I know how the older kingdom felt in the wilderness. This is bleak. But then they had ...*

He stopped. His foot hit something hard. *How about that. A rock. Out here by its lonesome.*

He took a few more steps, pointed in the air and turned. *The Ruler of the Realm is our rock.*

He picked up the round object and tossed it a few times. Then, holding the solitary mass in his hand, he thought *this rock may help me to get water.*

Rays of light filtered slowly on Shay as Migmah rotated on its axis toward the sun. The bright beams gave him an idea.

He carefully tore a piece of robe and covered the nugget. With crossed fingers, he laid the shrouded conglomerate of mineral at his feet. Seconds passed. He aimed his hand at the innocent target. *I hope this works.*

The white material glowed as the rock beneath it shriveled from the heat. *It's a good thing our robes don't burn.*

He waited, placed the tip of his finger on the material and pulled back sharply. *Ouch, that's hot.*

He strutted around his experimental stone with hands behind his back and whistled, nonchalantly. He looked up and fixed his eyes on the sky above. *It's got to cool off sometime.*

Moments later, he patted the cloth. With caution, he placed the treasured lump in his hand and opened the fabric like a prized gift.

There, below what remained of the stone, were droplets of condensation. *Water.*

His eyes sparkled as he held this precious commodity. As if it were delicious nectar, he brought it to his lips and drank with closed eyes. *I don't think I've tasted anything so good before.* As he relished this wonderful morsel, a thud resounded behind him.

Shay spun around. A boulder landed next to him. He attempted to see where it came from but the bright rays that streaked across the heaven prevented a good visual assessment.

Before he took a step, another one stone blasted in front of him. He didn't dare take a step as another and another began to rain upon him. A sheet of stones barraged the austere terrain. *What do I do now?*

An inner voice spoke to him. *He will cover you with His feathers and you can trust under his wings.*

Shay situated himself on the ground cross-legged and pulled his wings over his head. The rocks crackled as they crashed around him and he repeated, *He is my shield, my fortress. He is my shield, my fortress.* He felt secure inside his simple cocoon.

Moments that seemed like hours passed. Finally, he heard what may be the last thump. He peeked through the fluff of his feathery wing and studied the damage to Migmah's surface.

Across the vast expanse, what he surmised to be asteroids dotted the terrain. *Jumping Toledo. With this bombardment I can make tons of water.*

He straightened his frame and stood tall amongst the myriad of irregular shaped objects. *I've to get off this star or I may be buried by space junk. But how?*

The patriarchs came to mind. Hours on end, Shay sat under the instruction of those who endured trials and tests.

Job withstood the scourge released because of the evil one's request. His servants who plowed the fields were slain by Sabeans. Fire fell from heaven and burned the sheep and servants. Chaldeans attacked and stole the camel herd and slayed those servants as well. Job's sons and daughters died by what seemed to be a tornado that tore the four corners of the house. In one day, at one time, nothing remained of his family or life's work.

Shay picked small bits of meteoric matter and skid them along the landscape. *That was something else when he told us what he said. "Naked came I out of my mother's womb, and naked shall I return thither: the Lord gave, and the Lord hath taken away; blessed be the name of the Lord."*

He worshipped. I could never imagine what it must have been like losing everything. Well, may be in a sense, I can. I didn't have what he did, but I don't have what I had before. I'm separated from my friends. I'm alone and discarded on this forsaken star but I can worship.

Shay knelt on one knee and looked to the heavens. "Ruler of the Realm of our glorious abode, I let go. My acquaintances are yours as my place of habitation lies with you. I applaud your name."

Stillness encircled him.

He recalled Abraham, the Father of a mighty nation. A simple man, he traveled far to another country. Abram, as he was known before his name changed, met three beings while he sat at the door of his tent in the middle of the day. Shay recollected his testimony.

"I ran from the door and bowed to the ground. I said, My Lord, if now I have found favor in thy sight, pass not away, I pray thee, from thy servant: Let a little water, I pray you, be fetched, and wash your feet, and rest yourselves under the tree: And I will fetch a morsel of bread, and comfort ye your hearts; after that ye shall pass on: for therefore are ye come to your servant."

Abraham stood and watched the eager-faced audience. "What do you think happened?" He asked. His listeners waited.

"They did! They said yes. I ran and told Sarah and set the provisions before them. That's when the promise came again about my son Isaac."

The group loved to hear the story. Abraham continued. "But that wasn't all. Because the sin of Sodom and Gomorrah was enormous, two of the men left and, my dear ones, they intended to destroy everything if the cities were as dreadful as they had heard. That's when I pleaded for my nephew. This is the point I want to make this morning. The Ruler of the Realm has placed beings around us with which we are to have special relations. I'm addressing my fellow earthlings who have learned this lesson from families and friends in their mortal lives."

Shay mused over the special truths. *It doesn't apply to earth people only. But what did Abraham do? He prayed.*

Shay thought about Abraham's plea to save the city. *If there are only fifty,* he began. *Fifty, out of a multitude in two cities, he asked for only fifty. And there were not.* The countdown continued to ten as Abraham humbly begged, But there were not even ten.

The lesson from this talk filtered into Shay's spirit. Again, he knelt and made supplication. "Omnipotent One, I ask you save us. We're less than ten, but you pulled Abraham's family of four out before brimstone and fire hailed and destroyed the cities."

The scenery remained calm, without a whisper of wind.

He bowed his head. *What else can I do? I'm almost a full-fledged angel. I let Skotoo dupe me with stupid toys and games when my focus should have been on Lev and the others. I might as well give up.*

He thought of one of his favorite accounts from a Patriarch. Under Jacob's tutelage, this "plain" man told of his struggle with an angel.

"We grappled with each other. I wasn't a young man at the time. My body was lean because of work and I was determined. He saw he wasn't winning and caused the hollow of my thigh to be out of joint on my mortal body."

The students marveled. One would never know it to look at him now.

"He said to me, 'Let me go.' I answered, 'except you bless me.' Young angels, my message is don't let go of the vision, dream or assignment. If you are not fully determined and persistent, you cannot aid and assist those who need strength in their trial.

A flicker of faith ignited within Shay. *That's it. I can't let go of my belief that I'll be rescued in time to help Lev. That's what Joseph did. His brothers, bless their hearts, sold him to get rid of him.*

Joseph strode at the front of the atrium at the afernoon picnic. "After finding grace in the sight of the master of Egypt, I enjoyed a prosperous time. Even though I missed my family, I believed there must have been a good reason for this separation. Then the temptation came."

The lust of the eyes, the lust of the flesh and the pride of life. Shay's head hung. *I failed my temptation. Joseph didn't. He wouldn't hurt his creator.*

214

Shay vowed to never give in to his own desires again. His spirit felt warmed by his declaration.

But even when Joseph did right, they imprisoned him.

"My imprisonment lasted many years. Although I had favor in the sight of the keeper, I continued to feel the separation from my family. From time to time, I would think about how they most likely carried on with their lives. They married and had children. Although I could do the same, I felt disconnected, especially with relationship with my father and one another. I found, later, that my grandfather Isaac passed on. It pained me at the time that I couldn't speak with him before he departed. As you know, all is different now and we converse daily."

Shay thought, *will I be here many years?*

"My brothers came before me several times. I was so handsome they didn't recognize me."

The spectators chuckled.

Joseph took a deep breath. "This was most difficult although blessings had come to me. I had my wife and my sons, Manasseh and Ephraim were born. As you know, a part of my spirit dwelled on my departure, though my good fortune caused me to forget at times. This didn't happen on its own. For my Creator's hand was upon me. Manasseh means 'For God, said he, hath made me forget all my toil, and all my father's house.' Then there was Ephraim, which I named so because of its meaning. His name, 'For God hath caused me to be fruitful in the land of affliction,' helped me in my time of sorrowful separation. There is a point I want you to take with you this morning. I will tell you what I told my brothers. It was not them that sent me, but God."

Faith flamed within Shay as the words echoed within. *But what do I do?*

"Whoever lacks wisdom let him ask and it shall be given him."

Leaping asteroids, who said that? I guess it doesn't matter. All right, I need wisdom and I ask.

He stood wide-eyed and waited. Possibly two eyelash blinks later, the thought hit him. *The only thing that might work is a signal.*

He worked industriously and began to pile every rock

and boulder he could manage. He rolled them into a large crater, constructing a huge fire pit. Some were extremely bulky and heavy, even with his angelic strength.

Shay wandered about a fourth of a mile from the mound, which resembled a ball. His powers should work long-range.

He stretched his arms and pointed toward his homemade signaling heap. He didn't wiggle his fingers but projected them directly toward the heap of stones. Flames shot across the plains in a straight line. The rocks radiated at the first flash of fire. A light orange glow beamed at the start, which smoldered until they burst into a pillar of flames. The fiery blaze lit up his face. Elated, he danced his infamous flamenco step around the edge of the pyre.

There. That little puppy should summon someone.

"Greetings." Shay heard.

He spun about. A large angel stood beside him with arms crossed against his barreled chest.

"I knew someone would come!"

The angel smiled but didn't answer.

"You are from our side, aren't you?" he asked warily.

"Of course. Your instructor Jonathan inquired of me to help in the search operation. You are master Shay, are you not? I would have been here sooner except that a battle ensued."

Shay's face portrayed a quizzical look. He had heard of angels that battled but not first-hand. "Who? What? Tell me all about it."

"There's not much to tell, really. You've been instructed in warfare with the underworld, have you not?"

Shay remembered the classes and instruction they partook of when his existence began. "I'm an angel who has been a long time in the making and as you can see I have not become a full-fledged angel yet. Tell me, you fought knowing you would win, didn't you?"

"Winning is the foundation and essence of our education but to win, one must fight. Therefore, to answer your question, I fought with nothing else in mind."

"By the way, what's your name?" Shay asked.

The dark-haired angel flashed a smile. "Sunergos."

A smile flashed across the young angelee's face. "Sunergos am I glad to see you!"

basic facts 22

Shay sprinted to the classroom. The entire time, thoughts ran through his head. *Lev, don't you see? How can I make you comprehend?*

He collected himself as he entered the classroom. The others sat quietly as Skotoo whispered in Lev's ear.

He stood close to Lev and then stepped closer.

Skotoo moved nearer also.

"Lev!" Shay pleaded.

"Yes?"

"Lev, listen to me. Do you think that I or any one of us would lead you wrong?"

"No, I know you're all wonderful friends. We've had a great time together."

"Skotoo has transformed himself. You know, the scrolls tell us that it's 'no marvel for Satan himself to transform into an angel of Light.' He's tried to make himself look, like, well … like one of us. Please, listen to me. What you see before you is reality but isn't truth."

"What?"

Lev looked at the vision. In a half-hearted tone Lev asked, "But what about what Skotoo said about all the people he sees? Is he right?"

"I'm sure he does see people who are powerful and rich,

Lev. He goes to everyone, rich or poor. But we do too."

When he heard the words "powerful and rich," Lev became transfixed again. "BUT," Shay exclaimed loudly to bring him back to reality, "Don't focus on what's in front of you. Focus on what Skotoo's objective is and where those you minister to will end. The difference, Lev, is where they and you will spend eternity! Skotoo wants to entice mortals away from the Creator and to devastate them. That's why he has the word *destroyer* written on him. He injures beyond repair or renewal and once mortals' side with him and their spirit leaves their body, they're doomed. Skotoo goes to those who have received Arnion's invitation to the Magnificent City and tries to steal it from them. He wants to take their freedom and put them in bondage to the evil one. Do you think they should change their choice from freedom to bondage?"

Lev stood quiet for a moment and then meekly answered, "No."

"Then why should you?"

The thought troubled him and he thought about the freedom he had as he soared through the galaxy with Sunergos, which occurred earlier.

He felt a tug in his heart but remained bewildered. Since Skotoo mentioned, "the rich and powerful," he had lost his concentration.

Unexpectedly, he answered Shay and said, "So then, Skotoo is right, he will be with the more important people."

"Lev, everyone's important. The world regards people by categories and respects them for how much money, power or fame they have. We minister to the same people but our outcome is drastically different. The sad thing is more of them will listen to Skotoo than will listen to us. Your decision is not so much about whom you minister to but rather more about who sent you. Whomever you choose to serve is the one whom you respect, adore and love. He's the one you worship."

Lev rubbed his forehead. "I feel as if I'm being pushed and pulled in every direction."

Jonathan walked behind them and stood between them and Skotoo. His face didn't disclose his fears. He couldn't believe that

Lev, of all his novices, would have such a hard time and that the others, except for Shay, were quiet. Earlier, he believed they were the right team for this imperative mission.

Shay turned toward Jonathan and said in a muffled voice, "I'm trying my best."

Jonathan shook his head, patted Shay on the shoulder, and faced Lev.

"Jonathan, please don't lecture me," Lev pleaded. "

"Yes, please don't lecture the boy." Skotoo added.

"I'm not going to lecture you at all, Lev. Earlier you made a remark that surprised us all but one that I want to address."

"What was that?"

"You asked if you could go on a trial with Skotoo."

"Yes, I did. I wondered if it was possible to see what Skotoo is about."

Silence surrounded the group as they waited for Jonathan's answer.

"Lev," Jonathan said quietly, "we're not like mortals. Mortals are – well they're different."

"I know we're different," Lev said promptly.

"Yes," Jonathan continued, "but you don't know the biggest difference. It's in the choices we can make. Those on earth in essence may have a 'trial' as you put it because they have not yet accepted the Son. The awful thing is that many of them perish in that state. Their opportunity is lost and their fate sealed with the evil one. Granted some walk in darkness for part of their life and come to understand what the Creator has provided for them before their life is over but many, many do not. You who are here cannot afford to trifle and play with darkness and hope to return. No, the decision you make here and now will determine your fate forever."

He waited a moment to let the words sink in and then continued, "Do you remember when Gabriel came to us?"

Lev closed his eyes for an instant. He envisioned the angel Gabriel as he appeared to them and remembered the enormous joy he felt in his presence. "Yes, I remember," he said softly.

"When Gabriel came," Jonathan continued, "he said he came to impart wisdom and strength in your trials."

Lev gazed at his fellow angels.

"Myself, this unit of angels, and Gabriel. We're joined with you and we make a three-fold cord, which is not easily broken. It's strong, Lev. We're here to help you be strong."

Lev looked down. He wondered *how he got in this state. Why couldn't they continue the way they did before? They had a good time. Now it felt like a cross. Didn't Arnion carry a cross on earth?*

His eyes moistened as his face flushed. Tears fell. They dropped on his hand, a small thing compared to the enormity of his emotions. He glanced upward and saw his friends, with tears in their eyes.

Then Jonathan interrupted the silence. "Have you received wisdom, Lev? It's time for you to make your decision."

"Yes, Jonathan."

He wiped his face and thought about how angels and mankind were similar in their emotions. Even though angels don't reproduce, they love with a deep steadfast love, in the same manner as mortals.

He surveyed his fellow crewmembers and his love for them went to the core of his inner being. Surrounded by their presence, he felt his heart would burst. He thought about the guidance they had received together and all the knowledge they had gained about the king's plan and thought about being a part of that wonderful plan. He tried to imagine what it would be like to be away from them and then the thought struck him. *What would separation from the Ruler of the Realm be like?*

Jonathan watched Lev's face intently. "Lev, Did you know that you're from Venus?"

At the mention of the name, Lev took a deep breath, his memory flooded with his escapade with Sunergos. The universe and the sights astounded him when they traveled through their galaxy, Qodesh. It thrilled him to know where he came from, but more importantly, he needed to solidify where he would spend eternity.

He straightened his shoulders and with his jaw firmly set said quietly, "I don't know where to begin."

"Just begin at the beginning." Jonathan answered.

"I realize now that somewhere back there I went wrong."

"It's where you end up," Jonathan responded.

I should've known and I'm very ashamed but I am sorry and all I have to say is … I'm sorry for the doubts I had. Please forgive me."

"Of course you're forgiven."

The quick response caught Lev off-guard. Then he felt as if an extreme weight lifted. Relief rushed through his inner core.

They waited eager to hear what he would say.

He clasped his hands together and pointed at his colleagues. "Then, I'm with you."

"Yahoo," they shouted in unison in an eruption of joy. They jumped up and down as one would if their team scored. As a tethered balloon cut loose, they leaped into the air. A choir of shouts resounded throughout the City.

"I knew it!" Jonathan roared.

The group had never heard him raise his voice above a normal tone.

"I knew it!" He continued to yell, beaming from ear to ear.

"Right on!" Shay yelled. He leapt into the air and unexpectedly heard a flutter behind him.

"Oh, my!" Elizabeth shrieked as she hugged Abigail. They too felt themselves go up in the air. They held onto each other's hands and rose higher and higher.

Abigail pointed to Elizabeth's back and cried out, "You're flying, you're flying!"

"You are too!" Elizabeth shouted.

Nathan, Gordan and Jonathan locked arms and lifted into the air. They soared and shouted, "Yo!"

Huge smiles covered their faces as they blasted into the air and catapulted through the atmosphere.

"Cucamonga," Shay roared as he ascended.

Lev flew on his own, flying up, down, up and down again in the shape of a heart.

They were caught up in their exuberance when they heard a loud howl.

"AGGGGGGH." The sound shook the angelees. They glimpsed and saw Skotoo with his fist in the air.

"You'll be sorry!"

They stared at the figure that had reverted to his original state. His features constricted as if under extreme pressure. Saliva drooled out of both sides of his mouth. His eyes were wild and bloodshot and his veins popped out as he stood and shouted, "You'll all be sorry, just wait and see! I'm going back to my hole; oh, I know, you all find it a despicable place but I love it. I wouldn't stay around here with your joyfulness and love. You all make me sick. We'll see how sweet you are the next time I see you. I declare war! I have authority to do this and I declare war against you all. It will be like one you've never seen before. You thought I was evil before, well now you'll see what EVIL is!"

He disappeared in front of their eyes as blown up in a puff of smoke and the scent of sulfur reached them as he disappeared.

It amazed them to have their wings in operation for the first time and they descended slowly as they chattered amongst themselves. A peace prevailed even with the threats from Skotoo.

Jonathan beamed with pride. Not the type of pride that said, "Notice me," but gratification that they were victorious. They confronted the evil one's ambassador in battle and came close to defeat. They were ready to continue now. "You did it! You did it!" he hollered.

"Did it?" Lev said. "Did what?"

"You're a team! You're the Teleiotes Squadron. Now you can prepare to prepare."

Shay and the others were elated but perplexed about the remark.

"The Teleiotes Squadron," he said. "You are the angels that will be sent forth to summon the end of the age. Think of it. The World system, as comprehended by all up to now, will end. Nevertheless, know this, you have much preparation yet. You will have assignments to perform before this takes place."

They gaped at one other as they absorbed Jonathan's words and the enormous responsibility. Now they understood why they had to endure this opposition. This trial strengthened them and affirmed their loyalty.

Along with the enormity of their responsibility, an inner

sense of joy filled them to their core. The end of the age! They smiled gleefully and embraced each other in a circle around Jonathan.

"We're the Teleiotes Squadron," they chanted.

Jonathan gleamed. The call on these young Angels seemed so large yet he thought they could make it. He felt 'in his wings' from the start that they would be the ones.

They rose up and flew in a circle around Jonathan. He thoroughly enjoyed their happiness. Then his mode of responsibility took over.

"Angelees," I mean, Teleiotes Squadron, I need your attention."

Then Jonathan heard his name. "Jonathan! Jonathan!"

He looked to see who called him and Lev fluttered beside him.

"Yes, Lev?"

"Jonathan, we are the Squadron aren't we?"

"Of course!" he answered with a hearty laugh.

"Aren't there seven in the Teleiotes Squadron?"

"Yes, yes there is," Jonathan replied exuberantly.

"Where is the seventh angel?"

Jonathan's broad smile widened. "We'll meet with him in the Temple."

Lev's mouth dropped, and the others followed.

The Temple.

"Yahoo," they shouted. They took off, led by Jonathan, and flew over the city.

An exuberant brilliance surrounded them, as if the jeweled wall sparkled brighter on this special occasion. The City seemed to celebrate with its own fireworks.

They glided upward toward the outer heaven.

They ascended higher and higher and Lev shouted back to Jonathan, "Can we visit our neighbor planets?"

Jonathan smiled and answered, "Lead the way."

They entered the outer atmosphere exhilarated by their freedom. Immediately colors flashed around them and they flew between the hues that radiated and lit into the darkness. They were ecstatic and as they circled up Shay pointed to the sky and shouted,

"Look!"

Unexpectedly, a blue star shot across the sky. The angels watched it cross its trajectory.

Lev pondered that it might be the birth of another angel.

sweet sleep 23

"Austin." The barely audible whisper hung in the air.

"Austin," she repeated. Quietness loomed around her, and she laid wide-eyed, flat on her back. An eternity seemingly passed and she whispered, a little more fervently, "Austin."

The rhythm of his breathing demonstrated his deep sleep. She looked at the clock. It read three thirty-three.

Normally, Anna emerged from sleep at a slow and dreamy pace. Here, in the early hours of this morning, she was wide-awake for no reason at all. She held her breath and lay still for a few more moments. She strained to hear anything out of the ordinary. All she heard was Austin's heavy breathing.

Her heart began to pound as she grasped at thoughts that ran through her head. *Was it a dream or something else?*

Austin rested on his back. His breathing became heavier and deeper. Anna didn't know if she should nudge him or let it go.

"Austin," she tried once more. He moved slightly as he turned to his side. Half asleep, he mumbled. "Hmmm?"

She leaned toward him and said in a low frantic tone, "I think I heard something!"

He remained undisturbed and muttered, "It's probably just the wind."

He turned on his side, facing the wall and announced in a clear tone, "You're probably suffering from residual fear from what happened. Go back to sleep, Anna. I'm sure it's nothing."

Nothing? How could he be sure? Unaccustomed to waking this way, she fretted all the more. *How can he go to sleep so easily when there might be someone here?*

She laid back, looked at the ceiling, and pulled the covers tightly up to her neck. She glanced at the window and half expected to see someone there.

A slight shaft of light from the street came through the side of the blinds. Curiously, it brightened. She thought it might appear that way because her eyes adjusted to the dark.

Nothing's out of the normal. Her body heaved a sigh, and uttered the name, Jesus, to herself. She tightened the covers around her body like a shield, turned and burrowed against her pillow.

Anna peeked at the digital on her bedside table. Ten minutes had passed. *What's wrong with me? Why am I still so awake?*

She remembered her friend Lisa told her about the prayer time she had with the Lord in the middle of the night. Lisa said she prayed for about a half an hour in her spiritual language and never knew what she prayed.

Is that it? Am I awake because that stuck in my mind or because that's what I'm supposed to do?

She peered at the clock again. Five more minutes had passed. She began to pray. After about ten minutes, something began to lift. Verses from a song ran through her mind and soothed her spirit.

"Consuming Fire,
Sweet Perfume.
His Awesome Presence,
Fills This Room."

The refrain permeated her being as she lay there. A sense of peace overcame her and confusion melted away. She enjoyed her interlude with the Lord for a while and slowly her mind became cluttered with future events. School would end shortly and preparations for Haley's last year were around the corner.

Her last year of high school. She could hardly believe how fast time had flown by. It had been such an eventful one and it seemed that they no sooner completed one thing, than the next one came along.

Anna became involved with a group that helped feed the homeless. She and her sister worked with a team that ministered on Seventh and Walton Streets. At times, it seemed dangerous because they were in an undesirable part of town but her desire to help prevailed over her fear.

Anna recalled her first trip. They parked the car and walked briskly with loaded arms from the lot. As they turned the corner, her eyes met the line of people that waited for a meal. The formation, made of mostly men, stretched down the block.

Used would be a kind term for their drab clothes. Though clean, they were well worn, and revealed their rank in life.

The second and third time that she went, she experienced the same thing. When she returned the fourth time, she realized most of the same people came repeatedly. After about eight months, she became discouraged and Anna remembered she asked Mackinsey, "Do you think we're going to see any good come out of this?"

Mackinsey pondered her question, and then said brightly, "Yes, I do. I believe I remember you telling me some time ago that we need to stand in faith."

Anna blushed. She recalled that she did. Change may not be evident on the outside and Anna recognized she needed to continue to trust and keep doing what she considered her 'assignment.'

Months past, and the question mulled in her mind once again. She chuckled to herself as she lay there. *I was such an anxious ninny. If I had pulled out, I would never have gotten to know Gee.*

"Gee" never spoke at first. Her umber shade of brown eyes darted back and forth untrustingly when she passed by. The first moment Anna saw her she wondered what those eyes must have seen in her lifetime.

Gee had long matted black, straight hair, tied with a rubber band behind her neck. It stuck out of a black cap that sat snugly on her head. The cap was the only thing she had to help defend her from the chill of winter.

The woman passed by Anna for several months. "Would you like a box of cereal?" she exclaimed with a pitch of cheer. Gee looked up, shook her head and snatched the box from Anna's hand. Her gloves covered only the palms of her hands and Anna recoiled at the sight of her soiled fingers and dirty nails. Gee shoved the box into the plastic bag and Anna attempted to smile.

Their first encounter turned into weeks and then months, until one day.

Anna worked at a steady pace lifting and loading the donated goods onto tables. Without notice, Gee stood in front of her. Her hair didn't look as tangled as it did before and her hands seemed clean. She didn't have her familiar cap on either. Anna almost didn't recognize her.

"I've been talking to the Pastors there," Gee said as she pointed behind her. "I'm gonna' get a job soon." The expression on her face was one Anna had never seen before.

"That's wonderful. I'm happy … it's … it's just wonderful."

Anna noticed a different look in Gee's eyes.

"Thank you, ma'am." Her crooked teeth were revealed as she smiled but she couldn't have been more beautiful to Anna.

She shuffled off and nodded to the others, "Good morning. Good morning," she said as she moved past the line.

Anna remained entranced with what she had just seen. A rush of joy overwhelmed her and she thought she would cry.

She wished she could run behind Gee, grab her and give her a big hug, but she knew that she would have to wait. Maybe someday she may express how thrilling the changes were.

She lay in bed, and joy flooded her spirit. She breathed a quiet, "thank you." *Maybe that's who I prayed for.*

Becky crossed her mind. *Now why didn't I think of my niece first?*

She asked her sister the other day but Mackinsey hadn't heard from Becky for almost a year. *I hope she isn't in trouble. Mackinsey has had such a time with her being out on the streets. She's been waiting for Becky to change for so many years.*

Anna turned in her bed. Her lips moved softly as she entreated protection and favor for her niece. After some time, she drifted into a sweet sleep.

Two Aman, or guardian angels, watched as slumber reclaimed her.

Shamar and Phileos were there since Anna whispered the

name of Jesus, with weapons drawn. They would stand and protect both Anna and Austin from any spiritual intrusion.

Since before man's creation, they had served the kingdom. Their assignment to Anna and Austin existed since their birth. They were the spiritual beings referred to where it says, "Take heed that ye despise not one of these little ones; for I say unto you, That in heaven their angels do always behold the face of my Father which is in heaven."

Shamar replaced his weapon into his sheath, and Phileos followed suit. They had not had been in combat since the Babylonians propelled Daniel into the den of lions over 2,600 years ago.

"Is it time for the message to be delivered to Becky yet?" Shamar asked.

"There has been so much opposition to this one's revelation of truth." Phileos answered. "I understand there are some, which are part of a squadron, sent on a special assignment for that very reason."

"It's a good thing she's supported by these pleas. Who knows what would have happened to her by now."

They sat intently and viewed the earthlings in deep slumber.

"A special dispensation is a lot to support one mortal," Shamar responded after a moment.

Phileos chuckled and answered, "Well the whole squadron won't minister to her, but as I understand, two of them were sent and will join her guardian. It's time for her to make a decision."

"What about her cousin, Jacob?"

"He's also very close to his final hour."

"By his own hand?"

"No. He's not going to commit suicide but his time on earth is limited."

Phileos let out a sigh. "We can only do what we're sent to do. Sometimes I'd like to shake these earthlings and tell them to shape up."

"Have patience, Phileos."

"I have patience," he said swiftly. Then he sheepishly looked down and added in defense, "I've waited for thousands of years for the final hour, haven't I?"

Shamar looked pensive for a moment and then answered, "Yes and we'll continue to wait since we don't know when it will happen."

"No one knows, except the Ruler of the Realm and I think that is what unnerves the old dragon. You know the one we rebuke in the Son's name.

They pondered the constant horror that myriads presently experienced at the mention of the leader of the underworld. "He knows it won't last forever. He knows his reign is imminent," Phileos said determinedly. "It must be dreadful to know that final destruction is on the horizon but not to know when."

"That's not all. I know Skotoo lost his bid for the squadron in the Magnificent City and the old serpent is … well, angry is a mild word. I guess Skotoo thought he could undermine the training once again but he failed."

"Yes, I imagine there is going to be a lot of anguish spilled over this last episode. If Skotoo isn't destroyed by this he may be the old serpent's best tool, he'll be so full of hate."

"We'll have to be on guard all the more. All the stops may be pulled out."

"I'm ready. I hope our wards are," he answered as he watched them sleep.

"Yes," Shamar answered. "And not only they but those they have tried to build up. We'll see if they've put on the armor of God and whether they will fight."

Gee entered the hallway and almost tripped over the woman seated at the landing of the stairs. A dark blanket over her head and across her shoulders concealed her well in the unlit corridor.

"Sorry, I didn't see you." "It's okay."

Gee offered apologetically.

The girl glanced at her and muttered, "It's okay."

As she began her climb, she stopped mid-flight. "Do you live here?"

"No."

She turned to continue her trek upstairs and heard a squirming sound. "What was that?"

"That's my baby."

"You have a baby?" Gee bounded down the steps like a gazelle.

She eagerly lifted the blanket. A toe-headed charmer lay in the woman's arms. Even at this late hour, the child appeared feisty.

"If you don't live here, then where do you live?"

Her head dropped. "I … I don't live anywhere. I mean, I kind of hang out in different apartment buildings, you know?"

"Yeah. I do."

Gee stroked the child's arm, her skin feeling like soft cotton. "Com'n. You and the kid can stay with me tonight."

"We can? That's really … kind."

"Yeah," she went on, "I have a couch you can sleep on and I think a box and some pillows will work for the little munchkin."

Gee, climbed the steps and rattled constantly. "By the way, what's your name?"

"Rebecca."

"Rebecca, I like that."

"Thanks. You can call me Becky if you want."

Pam's eyes darted from one side of the street to the other in search of Becky. He completed his fourth trip around the block and still no sight of her. He hadn't seen her for months.

He turned the next corner and caught a glimpse of her back. *There she is.* He pulled the car over and hastened to catch up with her. The car window rattled when he slammed the door closed and he ran down the street. "BECKY!"

She didn't turn around.

"BECKY," he bellowed again.

The woman turned.

Panting for breath, he reached her and stood towering over the woman. "I'm sorry," he muttered. "I mistook you for someone else."

"That's okay, handsome," she replied.

The woman, dressed in a skimpy outfit, flashed an all too familiar smile at Pam. She sashayed her body toward him with her hand on her hip.

"Um, no thanks, sweetheart, I'm not interested."

"Oh, but we could have a good time."

"No, thanks, you see I really did think you were a friend of mine. Her name's Becky."

"No, don't know her."

Her hazel blue eyes softened and she added, "You know, I've had a hard time getting along lately."

Pam looked up and down the street. "Maybe I can help you in another way," he said taking her arm.

She smiled sweetly and leaned close to him. "Thanks mister. I'm not expensive. Twenty-five will do."

Her request pained his spirit. *Twenty-five dollars? Lord, what was I thinking when I panhandled jobs for Becky and the others?*

"Oh, I'll have to have the money up front."

"What? Listen, honey, no one gets it up front."

"Up front, or it's no go."

He looked at the woman and knew she wouldn't begin to understand if he tried to explain. Perspiration began to form on his forehead. *Maybe it would get her off the street for a while. Maybe he could talk to her about God.*

"Okay. I'll give you the money but I just want to talk, that's all. You got that?"

"Sure, anything you want sweetie," she replied, with an outstretched palm.

Pam popped his wallet open. The rumpled five and crisp twenty-dollar bill seemed made to order. He pulled them out and gave them to her.

She took the money as her gum cracked between her teeth. "Thanks," she replied as she stuffed it into her handbag.

Without warning, two men spun Pam around and grabbed his arms. Cuffs tightened swiftly around his wrists behind his back. He struggled against them with widened eyes of disbelief. "What's going on?"

"You're under arrest."

"Who are you? You don't look like cops."

"We're undercover," the tall, blond policeman in torn jeans and a polo shirt announced.

"You don't understand," he countered, "I just wanted to talk to her."

"Sure, buddy. We know all about it. You have the right to remain silent …," they began in a monotone. The rest of the 1963 Miranda rights droned on in Pam's astonished ears.

The officer placed his hand on his head as he shoved him into the back of the patrol car. "Hey, what about my car?"

"That's not our problem. You should have thought about that before you tried to pick up our decoy."

Pam leaned back against his muscular arms, uncomfortable. He gazed straight ahead. *Well, I'll tell the truth. That should get me out. I didn't do anything wrong.*

In a corner on the busy street, a demon named Pach snickered as he watched them lead Pam away. The demon lived up to his name, which meant *trap.* Thoughts rushed through his devious mind of how the successful snare of this newly reborn Christian would please his master. *This is going to take me up the ladder a couple of notches!*

His chest expanded as he triumphed in the thought for a moment. Then suddenly, as if someone let the air out of a balloon, he realized this wouldn't bring him any recognition or commendation. His master didn't work that way.

Pam arrived at city jail. They ushered him into a room that resembled a school classroom. The detectives left and Pam thought about the incident until his head swam. *Lord, I don't understand. Why didn't you stop me from talking to this woman? Of all the people on the street, why did I, at that particular time, have this conversation with her?*

He remembered the times he slipped through their fingers, the drug sales, pimped deals and thefts. *Maybe this happened because of some kind of law of averages or justice.*

They returned and escorted him upstairs. The large office looked business-like with computers and desks.

The plainclothesmen were nonchalant when they booked him. They took his cuffs off and sat him down for his mug shot.

Detective Owens walked by. "What do you have here?"

"Just a John Doe," the man replied.

"They should throw the book at him," Owens retorted.

Pam hung his head. *Lord, I feel so bad. All the times I took money from these ladies on the street. I didn't see this side. Lord, I'm on your side now and I'm asking you to help me.*

"Like I said, book him for something. Vagrancy, shoplifting or whatever you can find. He probably has warrants."

The eager undercover cop scanned the records carefully. "What do you know? He's not in the system," he answered sarcastically.

Pam stared straight ahead. *How am I going to get out of this?*

"You can find something. And if you don't, make it up."

"What do you mean?"

Owens leaned closer to the officer that made the arrest and spoke in a mumbled tone.

"I can do that?" the officer said with a sly smile.

"Yeah. It's been done."

Owens walked away with an air of satisfaction. In his mind, he thought he got someone off the street that would otherwise be doing something wrong.

"Okay, buddy." The man guided Pam past the busy desks that filled the large room. Phones rang at intervals while he pushed him along.

"Where am I going?"

"Somewhere to cool off."

"But I didn't do anything wrong. I'm innocent."

"Don't worry, pal, we've got someone who will testify about your 'innocence'."

"Yeah, I think it's going to be some time before you see daylight again. You might as well settle for some sweet sleep."

high places brought low 24

Skotoo received information his underling had been removed. He heard she kicked and screamed upon the news of her demotion. *Pity* he thought. But then there were far weightier circumstances that occurred.

His return from the Magnificent City was long and arduous and not the first mission he failed.

He strained to remember exactly what happened the last time and he wrestled with the recollection as he scuttled as fast as he could to his master's throne room.

The details drifted back and they weren't pretty. His assignment was a pastor who led a large congregation. If he caused him to fall, it would create havoc and have a domino effect.

Skotoo didn't even have to appear in person. He utilized his craftiness from behind the scenes. Attempt number one was outright. *Too obvious, that's what it was.*

He maneuvered one of their own to entice the pastor into an illicit affair. She was to appear a helpless member of the church and appeal to the shepherd's caring side. It had worked many other times but not this time.

Attempt two, continued with trials and tribulations, one after another. Sickness, debt and parishioners that fell away from the fold attacked the innocent believer.

The pastor persisted through it all and kept his faith in his creator.

There has to be something Skotoo brooded.

His epiphany finally came. *That's it. I'll get the closest thing to him, his family.*

Skotoo proceeded and pulled strings. The clergyman's brother was superficial enough. The argument was classic. Skotoo was pleased. *Now we'll see what will happen.*

Unforgiveness settled. The festering sore fed it even more.

Then something strange happened. A child entered the picture.

It happened as the pastor prepared his six-year-old for bed. "Dad, how much is seventy times seven?"

"Four hundred and ninety."

"Wow, that's a lot of times, huh."

The pastor sat on the end of the bed. He knew the passage his son referred to and sat quiet.

"Is that what you do, Dad? Do you forgive that many times in a day? Would you forgive uncle Charles that many times?"

The pastor thought, smiled, and scooted the blanket around his son's chin. "Yes, son, but the first one seems to be the hardest."

The rat. He had to go and repent and leave me with a bad report.

What's going to happen to me? If he throws me out from the inner circle, it'll mean I'll have to join the rest of the masses in the pit and probably shovel lava.

In a stage of fright, Skotoo reached Nachash's throne. This time, the master surrounded himself with hordes of what he called "advisors." This could be worse than if no one were around. His plan could be to use him as an example.

Skotoo's wings dropped and his head lowered as he moved before his superior. It can't be long before he unleashes fury.

"IDIOT!"

The others snapped to attention as fear quaked through them from the resonance of his shout. Skotoo expected the rage and remained calmer than the others.

"Haven't you learned anything after all these years? Any one of these other morons could have done better!"

The words blasted hotly and Skotoo wanted to back away but didn't dare move.

"How could you let those pampered, juvenile sniveling ingénues get away from you? You've been taught better," he snarled.

Flames exuded from the old dragon's mouth with his words, a new interpretation to the phrase, "tongue lashing."

Skotoo winced in rhythm with each syllable. Until now, he had some pride regarding his abilities. What was the old proverb, "pride goes before destruction?"

He hung his head low and wished he could slither away. A sorrowful, piteous expression came across his face.

"Don't give me that wretched look," the creature growled.

Skotoo's eyes glanced downward. Not one of his muscles shifted. He remained as if frozen. One false move and unbearable torture could be imminent. The General controlled deception like no one else, making it his greatest weapon. He hid issues of every type. When he used truth, it was to do exactly that – use it. Skotoo knew he would not be able to mislead him.

As his right-hand man, Skotoo knew that Nachash hid the fact that sin existed from many mortals on earth. He spoke to their inner beings and told them 'wrong' didn't exist and that they could live however they wanted. He told them 'all people are good.'

Quietness crept in. Skotoo remained idle and finally worked his nerve up to look. He peeked through his eye slits.

Nachash no longer appeared in his warfare mode, but as an anointed cherub, his former nature.

"I have a thought," the dragon said blithely.

The tone caught Skotoo off guard. *What could he be thinking? Does this mean torture?*

He wondered if it meant banishment from his assignments on earth above or in the realm of the emperor and creator of all creation. His escapades, even though evil in nature, were what kept him sane. *What will I do if that is taken away?*

The being gushed, "Don't worry." "I have a plan that might work quite well. Not all is lost. We aren't done with our little angelees. I'm not one to give up and I've decided you have another chance."

Skotoo reeled with relief to the point that he almost passed out. *This is exactly what I wanted.*

A crooked smile crossed his face, his eyes dreaming of a conquest.

This is what I exist for – vengeance.

first visitation 25

"YAHOO!"

The gregarious shout sank into the vast expanse of the Universe, their first trip together.

Gordan giggled and spun in circles. Their journey through this glorious expanse of the cosmos would take them to the earth. Finally, they could experience first-hand their long-awaited destination.

Nathan and Abigail flew closely to each other with Lev in the lead. The astounding sights reflected in their faces.

Shay and Gordan followed and last, Elizabeth.

An array of marvelous colors displayed throughout the heavenly bodies. Brilliant younger blue stars with orbiting planets and moons emitted vivid and vibrant shades of not only blue, but also yellow, purple and pink as well.

Lev and the others recognized the Milky Way galaxy from their studies and a surge of peace and fulfillment captivated them as they approached the outer limits.

They flew in a straight shot until they drew nearer to earth, and reached its atmosphere.

"Gosh," exclaimed Abigail, "look how it glows in the dark heavens."

Nathan surveyed the majestic blue bubble. "It turns like a gracious ballerina. Look at how the colors weave across its mass."

Nathan referred to the land that appeared dark against hues of blue water, both deep and shallow; and white clouds and glassy ice formations that formed a magical swirl around the sphere. Only a handful from earth had ever encountered this regal sight.

"It's too bad Jonathan couldn't come with us," Lev said, even though it thrilled him that Jonathan chose him to lead their small entourage for their first hands-on mission. At the time, Jonathan acted low-key about the assignment, although he longed to be with them.

Jonathan had wondered, *were they capable of this mission?* It didn't take him long to attest, yes. He had no doubt they were, but he wished he could go with them to experience this fresh, new encounter. Not being with them on their first assignment away from the City, which promised to be spectacular, would be hard. However, *how else were they to grow if they weren't away from his watchful eye?*

As the squadron drew nearer to earth, the intensity of their exhilaration mounted. Their expressions exhibited the thrill of their first Visitation.

"Are we supposed to get involved with the inhabitants," Shay said.

Gordan responded quickly. "I believe we can as we observe. In certain instances we may have to intervene but we can't take matters into our own hands." They had learned much about the inhabitants of earth in their classes. The time had come to gain knowledge through practice.

Elizabeth looked across the horizon of the wondrous blue ball as they drew closer. She thought about how humanity began in what one may consider a tiny drop in this huge spectrum called earth. It amazed her that two earthlings could make such a difference on this immense planet. "I can't wait until we reach the cradle of civilization in the Garden. We've talked about it so much in our studies and I've imagined what it looked like for so long. It takes my breath away to think we're going to be there."

They flew through a mass of a cumulonimbus cloud before them. The height reached fifty thousand feet above the ground. They swirled through the cloud and descended in a cone-shaped trajectory.

They soared through the huge billows and realized that as they did, the soft form changed shapes.

"This is going to be fun," Shay commented as he altered the gigantic puffs. He fluttered through more of them and played with the ethereal patches of white curls. It started to take the shape of an animal.

The squadron cheered when they saw Shay form the neck of a giraffe.

Elizabeth caught on. She began to work on the mass next to her. "This one's go to be a bear," she announced.

"I'm making a camel," Abigail proclaimed as she rounded out the hump.

Nathan worked hard on an elephant, but he didn't say anything about it. He laughed as he darted past Lev.

Engrossed in their glee, they didn't realize how close they were to the ground.

"Look out!" Gordan yelled.

Shay caught a glimpse of the fast approaching tree. Quickly, he darted to the side and luckily avoided the collision. "Whoa!" The others chuckled as they roared passed him and narrowly missed it themselves.

"We'll get the hang of flying, yet," Lev teased.

One by one, the angelees landed until they were all firmly planted on the ground.

They stood in a circle with their faces outward, speechless as they soaked up the array of plants that surrounded them.

"Look over there!" Lev said, pointing ahead of him.

A bright gleam of light flashed. It beamed on and off like a signal. They took off into the air all at the same time, veered left and took great caution as they flew toward the light. Below, a massive amount of trees formed a thick solid wall of forest.

How does that light come through? Lev wondered. "There's a clearing," he cried out.

"This could be it!" Gordan shouted elatedly.

"That's it. That's it," Elizabeth and Abigail shouted together as they descended.

"Wait," Nathan said. "We need to scout the area and see

what's there first."

Abigail and Elizabeth resignedly shrugged their wings. "I guess that's best," they sighed.

"I'm itching to see," Elizabeth added.

Lev realized their mistake. "Hey you guys, we don't have anything to worry about. We're invisible!"

They laughed when they realized they didn't have to worry. Relaxed, they wove back and forth above the light.

KABOOM! A loud sound echoed across the treetops.

"What's that?" Abigail asked.

"I believe a war is currently being engaged," Nathan answered.

Shay shook his head. "Won't they ever learn?" As he finished speaking, he realized the light diminished. The small peephole of a beam led them to an insignificant opening in the midst of the dense trees.

"We can't make it through there," Abigail declared.

"Yes we can," Lev asserted. "Don't you remember we can go *through* walls? We don't have to here. A small space has been provided for us and we just have to slither in."

One by one, they constricted their spiritual vapors and oozed through the small speck of a hole. On the other side, they were astounded to see a huge open space bounded by thick woods. A bright green lush field before them and trees that towered into the heaven encircled the luxuriant meadow.

They heard what sounded like a stream or brook close by and walked toward the sound.

They pushed through some brush and emerged on the other side where the water sparkled crystal clear.

Spectacular beauty of foliage and flowers lay before the angelees.

It reminded them of their own river of life.

"This is incredible," Lev declared. He marched around as he sought clues about its previous existence.

A gigantic flame, in the form of a blade, flashed over their heads.

The creatures that appeared above them resembled the form

of a man but had four faces and four wings.

Their feet were straight and the sole of their feet was like a calf's foot that sparkled like the color of burnished brass.

They had the hands of a man under their wings.

The curious creatures with the four faces astonished them, even though they had seen cherubim before.

One of the creatures came nearer and turned so that each of his faces looked upon the dumbfounded group.

Nathan spoke quickly. "Sir, we are from the Sanctuary Qodesh here on a mission."

As the being continued to spin, he raised his fiery sword and said in a voice that quivered, "Yes, we know. We have expected you. Your group is here to investigate the beginnings of Man in order that you may serve them better. Your leave to do so is granted."

Swords swirled above their heads once again. They could reap demise of a legion of angels if they desired but they left as quickly as they arrived.

"Whew," Abigail heaved. "It's a good thing they're on our side."

"I'll say," they chimed together.

"This is where it all started," Elizabeth exclaimed with her hands held out. She twirled around and danced with joy to know they were at the very place where life began. "I bet Eve stood right about here beneath this large tree," she exclaimed. It reminded her of the vision she experienced of Adam and Eve in the Garden.

The others replied, "Sure," and "Maybe," but walked ahead to explore the spectacular estate.

Elizabeth stood enraptured. *Six thousand years ago the Ruler of the Realm formed man and woman.* She walked slowly through the lush and magnificent garden.

She looked sharply to the left and found a tree, about a hundred feet high, that stood out from all the rest. It had deep green and yellow gloriously colored leaves and she noticed it bore strange fruit – such as she had never seen before. Her curiosity led her toward it and she stood transfixed.

Moments passed as she stared longingly at the superb specimen. She remained motionless and then in her innermost being she could almost hear, "Isn't it wonderful? This fruit can make you like the king and you will be wise and know the difference between good and evil."

The luscious fruit beckoned to her. She had an extraordinary urge to take hold of this magnetic . . .

"NO!" She yelled. Startled by the force of her own voice, she jumped back. *This might be the same tree Eve partook of.*

Her eyes guardedly pierced the neighboring trees. No one else appeared.

Her heart pounded in her chest and she turned and ran across the garden. A residue of this strange desire lingered and she ran as fast as she could. The words "resist the devil and he will flee from you," invaded her mind.

But she was the one who ran. *Maybe this is how it should be. Run, Liz, run.*

Hurriedly, she sprinted, eager to catch up with the others. She didn't want to take another chance and looked back continually to make sure no one followed her. *What if there are unfriendly spirits and I have no one to help me fight.*

What a sight. The most important historical site of all-time, seen by only two people and uninhabited for 6,000 years stood before the six young angels. The cradle of civilization – where the first two living creatures of humanity were fashioned – glowed as the sun gleamed on the immense river. The angelees found themselves at the intersection of the rivers.

They stood at the junction and surveyed the wonder before them. The Garden existed in the geographic center of the Eastern Hemisphere, the larger of the two Hemispheres.

Nathan stood at the intersection where the river that watered Eden split four directions. The Pison flowed into Havilah (Arabia) where gold exists, precious bdellium and onyx. The Gihon flowed around Ethiopia and Egypt, the land of Cush. The Hiddekel (Tigris) streamed east of Assyria. The Euphrates, the fourth river, has been competed over by Turkey, Syria and Iraq for hydroelectric power and irrigation.

Abigail came alongside Nathan. She pointed in the direction of the Euphrates. "Isn't this is where four angels will be bound and released at the sound of the sixth trumpet?" Nathan nodded. They had been diligent to learn their lessons.

"Jonathan said that's when our true assignment begins, after the sixth trumpet."

The rest of the team lined up on either side of Nathan and Abigail. Lev, Abigail, Gordan – Nathan, Shay and Elizabeth had not been totally versed yet as to their final assignment. They knew they came to earth to receive thorough education for that ultimate mission.

They knelt and sipped the water. The cool, wet liquid satisfied their avid thirst.

"Let's go hunt," Shay declared. Gordan and Lev's ears energized.

Unaware of what they were about to hunt for, Elizabeth went and foraged about. When she returned, she found them seated with mounds of, pears, cherries, peaches, and olives; produce of every type heaped around them.

"You guys, what are you doing! You aren't going to eat those are you?" She cried out.

"Don't worry," Nathan said with a big smile, "We left some for you." He had especially enjoyed the dates and almonds.

"Here, here's some quince," he said as he handed her the bright yellow-skinned fruit.

"But we shouldn't eat these," she said with widened eyes. "The fruit Adam and Eve were told not to eat may be one of these."

Abigail threw hers on the ground. "You think so?"

"Yes!"

Gordan stood up and with a hearty laugh said, "What's with you two? Don't you know we're not the ones who were told not to eat of a certain tree? We're different. It doesn't apply to us."

Elizabeth surveyed the luscious food before her.
"Are you sure?"

"Of course. Would we eat it if we weren't?"

She sat down hesitatingly next to Abigail, who picked the half-eaten pear back up again, wiped it off and enjoyed the delicious flavor again.

"Well, if you don't think it'll do any harm," Elizabeth coaxed.

She reached over and took a mango from Shay. He glanced at her from the side, eyed the quince in her other hand, and shrugged his shoulders. "There's more where those came from."

Shay had changed since his encounter with Skotoo. He exhibited such strength of character that even his outer physique changed from what could have been thought of as robust to that of a more sophisticated, slimmer angel. Now he could eat without adding to his form.

"Do you know where we're expected to arrive next?" Abigail asked Nathan as she munched away.

"I don't know for sure but I know we are to split up in pairs."

"Pairs? Why do we have to do that?"

"Since this is our first expedition, it's better that we team up. Not that anyone can harm us but we'll be able to confer if we have a question about how to proceed."

"What about morphing?" Shay asked with a gleam.

"I expect we'll be able to," Nathan answered.

Angels possessed the power to become like human beings and disguise themselves, if necessary, to carry out their mission. At times, people entertained angels without knowing.

"I want to be a football player," Shay announced, thrilled with the thought of interacting with those on the planet.

Nathan chuckled. "Well, unfortunately, we don't get to pick and choose."

His mouth dropped. "What? I thought we could be who we wanted to be."

Nathan shook his head. "Sorry about that but it's as each situation arises. Remember, there are many ministering angels already here and we're called for special cases. Besides, they don't play the same manner as we do. They're rough you know. Not that you couldn't handle it, but I know you wouldn't want to hit some of these mortals the way they hit each other."

Shay pondered the thought. "I guess it's probably for the best then. I know I don't want to hurt anyone. That would look great on our report, wouldn't it? 'Angel knocks out mortal – mortal in coma.' No, I think I will pass on the football thing." He picked up another scrumptious piece of fruit and bit into it heartily.

"I believe that whatever the king has ordained will be memorable so I don't think you'll be disappointed. We have to remember, if you don't know what to do for sure, don't do anything."

"Don't know, don't do, huh?"

"Right. You'll have a 'witness' inside of you and you'll know what the 'go ahead' feels like."

"Okay. That sounds …

A high-pitched whistle shrilled through the air, ending in an explosive bang.

Shay whirled around with his hand on his sword, ready for combat. "What was that?" His eyes darted across the landscape. The others followed suit.

A second shot fired, but this time it sounded farther away.

"We're far from our homeland, aren't we," Abigail stated.

"And these battles never end, do they?"

"No, and they won't until the Ruler of the Realm places his Magnificent City upon earth."

Lev interjected, "Is everyone ready?"

They concurred and rose to their feet.

They appeared curious, as they stood in the green field in their luminous white robes.

Larger than the average individual on earth, if they were visible they would have frightened anyone.

"Before we continue, there's somewhere we need to go first," Gordan announced.

He took the lead for the first time and the others followed, trustingly, not knowing where he would take them.

Abigail, Nathan, Gordan, Elizabeth, Lev and Shay, whisked into the clouds.

Unquestionably they were -- *The Making of Angels.*

"Wings"

I used to dream of Angels
Snow-white would be their wings,
And I could hear their voices
And praises they would sing.

But as for me, I walked alone
Paths of destruction, didn't see,
Headed to the darkest parts
My sins had blinded me.

Now Jesus spoke that once His own
No one could pluck me from His Father's hand,
He knew how once that I was His
And proceeded with His spiritual plan.

Then I repented, turned from my sin
Set clearly to see His face,
And at His beauty, I let out a gasp
Lifted into a heavenly place.

Then I sang the songs of Angels
As one took my hand in his own,
And off in flight we proceeded
As my wings had finally grown.

Ereina Rubino 1998

In this story, Doug paid a price. How about you? Will you pay a price or receive a reward?

The Bible says if you believe and receive, you will be saved (Romans 10:9:10).

Pray this prayer now and assure your place in heaven:

"Father, I know I'm a sinner and I ask for, and receive, your forgiveness for all the wrongdoings I committed. I accept Your Son, Jesus Christ, as my Lord and Savior."

Welcome to the family.

God bless.

Breinigsville, PA USA
12 October 2010
247191BV00002B/4/P